For everyone we've lost too soon.
And in particular, for Cheryl:
I wish you could have read this.
I think you'd have liked it.

1

THE LAST TIME I saw my sister alive, I told her I didn't love her anymore.

I didn't say it in those exact words. I didn't say, "Fiona—I don't love you anymore." What I actually said, as she was walking away from me, was "You're no better than Mom."

But in our family, that means the same thing.

I'm thinking about that again, the parade a blur in the background, Fiona's blond hair flying around her shoulders as she spun off and headed toward the woods. To the ravine.

In my mind, I go after her. I tell her I'm sorry. I bring her home safely. I don't wander off to drink my problems away with Seth Montgomery on the star-watching rock. Don't wake up with Seth's arms around me and the stale taste of cider on my tongue. Don't stumble home in the early morning to collapse into bed, only to be woken up a few hours later by the police letting me know my world would never be the same.

In my mind, I'm always a better person than I actually am.

A whistle sounds, startling me back to the present. I'm at the edge of the park with my bike, in the shade of a maple tree, waiting for my brother to finish soccer camp. On the far side, next to the woods, a group of teenage boys disperses from the field. Davy is easy to spot: taller than most of them, skinny, blond hair sticking straight up at the back of his head. He shot up this past year, so he can actually pass for sixteen now, even though he still has that round baby face.

I wave to get Davy's attention. When he sees me, he jogs over, frowning slightly.

"You didn't have to pick me up," he says. "I can ride my bike home on my own."

"I don't mind. Besides, Dad's working late again. He asked me to pick up pizza. Come with?"

He's about to respond when his head whips to the side. I turn to see a girl on a bike riding into view—a white girl with brown hair.

"It's not Marion," I tell Davy for what feels like the hundredth time. I try to sound patient; he's not the only one seeing last summer's ghosts. "They're not coming back."

Davy doesn't answer me, just looks pissed, the way he always does when his ex-girlfriend gets brought up. He hops on his own bike and takes off.

We pedal down a few residential streets, and soon we're on the outskirts of downtown. Bier's End, in the northwest corner of New Jersey, was once a retreat for wealthy Manhattanites, with lavish mansions on huge pieces of property spread out along the edge of the woods. Now most of those mansions have been knocked down, their giant plots of land divided up, turned into the stretches of middle-class blocks like the one my family lives on. Pieces of downtown remain from that bygone era: the old theater with its velvet seats that plays vintage movies, the one nice restaurant that used to be a country club. But those are now interspersed with the deli, the dollar store, Fiona's old dance studio. Middle-class things for middle-class people. The pizza place is next to a Wawa.

I stop my bike just outside the pizza place's big window, behind Davy.

My throat tightens as I peer through the glass, trying to make out who might be in there.

"I'll get it," Davy says.

I clutch the gold ballerina necklace at my throat, the only piece of jewelry I wear. "Thanks."

He leans his bike against the wall and disappears through the glass doors.

I stay there in the shade of the building. The hair under my helmet feels sweaty, so after making sure no one's looking at me, I take it off. I drum my fingers against my handlebars, recite prime numbers in my head. *Two, three, five, seven.*

Davy walks out, pizza box in his arms.

And then he stops and stares at something over my shoulder.

I turn, expecting another Marion look-alike.

But what I see makes my heart stop.

Parked five spots away is a black BMW X3. License plate BONES05.

Seth Montgomery's car.

They're back.

The Montgomerys live in the city during the year, but they've been spending their summers in Bier's End for as long as I can remember, all of them up at their grandmother's big old mansion on the dead-end street that gives the town its name. But when June rolled into July and there was no sign of them, I thought they were actually skipping this summer. Not that they've ever done that before. But then, I've never accused any of them of murdering my sister before, either.

The sweat on the back of my neck has turned cold, and at the same time, I'm mad at myself. I should have been able to feel it. There should have been a ripple in the air, a thunderstorm, *something* to warn me. So I could prepare.

Seth isn't even the one I want to talk to. In fact, he's the *last* Montgomery I want to talk to. But if he's here, it means they all are.

I can't see Seth right now. "Let's get out of here." I swing a leg over my bike—just as the door to the Wawa opens.

And there he is.

Tall, broad-shouldered, shock of black curls. Stubble thicker than I've ever seen it. White collared shirt with little blue stripes, untucked. Khaki shorts. Loafers, no socks.

Seth Montgomery.

My heart flips over in my chest.

Seth looks shocked. I don't know why; *we're* the ones who live here all year. But then he pulls himself together.

"Addie." He says my name like an accusation.

I swallow. "Seth." I say his name the same way, put my foot on my pedal, ready to ride off, even though my helmet's not on and Davy hasn't strapped the pizza to his bike. "If you'll excuse us—"

"I need to talk to you."

I steel myself. "I don't have anything to say to you."

His brows come together. "Well, I have shit to say to you."

"That's too bad. Now, can you please—"

"Addie—" Seth's eyes dart up and down the sidewalk, but the only person within earshot is Davy, staring at us wide-eyed. Seth drops his voice. "Can we talk? It's important."

"Is Marion here?" Davy blurts out then. Marion is Seth's cousin.

Seth turns briefly. "Yeah. She's at the house."

Davy's head whips around, even though their house is miles from here.

"What about Thatcher?" I ask. Marion's brother, another of Seth's cousins. The one Montgomery I *do* want to talk to.

Seth holds my gaze for a long moment before answering. "We're all here. Our grandma passed away."

I'm temporarily speechless. I haven't seen Mrs. Montgomery in forever. All our time running around in their backyard, we barely went inside the mansion, and in the past few years, Mrs. Montgomery stopped coming outside altogether. I should feel sad; that's how you're supposed to feel when people die. But I never knew her all that well.

And my mind is more caught on the fact that Thatcher Montgomery is here, on Bier's End, for the first time since last summer.

I need to think this through carefully. I can't just hop on my bike, pedal up to the Montgomerys' front door, demand to see Thatcher, and ask him, face-to-face, if he pushed Fiona.

But I *do* need him to see me. Maybe after a whole year of stewing in his guilt, it's eating away at him. Maybe all he needs is someone to come along and drag a confession out of him. I could bring my phone, secretly record him, take it to the cops—they'd have to listen to me then, wouldn't they?

Straight-up confronting the boy I suspect killed my sister isn't the smartest plan, I know. But I've exhausted every other option. I told the police what I thought. Over and over. And they didn't do a thing about it. Thatcher went back to school in England, his family name and his money protecting him. No one was ever arrested. They called Fiona's death an accident. That, or suicide.

No one would listen to me, no matter how loud I was.

"I'm sorry about your grandma," I say to Seth. "But you and I have nothing to talk about." I jerk my head at Davy. "Strap the pizza on and let's go."

But Davy doesn't budge. "Is Marion okay?"

"It's been a hard year for everyone." Seth looks at me again.

"Davy. We need to *go*."

I don't like the look on Davy's face—like he's already calculating how he's going to run into Marion—but thankfully, he does as I say.

I'm half-afraid Seth will try to physically stop me from riding away. Block my path, demand to know why I never returned any of his texts or DMs. But he doesn't move. Just watches as I fasten my helmet, despite my shaking hands, and start down the sidewalk—nearly toppling over as I do.

On the ride home, Davy and I don't speak. We glide past small suburban houses and maples with their leaves drooping in the heat. To the west, the sun is sinking into the tree line. Somewhere, someone is mowing a lawn, the steady buzz of it like the drone of an insect.

I barely see any of it. All I can see is Seth's face, that expression: surprise, anger, determination.

Desperation.

I need to talk to you.

On Bier's End there are summers when nothing happens, and summers when everything does.

I touch the gold ballerina at my throat.

When we were little, Fiona and I lived for summer. Running through the tangle of woods that separates our house from the Montgomerys', meeting the Montgomerys for the first time. Thatcher was two years older than Fiona; his sister Kendall and their cousin, Seth, were both Fiona's age. When Davy and Marion got old enough, they'd tag along, too. And summers became synonymous with the Montgomerys: manhunt in the woods between our houses, cannonballing into their giant pool. Daring one another to hop the old stone wall to the abandoned Bier mansion next door and screaming when the ivy brushed our ankles.

Searching for treasure. Legend has it the last Bier took what was left of the family fortune and buried it somewhere on their acres of land.

Sometimes, in my wilder moments, I think maybe that was what Fiona was doing on the Bier property the night she died. Searching for buried treasure.

Because I can't come up with any other explanation.

She must have been drunk, some people said, wandered off from the Founders' Day parade and fallen down the ravine. But Fiona didn't drink.

She must have been meeting up with a boyfriend, others said, and something went wrong between them. But Fiona didn't date.

She must have done it on purpose, more people whispered. But Fiona wasn't suicidal. She was leaving for the American Ballet Academy in a week. Her life's greatest dream realized.

It was an accident, the police finally said. She must have tripped and fallen. But Fiona wasn't clumsy.

I didn't believe the police's verdict. I'm not sure how many other people did, either. Someone saw Fiona and me arguing at the parade. Details from the investigation surfaced somehow: The only sign of another person near her that night was a strand of my hair on her tank top. Her journal had gone missing.

None of that proves anything, of course. My hair could have gotten there anytime. And I don't know what happened to her journal. I didn't take it.

It took me a little while to see past the murmurs of *I'm so sorry for your loss*, the Cs on tests I should have failed. But the more time went on, the more things shifted. Once I told Jeremy what Seth and I were doing the night Fiona died and he broke up with me for good, I stopped talking to everyone except my own family. People started avoiding me, looking away when they saw me coming. Without Fiona, without Jeremy, without any of the Montgomerys here anymore—it was like the membrane that had protected me was gone. I became a hermit crab, coating myself in hardness.

That's who I am now. Who I need to be.

What I *don't* need is to hear whatever Seth Montgomery has to say about last summer. About that night or the morning after. I don't need the drama, I don't need his questions, and I definitely don't need him looking at me in that way he does.

It's only been a year since Fiona's death. Too soon for anything more to happen. Far too soon.

2

DINNER CONVERSATION IS stilted. I brace myself, waiting for Davy to bring up Marion. But he just stands there at the kitchen counter, shoveling pizza into his mouth like an automaton. So I stop trying to talk to him and let my eyes wander around the kitchen of our old farmhouse: yellow tile, linoleum countertops, wooden cabinets from the seventies. We moved here from the city when I was too little to remember. My grandma had already passed away; my grandpa lived here with us until I was ten, when he died, too. We should be grateful, Dad's always said. We'd never be able to afford a house this size without them. Never mind that it's dated and drafty in the winter and has no AC.

After dinner, Davy wants to take Sadie—our part golden retriever, part who-knows-what—for her walk. He never takes Sadie for her walk. I'd bet the value of the Montgomery mansion he'll end up walking her right up to their door.

"No, I'll take her," I say. "Can you clean up?"

He frowns but apparently decides it's not worth the argument and starts loading the dishwasher. I watch him a long moment, debating what to say. I really don't want him chasing after Marion Montgomery again. When Davy was a little kid, after our mom left, he had no problem listening to me when I told him what to do and what not to do. But in the past year, things have shifted.

I take Sadie out, turn in the opposite direction from Bier's End. The sky is pink, the sun already gone below the trees, the crickets chirping, the lightning bugs just starting to emerge. I can't stop thinking about Thatcher. Just on the other side of the woods.

I tried telling the police about the argument I saw between Fiona and Thatcher Montgomery last summer. The rage in his eyes.

They didn't listen. So I tried telling the world. Or at least the world that was true crime enthusiasts on the internet. Anonymously, of course. I was afraid no one would believe me if I posted my Thatcher theories as myself, since me-as-the-murderer was another theory on Citizen Sleuths, the biggest true crime message board.

Some people listened to me. But not enough.

I'd hoped that keeping Fiona's case alive on the forums might mean it would make it onto one of those true crime podcasts, with someone dissecting it episode by episode. That it would garner enough public attention—*rich white guy literally gets away with murder*—that the police would be forced to reopen the investigation.

But that didn't happen. Nothing came from the hours I spent posting my theories except that I saw so many comments speculating about me that even *I* started to question why the cops hadn't interrogated me more thoroughly about that night.

My sister is dead, and someone needs to be held accountable.

And that someone is Thatcher.

All I need now is to get him to confess. He has to. The boy I knew wasn't a cold-blooded killer; I don't know what happened between them that night, but I do know he has to be regretting it. Maybe he even *wants* to confess, and it's his family who's holding him back.

Just one confrontation, and I can get Thatcher Montgomery behind bars, where he belongs. Then all of this will be over. Davy and I will go on to have a boring summer, and I'll actually get to leave for Rutgers next month like a regular person with a regular life.

When I get back home from walking the dog, my brother is waiting for me. As I suspected he would be.

"I'm going to go talk to Marion," Davy starts. "Even though she didn't answer all last year, I should at least say I'm sorry for her loss. Or I should, like, bring her flowers. And a card. That's what you do when someone dies—"

"Davy, no," I cut in.

His head lifts, a stubborn tilt to his chin. "Addie, she's probably upset. She might *want* to talk to me now."

To me, Marion Montgomery has always been an afterthought. Short and skinny, the same big brown eyes and chestnut hair as her siblings, never speaking when we were very little, later only in whispers and only ever to Davy. Last summer, Marion and Davy were fifteen, and suddenly they were missing at the same time, holding hands at the park, DMing each other late into the night.

I was worried, of course. A Montgomery was never going to end up with one of us, and Davy fell for her in the Davy-est of ways, wholly and without reservation or safety net. I figured it was only a matter of when, not if, she broke his heart.

I was right.

"If she wanted to talk to you, she would have called you back," I point out.

My brother flinches, and a stab of guilt goes through me. Davy doesn't just look all wide-eyed and innocent. That's his personality, too. He literally wouldn't harm a fly. When he finds one inside, he opens the window to let it out.

"I'm sorry, Davy. I really think we need to stay away from them." But even as I say that, my eyes stray to the window. I'm not about to tell him that I'm planning on heading over there the moment I figure out the best way to confront Thatcher.

"How can we do that, now that they're back in town?"

"They're probably not here for that long." But even as I say it, I know it's not true. They're not only here for the funeral. They're here to fight over the will. Like rich people do.

Davy pushes his hands into his hair. "Addie—I can't stay away. I was still dealing with losing Fiona, and Marion just *stopped* talking to me and—I want to know why. If it was because of me or because—"

He looks at me, and again I feel the guilt rise up.

One of Davy's theories is that Marion stopped talking to him because of me. I admittedly didn't give any thought to Marion and how she'd react when I started spreading my Thatcher-as-murderer theory, or how that might put a strain on Davy and Marion's relationship. It wasn't until my brother came to me and burst out that I had to stop talking about Thatcher all the time that I realized what I was doing was affecting him, too.

So I stopped. Publicly, at least. Davy doesn't know about Citizen Sleuths.

I can still see Seth's face in my mind.

I need to talk to you.

He must have found out that I spent the past year accusing his cousin of murder.

I blocked him and all his accounts. I knew he'd defend Thatcher and didn't want to hear it. And he'd want to discuss the night we spent together, and I didn't want to speak to him about *that*, either.

And now he wants to talk to me.

More than likely, he wants to yell at me.

But if I want to confront Thatcher, I need a reason to be at the Montgomery property.

"I'll go see Seth," I tell Davy. "Find out what's going on. How long they'll be here. And I'll report back."

Davy's shoulders slump a little. The relief of having someone else decide. I miss that. "Tonight?"

I pull out my phone, unblock Seth's Instagram, and DM him.

Clearing. 8:30. Meet me there.

3

I WAIT UNTIL my dad gets home so there's someone to make sure Davy doesn't try to follow me. I don't tell him where I'm going, just that I need to go out for a run. Dad would not be okay with me being anywhere near the Montgomery mansion.

As I'm tying my shoes, Dad calls, "Stay on—"

"The main roads," I finish. "I know."

Bier's End isn't a dangerous town. At least, it wasn't before last summer. But losing one daughter obviously means my dad's a bit paranoid about the other and her habit of evening runs.

I poke my head into Davy's room to tell him I'm leaving. He's on his phone, probably staring at last summer's selfies with Marion. He looks up when he hears me. "Please just ask her why she wouldn't answer me."

"I will if I see her," I say.

It's a warm night, the air hot, suspended. The fastest way to get to the Montgomerys' is to cut through the woods to the back of the old Bier property and pass the ravine, where Fiona died. But I can't go that way anymore. So I stick to the street.

I pass house after house at a slow jog, the windows like eyes following my every move. Like they know I'm not supposed to be heading this way.

I reach the corner, pause at the old sign hanging on a wooden post. I don't know exactly how old it is, only that Bier's End the street was here before Bier's End the town.

There's a buzzing in my ears, an insect, cicadas, or maybe something else, some species found only here. At first glance the street looks the same—wild and dark, the few houses so far apart and set so far back from the road all you can see of them are their gateways, wrought iron, brick, stone. Old money. The old money that survived.

The Montgomery mansion is the third one on the left.

Brick columns frame both ends of the circular drive, the number and family name on a plaque. There's ivy everywhere. But it's not over-grown. There are flowers planted along the drive. The grass has been recently mowed.

For a second I just stand there, staring at the house. I think of the long line of money that built those high gates, those walls that keep them in, keep them safe—keep Thatcher Montgomery safe. And the anger rises in me again, and all I want to do is throw myself at it, claw at those walls with my bare hands, or maybe burn them down until there's nothing between Thatcher and me, nothing to protect him from what he's done.

I take a deep breath.

Before I reach the first column, I turn off the sidewalk and onto the dirt path next to the honeysuckle that skirts the house. The windows on this side are dark except one on the second floor, but I don't see anyone inside. I go past the porch, beyond the patio and the long expanse of mani-cured lawn. The pool, huge and elaborate, still covered up, even though it's mid-July. The pool house, bigger than my actual house, made of brick and filled with white wicker furniture, musty cushions, old paperbacks, deflated pool toys. The detritus of our childhood. I thought it all meant something once. That we'd built something here together. That we and the Montgomerys were important to each other. And now look at us. On opposite sides.

Behind the pool house is a barely there trail through the shrubbery. The grass is overgrown, the stones hardly visible. But my feet know where to step, the memories so sharp it's like it was only yesterday that I passed this way, instead of nearly a year ago. That curve in the path, that old pine tree, the blanket of needles that makes it smell like Christmas, bushes of forsythia, their flowers already gone—all leading to the clearing.

The place I was the night Fiona died.

I found the clearing one day when I was seven or so and decided it was my secret place. The summer grass was thick with wildflowers, buzzing with bees, and in the center of it all was a big blue-gray stone, like some kind of sacrificial altar.

In the days when our mom was still around, she'd go through phases of wanting us nearby, then telling us to go out and play and leaving us entirely to our own devices in a way I've since learned not a lot of parents do. The Montgomerys were under equally loose supervision, so it wasn't unusual to encounter one or all of them out in the yard on their own. I'd never seen them in the woods, though, so when I came back to this clearing and saw Seth here, too, we fought about whose it was. It's one of the earliest fights I can remember having with him, the precursor to hundreds more over the years. I told him it was mine because I was there first, and he countered it was his because it was on his property. He challenged me to a race, winner take all, which he promptly won. But then, in an oddly un-Seth-like moment, he told me I could use it when he wasn't there.

From then on, we'd occasionally find each other here at the end of a summer day. Whatever was going on between us when our siblings and cousins were around, whatever fight we'd gotten into, when we came here, it was set aside in favor of sitting on the rock and looking up at the sky and talking about anything that was on our minds.

And when I hit fourteen, we'd sometimes do more than talk.

I push that out of my mind.

As far as I know, no one else comes here. It's far back, almost to the state park, along the edge that runs up against the Bier property next door. The stone wall that separates the two is just twenty yards away, on the other side of the trees. You can climb the wall, follow a trail through the woods down to the ravine where they found Fiona's body. I think about it constantly—how close I was to my sister when she died.

I step around a tree and see it: at the center of the clearing, the sloping blue-gray rock.

And on that rock, a boy.

Seth's face is tilted toward the moon. His eyes are closed, one of his arms flung across his forehead like a shipwrecked sailor.

I don't make any noise. But his eyes open. He lifts his chin, props himself up on his elbows, and looks straight at me.

I cross my arms. "You have fifteen minutes before I'm out of here. So say what you have to say."

That twist of his mouth that is Seth Montgomery's version of a smile. He sits up, rests his arms on his knees. I can see the breadth of his chest under his shirt. His hair is its usual mess of curls. My fingers twitch with the memory of running my hands through it, tugging on it—

"You gonna stand all the way over there this whole time?" His tone, that edge of sarcasm laced with defensiveness.

I make myself walk forward. The grass grazes my ankles, my knees. This far back on the property, they don't bother mowing the lawn. No one ever sees this place except us and the deer.

Seth's looking at me: my athletic shorts, black running shoes, the ripped black tank top I cut the bottom off of, uneven and thready, matching my hair, which I also cut myself, dyed black myself. Last summer it was blond. I'm pale except for my nose and the tops of my shoulders, and I'm not as round as I was before; all the running I did this year turned my curves more angular. I like it better this way, even though I didn't really do it on purpose. I like being a human KEEP OUT sign.

I touch Fiona's necklace, then walk up to the rock. With Seth Montgomery, you can't show any fear. Not that I'm afraid of him. And he's not afraid of me. It's kind of a relief, having eyes on me that aren't speculating about whether I killed my own sister.

"I like the hair," he says.

I'm not sure about this. In town, he looked a little wild, a little desperate. Now he's almost . . . triumphant. Like in just getting me to come here, he's won some kind of game.

"I don't have time for that," I say. "What do you want?"

Seth's teasing look fades. "I want to know exactly what you told the cops about Thatcher."

I bite my lip. "He told you about that?"

A flicker of Seth's smile, but there's no humor in it this time. "No. But you just did."

Dammit.

He rises from the rock, comes to stand in front of me. "Thatcher barely talked to me at all this year. Hasn't been talking to anyone. My uncle and my dad tried to keep it under wraps, too. But I'm not stupid. There had to be a reason the cops called Thatcher in so many times, why he needed a lawyer. So one night, I eavesdropped outside my dad's study. Heard Thatcher had an 'accuser.'" His eyes don't leave mine. "You've known Thatcher as long as you've known me. Practically your whole life. And you really accused him of *murder*?"

Thatcher and Seth are nothing alike, in looks or manner. Where Seth is tangled dark curls and a surly expression, Thatcher looks like the rest of them: thoroughbred-brown hair, thin, serious-looking. He's unfailingly polite, has very white teeth, a politician's smile. He's majoring in finance, like he's supposed to, while Seth messes around at Columbia with art history and archaeology, pissing his father off. They have nothing in common. But they're close anyway.

Like Fiona and me were.

Seth would never believe Thatcher had anything to do with my sister's death. I didn't want to have to fight about it. But here we are.

His fists are balled at his sides, his eyes narrowed. He's angry, I realize. But so am I.

"I had—"

But Seth interrupts. "Thatcher had to fly back from Oxford to talk to the cops; my uncle was calling every top defense attorney in New York State. Meanwhile, no one would tell me what was actually going on. No one told me that it was *you*, making up stories—"

"Making up stories?" The rage courses through me and I have to physically stop myself from grinding my teeth. "So what do you think killed her, Seth? My sister, the dancer so good she got into the American Ballet Academy at eighteen, when normally they only take little kids, just *happened* to be walking along the edge of the ravine in the woods at midnight and then just *happened* to trip and fall?"

Seth's eyes dart around the clearing, then come back to rest on me. "I don't know. I was occupied all night. And so were you." My face flushes hotly, but I don't back up. "So whatever it is you think about Thatcher—"

"You have no idea—"

"So tell me!" He spreads out his arms. "You blocked me everywhere, wanted nothing to do with me after that night, but you went to the police and you accused my cousin of murder. The least you could do is tell me why."

This isn't smart. The smart thing would be to walk away. To tell him nothing. He's not on my side. He's on his *family's* side.

But I'm practically vibrating, I'm so angry. Because he's standing here accusing me of things without knowing *anything*. And some small, vicious part of me wants to see the look on his face when I tell him.

"Fine." The night gets hotter, the crickets louder. "A week before Fiona died, Thatcher showed up at my house, looking more pissed than I've ever seen him in my life. He banged on the door, yelling her name." Seth listens, not interrupting, even though he looks like he wants to. "I asked what was wrong, but he just shoved past me. He was about to go up to her room when she came down, looking freaked out. They got into Thatcher's car and hadn't even pulled out of the driveway when he started screaming at her."

Seth doesn't look surprised. Which makes *me* surprised.

"What were they fighting about?" he asks.

"I didn't say they were *fighting*, I said he was *yelling* at her. And I can't hear things when the windows are closed and the car's driving away from me."

Seth's expression doesn't change. "Fiona didn't tell you what it was about?"

I shake my head. "It took them a while to get back. I waited. She went straight to her room. Refused to talk to me about it."

I can still hear the bitterness in my voice. Fiona and I used to tell each other everything. All that changed last summer. If I'd only pushed her— insisted she tell me what was going on.

"None of that proves he killed her," Seth says.

I glare. "Yeah, I know that, thanks."

I went back to the police station a few times after the night she died. They had more questions for me. And I had more questions for them.

Why haven't you arrested Thatcher yet?

Detective Carter, dark brown hands folded in front of him, kind voice, serious expression that gave nothing away: *We cannot disclose details of this investigation to anyone, Miss Blackwood, even family of the victim—*

Detective Ramsay, squinty blue eyes that followed me across the room, lips that were too big for his face, a buzz cut he really should have let grow out a decade ago: *The only evidence we have that this fight even happened is your word.*

Because of course Thatcher denied it. And of course they took the word of the pedigreed Oxford rich boy over mine.

Seth runs a hand through his hair. "So that's it? That's the 'big fight' Fiona and Thatcher had that was all over Citizen Sleuths?"

It's my turn to be surprised. "You go on Citizen Sleuths?"

Seth nods shortly. "Let me guess. UnaOwen235711?"

I stare.

That's my username.

I don't confirm it, but the look on his face makes it clear he knows he's right.

"Goddammit, Addie." His voice is low, but I flinch as if he'd yelled. Because I know that tone. The yelling is about thirty seconds off. Once, when I was around ten, we got into a fight over who splashed who first in the pool. Thatcher, our self-appointed babysitter, sided with Seth, and I got so mad I took Seth's fancy watch and threw it in the deep end. He yelled so loud it made me cry. "Why didn't you just talk to me about this? Instead of posting all over the internet?"

I see red. "Maybe because you wouldn't believe me, like you're doing right now—"

"I believe you that it *happened*. Why would you lie about that?"

" 'To take suspicion off myself,' " I quote.

His eyes widen. "Who said that?"

"Detective Ramsay." I feel that rage again. At not only being dismissed like some dumb kid, but at the insinuation—the first time I'd heard it, but not the last—that I might have killed my own sister.

Seth shakes his head. "No one with any brain cells thinks you killed Fiona. Those posts on Citizen Sleuths are just people being stupid."

And my anger at Seth dissipates, just like that. It's infuriating the way he does that—works me up, makes me want to hit him, then says something to cut my anger down, make me think he might be on my side after all.

But I can't let him get to me. "Even if they don't really think I did it, one thing is clear: They don't give a shit." Seth stares at me, not interrupting. "If it was one of *you* whose body turned up at the bottom of the ravine, they'd be calling in the FBI to solve it. But not for us. Not for her. To them, Fiona's just another dead girl from a nobody family. They don't care that someone out there killed her. Just like—" My voice breaks, and I hate it. "Just like they didn't care about my mom."

Seth doesn't say anything for a long moment. Then, quiet: "Your mom left, Addie."

"You don't know that."

"She'd been telling your dad she wanted to leave, her stuff was gone—"

"They didn't even look for her. They—"

I break off. It's not like I have to tell Seth about my mom. The first summer without her, Fiona was ten and I was nine, both of us so fragile, a single misplaced word could break us. Davy, seven, was more bewildered than anything else. I pretended I was fine, for their sake, but the moment I was on my own, after a day of splashing around in the Montgomerys' pool, I came here to this very rock and bawled my eyes out. Seth found me, but instead of teasing me, he just sat next to me and let me cry.

I try to focus. "Whatever. I didn't come here to talk about my mom." I pause. "Where is Thatcher?"

Seth's mouth goes into a straight line. "I'm not letting you talk to him."

"Why not? If you really think he's innocent?"

His eyes dart in the direction of the mansion. "He's . . . not doing well."

I seize on that. "How so?"

"He's withdrawn. Tired. He lost weight this past year. I thought it was because he was upset about Fiona. And then I thought it was because he kept getting questioned by the cops. I asked him about what I saw on the boards. About their 'fight.' But he told me that it was all bullshit. That it never happened." His hands are on his hips, his body half-facing the house. The house where Thatcher is, right now. "He lied to me."

"And it didn't occur to you that it might be because he's guilty?"

He spins around. "*No*. I know Thatcher. He'd never— He was in love with her."

"Yeah, and she wasn't in love with him. Maybe the rejection finally got to be too much. Maybe that's what they were fighting about. Then maybe that night, at the parade, he tried to talk to her again. They went for a walk. She told him once and for all that it wasn't going to happen, so he got upset, and just—snapped."

Seth stares at me. There's a little scar over his left eyebrow that didn't used to be there. "That's the story you've been telling yourself."

I throw up my hands. "Because there *is* no other story! I looked into the other theories. Really, I did. I went to her ballet studio, talked to her teachers, her classmates. There were no 'jealous ballerinas.' No stalkers. No one at school had any issues with her. She wasn't dating anyone. Fiona had no enemies. Nothing else weird happened last summer. Except Thatcher yelling at her, and her refusing to tell me why. It *has* to be him."

He's shaking his head before I've even finished talking. "You're just looking for someone to blame. Someone other than yourself."

I feel like all the air has been punched out of me and, at the same time, like I'm burning so hot that it's a miracle I don't set the forest on fire. "Where do you get off—"

"I get off defending my *family*, Addie. Just because you can't think of anyone else doesn't mean you get to go around accusing Thatcher without any proof."

I close my eyes. Take a deep breath. This is pointless. I shouldn't have said anything to Seth. I shouldn't have even come here. I'm going to have to find a way to confront Thatcher without Seth's help.

I turn to go.

Then Seth's hand is on my arm. "Addie, wait."

It's the first time we've touched since that night.

I rip my arm away.

He holds up his hands. "I'm sorry. Just—can you wait a minute?"

I'm not sure why I listen, why I stand there as Seth runs another hand through his hair, paces back and forth in front of me. "Thatcher's been acting weird," he says.

"You already said that."

"No, I mean, even weirder. Just since we got here. The last time I saw him was last summer, so maybe this is just how he is now, but he walked into the house all . . . freaked out. Like there was a ghost waiting for him. Jumping at every little sound, holing up in his room. And more than once I've walked in on him on his phone, and he drops it the moment he sees me."

"Because he's *guilty*, Seth."

"Or because—"

Just then, we hear a shout.

Seth and I stare at each other.

The shout comes again. Loud. Male.

Coming from the Bier property.

4

I DON'T KNOW who takes off first. Only that Seth and I are tearing down the path to the wall, toward the shouts.

The trees are everywhere, branches reaching for my arms, scraping my skin. My breath is loud in my ears. I trip on something, a tree root, a rock. My hands barely hit the dirt before Seth is hauling me up. And then he's off running again, and I'm staggering after him.

We reach the wall—five feet high, made of flat, worn stones, covered in lichen in places, ancient-looking. Seth is over it impossibly quickly; I have to scramble up, my foot finding the hole I knew would be there. I jump down, the impact reverberating through my knees, and then I'm taking off after Seth through the trees on the other side.

I don't hear another shout. There's nothing but the crickets and cicadas and the sounds of our pursuit, our breaths, our feet scrambling over rocks and fallen branches. The dark presses in on all sides, hot and suffocating.

I round a bend, and there's the big stone circle we spent hours digging around as children, looking for treasure. I haven't been onto this part of the Bier property in years, not since our last treasure hunt ended the way they all did, in disappointment. I fly past it, after Seth, the woods loud in my ears.

And then I hear the trickling of water. The ravine.

My throat feels tight, my breathing shallow. Seth skids to a halt in front of me. I nearly run into him. A foot in front of us is where the land slopes sharply downward, culminating in a shallow, rocky stream twenty feet below. I strain to hear anything: that shout, that voice. But there's nothing.

I finally regain my breath. "Who was that?"

Seth's eyes are wild as he scans the landscape around us. He gulps in a breath. "I—I'm not sure."

I have no idea what to think. There's no sign of anyone here except us. But the darkness is full of unseen things, and I think of the other theories around Fiona's death, the ones I had no time for: that it was the ghost of the last Bier brother who killed my sister, that he still haunts these woods seeking vengeance on the brother who supposedly murdered him.

I am logical, practical, don't believe in anything I can't see with my eyes, feel with my hands. But I also grew up on Bier's End. I spent my childhood running around behind an abandoned mansion searching for buried treasure left by a cursed family, according to local lore. And one thing is certain: Something killed Fiona less than a year ago, right here, on a night like tonight. And standing here with the woods behind me and the hot, seething dark pressing at my back, the cold white moonlight making everything over into a silver-bleached world, it's all too easy to imagine I hear the slinking of something heavy through dead leaves, growing nearer.

The hairs on the back of my neck stand up. Someone is watching us. I'm sure of it.

I spin around, one hand grabbing Fiona's necklace, the other clutching on to Seth's arm. The crickets are reaching a crescendo, so loud I'm certain they'd drown out the sounds of anyone coming toward us. My heart hammers in my chest. I open my mouth, ready to let out a scream.

Seth's arm goes rigid under my hand. "There."

And he's running away from me, north along the ravine. I don't see what he saw, but I follow as fast as I can, not wanting to be left alone.

His legs are longer than mine. When I round the bend in the trail, I don't see him. "Seth?"

Just then I hear the sounds of scuffling.

"Seth!"

I stumble forward through the dark, aware of the empty space of the ravine to my left. I round another bend to find Seth at a rocky outcropping, staring over the edge of the ravine.

He inhales sharply, and I forget about what we heard to send us shooting through the trees, forget why we're here. I think he's seen something having to do with Fiona and hurry to his side to get a look.

At first I can't make sense of it.

Long legs, clad in khaki pants, contorted at an odd angle. Loafers. A button-down shirt, silvery blue in the moonlight. A shock of brown hair. Eyes, looking up at us, wide and staring.

It's Thatcher Montgomery.

And he's dead.

5

"MISS BLACKWOOD."

I blink against the fluorescent lights of the interrogation room to see Detectives Carter and Ramsay entering.

Déjà-vu. It's last summer, and I'm in this same room, under these same lights, looking at these same men. Except it's different this time.

With Fiona, I wasn't called to the police department until the day after. I didn't have to see her until the wake, when they'd cleaned her up, tried to make her look like she was only sleeping. I didn't have to see her body where it landed.

And I wasn't the one to call it in.

Seth and I had stared in horror at the bottom of the ravine. And then he darted forward. I woke up, grabbing his arm just before he skidded down the rocks after Thatcher. "Seth, no!"

He listened to me, frozen at the edge. But his eyes didn't move from the figure lying there.

"Thatcher?" His voice was a whisper, the question at the end of his cousin's name enough to break my heart. Because there was no question as to who it was. No question as to whether or not he was alive.

I held on to Seth, partly to keep him from joining Thatcher there, partly because I just needed something to hold on to. I finally got it together enough to pull my phone out of my pocket, call 911. Carter and Ramsay both arrived on the scene with the paramedics.

And now we're back here. They separated me and Seth immediately, pulling us each into our own rooms. I'm eighteen now, Seth nineteen, so no parents needed to be called.

Detective Carter settles his heavy frame down onto the chair across from me, while Detective Ramsay remains standing, leaning against the wall, arms crossed. Their classic stances. I haven't been in this room since October, and nothing's changed, not the coffee stains on the table, not the chip in the blue plastic chair I'm sitting in, not the relentless overhead light. It feels like a nightmare, one I'd woken up from, escaped, and then somehow been foolish enough to fall back asleep into.

Carter presses Play on the recorder next to him. "Detectives Carter and Ramsay, interviewing Adelaide Olivia Blackwood, July fifteenth, 2024, 11:04 p.m." He looks at me, folds his dark brown hands together. "Addie. Let's start at the beginning. Tell me what you were doing before you found the body."

"Thatcher." I hated when they said *the body*. They did that with Fiona, too. They should know by now how much I hate that. "We found Thatcher."

"Before you found Thatcher." Detective Carter has a deep, serious voice, the kind that should be narrating children's bedtime stories. Comforting in any other setting.

"I was with Seth," I say.

Ramsay lets out a loud exhale.

Detective Ramsay is not kind, not gentle, not comforting. I knew him before, sort of. He's my ex–best friend Gen's uncle. He's always made me vaguely uncomfortable, and I'd never been able to pinpoint why. Now I know: It's because he's a complete and total prick.

I open my mouth, but Carter holds up a hand. "Just walk us through your evening, please, Addie."

I swallow. "Fine."

I tell them about seeing Seth in town. Him wanting to talk to me. Deciding to hear him out.

"When did you leave your house?" Detective Carter asks.

"Eight thirty-ish."

"And then what?" Ramsay asks.

He's looking at me the way he did the last time. Like he knows I'm guilty and he's about to catch me in a lie.

But there's no way they can try and pin *this* on me. Seth and I were together when we heard Thatcher yell. There's no way it could have been me. *Or* him.

Of course, that means they'd have to believe both Seth and me. Something I'm not sure they've ever done.

I keep my voice and face calm, tell them about the fight we had. Being interrupted by the yell. Sprinting through the woods toward the ravine. Getting there too late.

Both detectives listen to my story with barely a blink. When I finish, there's a long pause.

Carter breaks the silence. "Did you see anyone else in the woods?"

I shake my head.

"Hear anything? Get any impression that there was anyone out there besides yourself and Mr. Montgomery?"

I hesitate. Almost tell them about that feeling. Of the dark pressing in, the sensation of eyes on the back of my neck. But it sounds silly now, in the bright lights of the interrogation room. I didn't actually see anyone. They'd think I was making things up.

I shake my head.

Ramsay eases himself off the wall. "We have techs combing the area now." His tone is almost conversational. "Same way we did last summer.

They didn't find evidence of anyone other than your sister then. With your hair on her, of course. What's the over/under on the chances they'll find evidence of anyone else this time?"

I stare at him. "I have no idea." I look to Carter then. "Do you think it was suicide?"

"People don't usually call out before committing suicide, Ms. Blackwood," Ramsay says.

My eyes flicker between them. "So you think someone killed him."

His eyes go lazily to me. "But how could that be? If you and Mr. Montgomery were the only ones there?"

The implication is heavy on the air. I dig my fingers into my bare knees. "We didn't . . . Why would we have called you, from the scene of the crime, if we were the ones who—"

"No one's accusing you of anything," Carter cuts in. "Now, can you tell me the last time you saw Thatcher Montgomery? Alive?"

That one's easy. "Last summer. The parade."

"You haven't seen or spoken to him since then?"

I pause. "I sent him a DM."

"What did it say?"

"*Did you kill her?*" I quote.

"Did he respond?"

"No. And then he blocked me."

"And what about Seth Montgomery?"

I shake my head. "We hadn't spoken, either. Until today."

Ramsay looks at me. "Really? You and your boyfriend didn't—"

"Ramsay," Carter says sharply.

I glare up at Detective Ramsay. How I wish I could just tell him to shut up. His fixation with the details of Seth's and my encounter last summer has always sent shivers of disgust rolling through me. I bet he's the kind of guy who watches weird, gross porn.

"Addie," Carter says, in his serious voice. "You hear how that sounds to us, right? You and Seth had a, uh, strong connection. And after that, you didn't speak at all for a whole year?"

I shift in my chair. "He DMed me a few times. Tried to call. I didn't answer."

"Why?"

"I was . . . trying to distance myself, I guess. I don't know."

Ramsay leans across the table, making me lean back. "You don't know—"

"Ramsay—"

I'm sick of this. "Okay. I do know. I didn't want to talk to the guy whose family was harboring the guy who killed my sister, who probably paid you off to never arrest any of them."

There. I said it.

Carter is, as always, impassive. Ramsay's mean little eyes get smaller and meaner.

"So your theory is Thatcher Montgomery killed himself?"

"I—" I falter.

We heard him yell.

"I haven't had time to think about it."

"Well." Ramsay leans back, looking satisfied. "Why don't you have a think on it, Addie? Think about how the only two people in the woods tonight were the same people whose only alibi for a nearly identical death were also each other?"

I stare. "That doesn't make any sense. Seth and Thatcher are—*were*—close. Like—"

I swallow. But I don't need to go on. Ramsay finishes it for me.

"Like you and your dear departed sister?"

The way his voice drips with contempt. The way this is all some game to him.

I don't even remember deciding to get to my feet. Just the rage that overtakes me. And suddenly Carter is standing, too, and in a flash,

Ramsay's leapt around the table and is twisting my arms behind my back so sharply I gasp, my eyes watering in pain.

"You are not to threaten a police officer, not verbally or physically—"

"Ramsay!" Carter barks. "Let her go."

The viselike grip on my arms is gone, though I can still feel the places where his hands touched my bare skin.

"I'll finish this up on my own," Detective Carter says.

I don't watch as Ramsay walks back around the table and out the door, shutting it behind him.

"Addie." Carter's voice is gentle again. "I'm sorry about that. Please sit down, and we'll go over your story again."

I sit, not looking at him, keeping my eyes on the table this time. I answer his questions. I rub my arms, imagining them starting to bruise where Ramsay grabbed me.

And I try not to cry.

6

I GET HOME around midnight.

Carter dropped me off, neither of us speaking on the way. The house is silent when I enter, except for my dad snoring in his armchair. I texted him and told him I'd run into Gen on my run and was hanging out at her place so he wouldn't worry. He doesn't know she and I haven't spoken in a year and a half.

I wake him, and as much as I don't want to burden him with this, I tell him a version of what happened.

My father's eyes widen. He's a tall, pale man, brown hair receding from a long, thin face. He's always been quiet, especially compared to my mom, and he got even quieter after she left. He was hardly home that next year, spending a lot of time at work, leaving Fiona and me and Davy with our grandpa. But then Grandpa died, and Dad was back, home every night by dinnertime. After Fiona died, he started coming home even earlier, asking us about our days, spending long periods in his chair on the porch, staring out at the trees, or peering at us like he was trying to see into our heads, make sure we weren't on the verge of leaving or dying the way Mom and Fiona and Grandpa did. It's only the last month or so that he's had some late nights at the office again, something about an insurance audit, leaving Davy and me alone to order pizza.

But something in his face tells me those late nights are over.

"And . . . you found him there?" Dad asked me. "At the ravine?"

I nod. "I—went to the Montgomerys'. Seth wanted to talk to me."

Dad doesn't yell. Not ever. When he's angry, he just speaks in this very low voice. "I didn't realize you were still in touch."

"We weren't. We just ran into each other at the pizza place earlier today, and he . . . wanted to talk to me."

"So he invited you to talk at the ravine?"

"No." I tell him we were in the Montgomerys' backyard when we heard Thatcher yell.

Dad closes his eyes, then opens them again. "It was foolish of you to go to the ravine with him."

"I'm sorry," I say. "Besides, Seth didn't do anything. He couldn't have. We were together the whole time."

"Addie—"

"I'm tired, Dad." I know he wants to talk more. Rehash it all. Assess me and see what kind of further damage I've sustained. I can't deal with it right now. "Can we talk about this tomorrow?"

After a moment, he nods. "Of course."

I leave Dad to double-check the locks on all the doors, then head up to see Davy, figuring he's waited up for me, but he's passed out on top of his bed, the lights on. I turn them off and pull a blanket over him, then after a short, hot shower to wash Ramsay's hands off me, I go to bed myself and toss and turn for hours. When I do fall asleep, it's worse than being exhausted and awake. I see Thatcher's unmoving body, his blank, lifeless stare, over and over, and then he transforms into Fiona. She's not still, though. She reaches toward me from the bottom of the ravine, trying to crawl up, her neck bent at an odd angle as she calls out, *Addie, look out— Addie, behind you—*

I wake up in a cold sweat before sunrise. My room looks ghostly in the gray light. It's on the first floor, an added-on room on the east side of the house. It has its own bathroom and its own door to the outside, making it convenient to sneak in and out of. Not that I've had many places to sneak off to this past year.

I check my phone to find a DM from Seth at 4:12 a.m.

I'd told the detectives the truth; about a week after Fiona died, Seth DMed me that he wanted to talk. I ignored him. He tried again a week after that, and again a few weeks later. Then he'd tried texting and twice he'd even called. No voicemail. I blocked him after that.

This DM just says, **You ok?**

I immediately feel like shit. Because I should be the one sending him that. He's the one who just lost his cousin who was like a brother to him.

Thatcher killed Fiona, I tell myself. I shouldn't be wasting time feeling sorry for Thatcher Montgomery. But the seeds of doubt Seth planted inside me have grown in the night. They're even bigger this morning.

We heard him call out.

The police aren't treating this like a suicide.

Those eyes on the back of my neck in the woods.

I shouldn't be talking to Seth. Detective Carter told me as much before I left. *During the course of this investigation, I advise you not to speak about any of this with Mr. Montgomery.*

But it's not like I have friends left to talk to anymore.

And I need to talk to *someone*.

I look down at Seth's DM. I'm sure if I was able to afford a lawyer, they'd also advise me not to answer. But Seth is grieving, possibly alone, the way I was last summer. And he would answer me. I know he'd answer me.

Not really. You?

The answer comes almost instantly. **No**

I'm sorry.

Then I type, **Do you want to talk?**

I pause before I hit send.

Seth and I have never been best friends. But we know each other in that way only someone who's known you since you were little can. We've spent every summer together since I was five years old. But we've never talked during the school year. As kids, we bickered and competed over anything and everything: who could run the fastest, who could climb a tree the highest, who could find the Bier treasure first. Seth and I would seek each other out in any game, from manhunt to our annual cannonball contest, and try to get the other to lose. I was happy to argue with him over whatever topic had come up. He was always fun to argue with.

Even more fun to kiss.

The first time it happened was the summer after eighth grade, on the star-watching rock, after drinking butterscotch schnapps straight from the bottle. No one was more surprised than me. We were arguing—I can't even remember what about—and suddenly we were kissing. I couldn't tell you who kissed who first. The next day, we pretended like it had never happened.

The only person I told was Fiona. I still remember her smile, that little eye roll. *Took you long enough.* How annoyed I was that she'd seen it as inevitable. I resolved to not let it happen again. That resolve lasted a month. Then another week. Before I knew it, we were making out almost every night on that rock, and I was coming home and stealing Fiona's concealer to hide the marks he'd left on my neck.

We repeated the pattern the following summer, and the one after that. Never going any further. Never talking about it around the others, even though Fiona always knew where to find her concealer when it wasn't in her room. *Just admit you're in love with each other,* she told me once. I told her never to use that word regarding me and Seth again. He could never actually *like* me like that. It was just a summer thing. Just a way to pass the time. It could never go beyond that.

When me and Jeremy started dating for real, midway through junior year, I decided to put Seth and his kisses out of my mind for good.

Until last summer, the night Seth and I became inextricably linked.

And last night, that link grew stronger.

I should never have set foot back on that street.

But I did. I can't ignore Seth now.

I hit send.

A moment later, a response.

My lawyer told me not to talk to you

I almost laugh. Of course his family's already called him a lawyer.

I'm about to type **Fine** when Seth writes, **Will you come to Thatcher's wake?**

I'm already shaking my head.

I don't think that's a good idea
Please?

I stare. I don't think I've ever heard Seth say *please*.

Before I can think it through, I write back, **ok.**

7

I SHOULDN'T HAVE come.

It's four days later, and my dad, Davy, and I are at Thatcher Montgomery's wake. The funeral, which apparently takes place tomorrow, is private, just for family, but the wake is open to the whole town. Davy insisted we come.

The morning after Thatcher's death, I told Davy what happened, the remains of our cereal in front of us.

My brother's eyes were round. "Is Marion okay? Did you see her? Did you—"

"I don't know," I said. "I didn't see her or talk to her. I'm sorry."

He looked down at his phone, then back up. "Was it . . . another accident?"

Davy has always claimed to buy the police's theory that Fiona's death was an accident. I'm not sure if that's what he really thinks, or if he doesn't want to believe his girlfriend's family is capable of murder. But he has to know that *two* accidents, almost exactly a year apart, is incredibly improbable.

"I don't know," I told Davy. Then I fixed my eyes on Dad. "All I know is it wasn't suicide."

I hated my dad's theory the most. That Fiona had grown up to be too much like our mom. That that's what probably happened to Mom, too.

Fiona was under a lot of pressure, he would say whenever we talked about it. *You don't know what's going on in someone's head. She could have just decided it was all too much.*

Or Thatcher could have pushed her, I would answer.

But then: Who pushed Thatcher?

Dad cleared his throat. "If the police want to talk to you again, I should be there."

"Dad, I'm eighteen."

"That doesn't mean I can't come with you."

"I think it does, actually."

His eyes went to his phone. "I could call— A lawyer would—"

"Dad." The last thing I need is him blowing our meager savings and my and Davy's college tuition on a lawyer. "No one's accusing me of doing anything to Thatcher." Yet. "I'll be fine." Probably.

Dad let it drop, for the moment.

The next day, Thatcher's death was all over the internet. All over Citizen Sleuths. Links to Fiona's death were obviously made. I saw theories about serial killers, forest ghosts, that it was a guilt-induced suicide.

That it was Seth. That it was me.

I know you're not supposed to read the shitty things people say about you online. But I needed to see what they were saying. There's this one user in particular, RdHerrng41, who just *loves* discussing their theory that I killed Fiona because I was jealous of how good she was at ballet.

I was jealous. But not of Fiona. I was jealous of ballet for taking her away from me.

Now RdHerrng41 was back, positing that I killed Thatcher because he had something on me. Someone else wrote that Thatcher actually *did* kill Fiona, and I killed him for revenge. I read all the threads about me until my head spun and my screen was swimming before my eyes.

I didn't want to go to Thatcher's wake. But there was no way Davy would be deterred from the chance to see Marion. And I wasn't about to make him go without me.

There was also the fact that I told Seth I'd go.

I haven't heard from him since that night. And if we aren't supposed to be talking to each other, I'm not sure if being in the same room is the best move. But I know Seth, know how close he was with Thatcher. He's going through what I went through last summer. And the only person who can understand that is me.

So the afternoon of the wake, it was with a mingled sense of dread, empathy, and obligation that I put on an itchy black dress, too hot for mid-July, slicked on tinted lip balm, and touched Fiona's little gold ballerina necklace before climbing into the front seat of my dad's car.

I can feel the eyes on me as we make our way across the parking lot of McCarthy's Funeral Home, a small, sad brown building with green awnings. Mrs. Rodriguez, Gen's mom, stands a few car lengths from us. Her brows come together the moment she sees me, and she leans in closer to whisper something to the woman she's standing with. I look away.

Mrs. Rodriguez is Detective Ramsay's sister. Rodriguez is her married name. She was never all that nice to me, even when Gen and I were little. I never really knew why. Is Ramsay allowed to tell people details of the case? I don't think so, but I also don't think Ramsay's the most ethical person in town. Like, how else would the detail about my hair on Fiona's shirt have gotten out on Citizen Sleuths if he hadn't told somebody?

More eyes turn toward us as we get closer to the funeral home. It feels like it's only been weeks since I was last here, instead of an entire year. People were looking at me then, too, but at Fiona's wake, it was in sympathy. The stares didn't come until later.

I do the same thing I did then: straighten my back, keep my eyes trained ahead, and recite prime numbers in my head.

Two, three, five, seven, eleven, thirteen, seventeen—

My dad is in front of me, showing no signs of noticing the heads swiveling toward us. Davy shuffles along behind. I know he's scanning the crowd, looking at everyone we pass, searching for Marion.

The line to get in starts before we even reach the steps. The whole town has turned out for this. And they're not just here to pay their respects to Thatcher and the Montgomerys, a family who's only ever here in the summer. No. They're here for the gossip. This thing that's ripped apart the Montgomerys' lives, and which I am absolutely certain has not finished messing with mine, is entertainment for most of them. I want to scream at them all to go home.

But I don't.

We join the line. I touch Fiona's necklace and try to only look straight ahead, but I can't help looking over at Davy, who's twitching like someone's put ants down his shirt.

I nudge him in the side. "She won't be back here. She'll be up front with her family."

My brother blinks at me. "Right. I know. I just want to be *prepared*."

I want to tell him I don't think there really is a way to prepare yourself for seeing your first love who entirely ghosted you ever since one of your siblings was murdered and whose sibling has *also* just been murdered in an eerily similar fashion. But you can't be flippant and sarcastic with Davy. He was a serious kid who's grown into a serious teenager, and it's not like life here has ever done anything to bring any levity to that.

The line inches forward till we're past the lobby of the funeral home. More people are turning to look at me. I stay between Davy and the floral wallpaper as we approach the main room, the one with the chairs set up in neat rows, flowers and photographs lining the walls. And up front, the family.

Davy stiffens. I have to stop myself from grabbing his hand, not only for him but for me. I clutch on to Fiona's necklace instead. Fiona's wake and funeral felt like a dream I had, not a thing that actually happened.

I remember this room being much bigger. I felt tiny in it, like a doll in a room of oversize furniture. I remember the floral wallpaper, lurid and too bright, blending with the actual flowers in the room, too many of them, a jungle, sickly sweet and green and pink and twisting out at me, carnivorous, ready to snap me up if I took my eyes off them. I remember not wanting to go anywhere near the casket, near whatever cold, waxy doll they'd put in there that was not Fiona, but Davy couldn't bear to be by it, and my dad looked like he'd collapse right into it, and so I stood closest to the casket, shielding them. I remember thinking it was the wrong color, too dark for Fiona. Fiona was light, the way I used to be, before; blond hair, blue eyes, pale pink leotard and skirt. But it's not like a pink casket would have made things any better.

There are still mornings when I wake up and my first tangled thoughts are of Fiona, if she has dance today or if she'd have time to hang out. My only sister and first friend. Just a year apart from me in age. Giggling inside our blanket fort on New Year's Eve, holding hands on the first day of school, plotting to marry brothers and always live near each other. I slept in her bed for six months after Mom left. She's the one I told when Seth first kissed me. When Jeremy first did. I missed my mom, of course I did, but Fiona was the one I knew I couldn't live without.

Sometimes I still don't believe it's true. That she's gone.

And now Seth will know what that feels like.

Before I'm ready, we're next in line. I wish suddenly, fervently, that I'd been a coward, that I'd stayed home.

Someone in front of me moves, and there's Seth in a black suit, black hair slicked down, stubble shaved away, handsome face impassive. He stands next to his petite, dark-haired mother as she nods at people giving their condolences. There's none of the grief hanging on him that I saw at the ravine. But I'm not fooled. He's good at hiding his feelings.

Someone else shifts, and then I see Seth's uncle and father, the brothers, the patriarchs. Thatcher Montgomery Sr. is an older, broader version of his son: gray-streaked brown hair, chiseled features, expensive suit over powerful shoulders. He looks older than I remember, or maybe that's the shadows under his eyes. Seth's dad, Harold Montgomery, is shorter than his brother, more stocky than muscular, has darker hair and less of it. I don't know either of them very well—they were mostly in the city during our summers together—but an ache goes through me when I look at Thatcher's dad, his mom next to him, trim and blond and botoxed, wrapped up in a dark navy dress. The end of her nose is pink where her foundation has worn off, and the thick eyeliner and obviously fake lashes can't conceal her red-rimmed eyes. I have a sudden image in my head of what my own mother might have looked like if she'd stuck around, if she'd cared enough to be standing here beside us while Fiona lay dead in her casket. Not for the first time, I wonder, wherever my mother is, if she's still alive, if she even knows.

The last of the Montgomery family comes into view. Marion and her sister, Kendall.

Next to me, Davy tenses.

Marion looks a little thinner, a little paler than I remember, but she's basically the same: brown-gold hair and big brown eyes. Today her hair's in neat, unnatural curls, and she's wearing too much makeup, thick eyeliner smudged from crying, foundation that tissues have rubbed away in places. The curls and makeup make her look older. And a lot more like Kendall.

Kendall Montgomery was Fiona's friend, never really mine. I can't blame her for that, though. I'd pick Fiona over me, too. Kendall has the same neat, unnatural curls as her sister, her makeup more artfully applied, the way it always is. But even through that, I can see that her eyes are the reddest of all.

I wonder how much Seth told her about that night. What she'll do when she sees me.

Right as I'm thinking that, Kendall's eyes go to mine and cut quickly away.

The woman in front of her says something, and Kendall leans forward to embrace her, giving her a smile I can tell is fake even from here. And then, so subtly I wouldn't have seen if I wasn't staring at them, she nudges Marion in the side. And Marion turns and sees us.

Sees Davy. Her eyes widen. Her lips part.

She still has feelings for him. It's written all over her face. It makes me think it wasn't Marion's choice to cut Davy off after last summer. Someone else made it for her.

Kendall murmurs something I can't hear to the woman, then grabs her sister's arm, and the two of them walk out of the room.

I blink. They just ran away from us.

But I don't have time to see Davy's reaction. The woman in front of me is gone, and now I'm face-to-face with Seth.

"Sorry for your loss." I echo the words of everyone who came before me.

"Thank you." His voice is odd, formal and without its usual inflection of sarcasm. We don't touch, just nod, but his eyes are locked on mine.

Then Seth stumbles, grabbing on to my arm for balance. I'm taken off guard but manage not to fall into Davy before Seth straightens up.

"Sorry," Seth says. He gives me one last look, and then it's time to move on.

That was weird.

I repeat the empty words to his mom, barely hear her murmured thank-you. Then to his dad. I glance up and am surprised to find Harold Montgomery staring at me.

He seems angry.

My heart drops to my shoes.

Does he know I was there that night? Does he know about last summer? Does he resent me because he thinks if it weren't for me, Seth would have been safely tucked up inside his house both times, nowhere near any murder investigations?

Or does he think I killed Thatcher, too?

I can't think on it anymore. Thatcher's parents are next.

I step in front of Thatcher Sr. "Sorry for your loss."

I feel the family patriarch's eyes on me. I glance up, afraid I'll find him glaring at me, too. But his expression—it's not anger or anything close to that. He looks like he's searching for something in my face. I don't understand it.

Virginia Montgomery's face is steely as she gives me a stiff nod.

And then there's no one left to offer condolences to, and we're at Thatcher's casket.

It's open. I don't want to see him, but I can't help it.

I knew Seth's cousin as long as I've known Seth, but it's not like we were ever close. He was three years older than me, but it always seemed like more than that, probably because he was so serious all the time. My memories of Thatcher are of him frowning at his phone, playing chess on the patio with his friend Caleb Jones. Bickering with Kendall, horsing around with Seth, telling Marion he needed to walk her back to the house, it was past her bedtime. Talking to Fiona about ballet, actually seeming interested when she launched into her detailed explanations on the differences between a temps de l'ange and temps de poisson.

Screaming at her, inside his car, last summer.

Lying dead at the bottom of the ravine.

The boy in the casket is too thin under his suit, his skin waxlike and too pale. I glance away as fast as I can, but it's too late; the image of Thatcher lying there is stamped on my brain. Like the image of Fiona always will be.

Davy still looks dazed. Dad is just behind him, his face blank. I wonder if coming to these things makes him think of Mom. Wonder if he'd feel better if he'd been able to put her to rest instead of wondering where she is.

Suddenly I'm too hot, itchy. The floral stench is choking me. I need to get out of here.

The outer room is crowded, and it slows our way to the door. Someone bumps into me, and I trip over my own feet. Two hands catch me just before I hit the ground.

I whip my head up to see Jeremy Reagan staring back at me.

My ex-boyfriend.

He looks ridiculously good—he always does, but especially now, in a suit and tie. It's bizarre being this close to him again. His hands are warm on my bare arms. He realizes he's still touching me and drops his hands, then pushes his moppy brown hair out of his face.

"Addie. Hey."

Jeremy, Gen, and I used to be best friends. Gen lives in the same trailer park as Jeremy, just a block away, less than a mile from my house. Her dad ran out on her family around the same time my mom left us, and a month later Jeremy's dad died of lung cancer. It was also the year Fiona's dance lessons got more intense. Jeremy, Gen, and I would sleep over at each other's houses at least once a week, talking late into the night, dubbing ourselves the "One-Parent Club," and trying not to cry. We were nine.

Sophomore year of high school, Jeremy became starting quarterback on the football team. He went from my friend Jeremy to Jeremy Reagan, the hot star athlete raised by his heroic single mother, her just barely able to afford the trailer they lived in on her waitress's wages, him promising to buy her a big, beautiful house once his pro football career started. It was so Hallmark Movie it sometimes made me cringe, but I couldn't fault Jeremy for that. There were new friends, and there were girls, so many of them, everywhere.

Of course I was attracted to Jeremy. Everyone was. When, in the spring of junior year, he told me that he liked me—I couldn't say no. I didn't want to. Finally, here was someone who was right for *me*. We were from the same town. We had been best friends forever. He wouldn't want to keep me a secret. Just being with him made me feel better about myself. Like I was worthy of a real relationship. Of real love.

We'd never talked about it directly, but I knew Gen wouldn't be happy about me and Jeremy. Two of us dating would change everything. But I thought we could survive it. I decided to be honest with her. I told myself I wasn't doing anything wrong.

But Gen didn't see it that way. She screamed at me that I'd messed everything up. Our friendship ended after that. Jeremy stopped talking to her, too, either in solidarity with me or because she wasn't talking to him, I wasn't sure. Gen became an open wound; I did my best not to poke at it.

Jeremy and I were together for six months. And we were happy. Until I ruined it.

A little over a month after Fiona died, I confessed to Jeremy what Seth and I had done, giving him an excuse to leave me. When I saw him at school, I always looked the other way. I ate lunch alone in the library. I didn't go to any more football games.

"Um, hi," I manage. It's the first thing I've said to him since we broke up.

He runs a hand through his hair, his eyes shifting away, then back to me. "Is it true—"

"Jere, there you—"

And then Gen is standing next to him.

Putting her hand on his arm.

Shock and anger jolt through me.

I didn't know he and Gen were talking.

Were touching.

Gen looks at me, and her eyes widen. I think I see a faint bloom of color on her tan cheeks. But she doesn't say anything to me, just leans in to whisper something in Jeremy's ear.

I can't think about them right now. About whether or not they're together. I can't.

I catch up to Davy, grab his arm, and hurry us the rest of the way out of the funeral home, not caring that I'm bumping into people.

Dad is outside, talking to a woman I don't recognize. I don't see anyone else I know. But there's still a prickling at the back of my neck. I need to get out of here.

"Let's wait for Dad at the car," I say to my brother.

He's looking over his shoulder. "Do you think Marion—"

"She won't be coming out until after everyone leaves. You can't talk to her here." I tug on his arm. "Come on."

Davy's shoulders slump, but he stops resisting. Together, we weave our way through the parking lot until we reach Dad's car. He has the keys, so we just wait there in the gray midmorning, summer heat trapped under the gathering clouds. I wipe my hand across my forehead. I'm sweating. My dress feels heavier than it did when I put it on.

A buzz comes from my dress pocket.

I frown. I thought I put my phone in my bag.

I reach into my pocket and pull out an iPhone that is not mine.

There's a Post-it attached to it that says simply *070520*.

Seth, bumping into me.

I rip the Post-it off and enter the passcode into the phone, where a text message pops up.

It's Seth. Use this to message me

I look at Davy, but he isn't paying attention; he's still glancing back at the funeral home.

I close out of the message before he can see. "I'm getting Dad. We need to go. Now."

8

SETH WASTES NO time.

Need to talk to you ASAP, he texts me on my new phone moments after I get home. **The clearing? 9?**

I set out after dinner, under the guise of another late run. Dad tried to stop me, but I begged him, told him how important it was to me, how much I needed normalcy. I promised to stay on the main roads. To not go near the Montgomerys'. I feel bad for lying. But I have to know what's so important for Seth to sneak me a phone.

Plus, I know *Seth* isn't dangerous.

The sky is the deep blue of dusk, and a waxing moon is rising. When I emerge from the forsythia, he's already there on the rock. His fancy mourning clothes are gone, though his face is still unnervingly smooth, making him look younger. He's in his usual city-boy outfit, white collared shirt and expensive brand-name shorts, sockless loafers.

He sits up straight when he sees me. "Hey."

Up close, I can see the red rims around his eyes. I was right. He held it together in public but let it out when he was alone. I don't know what it says about us that he doesn't have a problem with me seeing him this way. Maybe it's because he's seen me like this before.

"How are you doing?" I ask.

He makes space for me on the rock, runs a hand over his face. "We need to talk."

I climb up next to him. "Thanks for the phone, by the way."

He nods. "My dad, my uncle, and my lawyer all told me not to talk to you. And maybe I'm being paranoid or whatever, but they could be monitoring my phone. So I called up this guy who gets people stuff like this. It's pay per month, not supposed to be traceable. We can talk freely on it."

"Why don't they want you talking to me?"

"They're . . . worried."

"About me?"

Seth hesitates. "You can't tell anyone any of this."

"You can trust me," I say, and mean it.

He lets out a laugh that sounds more like a bark. "I think you may be the only person I can."

I exhale. "Being each other's alibis has its advantages."

Seth looks at me. "Addie, it's not just that. Even if I had no idea where you were those nights, I would never think it was you."

I hug my knees to my chest. "I know what they're saying. I'm on the boards. Before, they were suspicious because my hair was on her body. Or because her journal was missing from our house and there was no sign of a break-in. Or they thought I was jealous of her dancing, because I'd dropped out of ballet lessons when I was six. And *now* they're saying I killed Thatcher to avenge her."

"It's only a few random idiots," Seth says. "Not everyone."

"That doesn't mean everyone isn't thinking it. People were looking at me at the wake today."

"No one was looking at you. No one even knows you and I were there that night, except the cops. Stop going on those boards, it's making you paranoid."

My laugh is short. "I'm a big girl by now, Seth. I can handle it."

"I know." He rubs at that new scar by his eyebrow. "I just . . . don't want things to be worse for you."

I look at him, his brown eyes leached of color in the moonlight, the way his curls shine silver. Something has changed between us. All the anger of our initial meeting a few days ago is gone. If Fiona's death tore us apart, in a weird way, Thatcher's might be bringing us back together. Maybe because I know what he's going through. Maybe because he's the only person whose whereabouts I can account for during both murders. But whatever it is, there wasn't a part of me that didn't consider coming here to talk to him tonight.

Seth lets out a breath. "So, according to my lawyer, judging from the questions they were asking—they're looking at me. For sure."

I close my eyes. Of course Ramsay and Carter didn't believe my testimony.

Then I open them. "Why do they think you'd kill your own cousin?"

Seth's jaw flexes. "My grandmother's will," he says flatly.

I stare. "What about it?"

"She left us money, all the grandchildren. But the wording is weird. It specifies that the oldest grandchild gets more than the rest."

I let that sink in. "Your birthday's a month before Kendall's."

He nods. "Yup."

"But—did you even know about that before?"

He lets out a breath. "Yeah. I did. It's one of the things my dad and uncle have been fighting about. Along with their own inheritances. I didn't care, I mean, Thatcher was always her favorite, and it's not like I even need—"

He cuts himself off, looks at me sideways. I know he's thinking of all our childhood arguments over the Bier treasure, how mad I used to get at the idea that Seth or his cousins would get any if they found it, because they would never need it as much as Fiona and I did.

"So that gives you a reason," I say.

"Otherwise known as a motive."

"But—our stories must have matched. Which means we were telling the truth."

"Or it means we did a good job of making sure our stories would match." He looks at me.

I blink. "They think I *helped* you? Why?" But it comes to me before he has to say it. "Do they think I was getting revenge or something?"

"Just three days ago you were certain Thatcher did it," Seth says. "And you told the cops that. More than once."

"But then—do they think Thatcher killed her, and then you and I killed him? For different reasons?"

Seth runs a hand over his face. "I don't know. All I know is they're looking at me, so it makes sense they're looking at you, too. We were the only people they know were in the woods that night. Our alibis for both murders are each other. We have an existing relationship we told them about." He rubs one eye. "I'm not sure they're about to immediately throw us in jail without any actual evidence. But being the suspect of a murder investigation doesn't look great, as my dad keeps reminding me. Colleges can kick you out for stuff like that."

I blink. That hadn't even occurred to me. "Even if you never get arrested?"

"Yeah, they have these morality clauses where they can make you leave if you do something they consider wrong. My dad said with the money we're paying, there's no way that'll happen, but . . ." His voice trails off.

I feel ill. "But a scholarship kid might not be so lucky." I put my hands in my hair. Another way life is easier for him than me. Just because he was born into a family with money and I wasn't. "So if I ever want to make it to Rutgers, and then Stanford, I can't have anyone suspecting me," I say dully. "Like, not even a little bit."

"That might not be the case. But someone else getting arrested for this and having the question answered once and for all would help, yeah. Not to mention, the cops are going to be wasting time looking into you and me. And in the meantime, the real killer's still out there."

A chill goes down my spine. I spin to look behind me, but there's nothing there except the trees and the dark.

Teaming up with the person whose family I thought was responsible for this all year might not seem like the best move. But I *know* it wasn't Seth. And I don't think his family is behind this anymore, since Thatcher was one of them. Which means it's someone else out there, someone I haven't even considered.

Someone the police won't be considering, either.

"So you have about as much faith in Carter and Ramsay as I do," I say.

"If by that you mean none, then yeah." Seth scowls at the darkness. "They've had a whole year to find out who killed your sister. They came up with *She must have tripped.*" He shakes his head. "No way. I think someone killed her. And now someone's killed Thatcher, too."

I close my eyes. Feel that familiar rage rise up in me.

But this time, it's not directed at Thatcher.

It's directed at me.

A touch on my shoulder. "You okay?"

"I'm so stupid," I whisper. "I spent the whole year fixated on him, and it was someone else this *entire time*—"

"You're not stupid," Seth says quietly. "It did make sense, as far as theories go."

"Oh, now you think it made sense?"

"If someone didn't know Thatcher, didn't know he'd never do

something like that, it would make sense," he corrects. "I was so pissed at you because I thought you did."

"I thought I did, too," I say. "But if I've learned anything, it's how much people can change." I'm thinking of Fiona, of Gen, of Jeremy. "Nothing stays the same around here."

"Nothing stays the same anywhere." He shifts next to me. "But what I was about to say right before we heard Thatcher yell—what if he didn't do it, but he knew who did?"

I stare at him. "What makes you think that?"

"The way he wasn't talking to me—I chalked it up to his grief, or the stress of being questioned by the cops. But then when we all came back here and I saw him, he was acting like—like he was afraid of his own shadow. Like he was keeping a secret. A big one. And now . . ." He turns to look at me. "What if whoever it was killed him to keep him quiet?"

"But then, why wouldn't he *tell* anyone?"

"I think he was afraid of them, whoever they are." Seth picks up his phone. "We need to get organized. Make lists. What we know. What we don't know. Suspects. Motives. Things to look into. The way I see it, we have three main questions: Who killed Fiona? Who killed Thatcher? How are they connected?" He pauses. "And are any of us next?"

"That's four questions." I feel prickly, unsettled. Everything is in a giant tangle, and I have no idea how to unravel it. This is why I like math. It's never this complicated. I frown at him. "Are you, like, actually *into* this true crime stuff?"

Seth looks offended. "Hey. I don't make fun of your hobbies."

"What hobbies? I don't have any hobbies."

"Your running—"

"You do actually make fun of that."

"And your numbers—"

I freeze. "What do you mean?"

He narrows his eyes at me. "You recite numbers when you're nervous."

"How did you know that?"

"Because I've heard you?"

"I do it in my head!"

"And sometimes out loud. What's the big deal?" He blinks at me.

I had no idea I did that out loud. Enough for Seth, of all people, to notice.

He clears his throat. "Let's start with that night. Did you see anything or anyone weird? Before or after your fight with Fiona?"

I close my eyes.

Fiona died the night of the Founders' Day Parade. It was exactly one week before she was leaving for the American Ballet Academy. It was tradition, our whole family going to the parade together. Things had been off between us for months at that point. Fiona had always taken dance seriously, but ever since she'd gotten into that school, it had become her whole life. I felt her pulling away from us as surely as if it were something physical, dragging my heart out of my chest. She never hung out with me anymore, didn't want to stay up late talking. She was keeping secrets from me. I used to wonder if she was doing it on purpose, pushing all of us out of her life. I told myself we had time. To repair whatever was broken between us. It never occurred to me that time would run out so fast.

That night, instead of coming to the parade, she wanted to stay home and pack for school. In the end, I convinced her to come, but once we got to our spot on the parade route, she wouldn't stop fidgeting and checking her phone. It was clear she didn't want to be there. So I snapped at her.

Just admit you didn't want to come.

Fiona, closing her eyes and then opening them, like I was some kid who didn't understand. *I didn't want to come, Addie. I told you I have a lot to do before I leave.*

And packing is so much more important than spending a few hours with me and Davy.

That's not what this is! She actually raised her voice, and I felt a twist of satisfaction from getting her to get mad, to react, to do *anything* other than dance away from me.

She paused. I remember it so clearly. For a second I thought she was really going to tell me why she'd been acting this way. What that fight with Thatcher was about. Why she'd stopped confiding in me.

But then she shook her head. *You wouldn't understand.*

So explain it to me! I shouted back.

By then, people were looking. But I didn't care.

Fiona kept her voice low. *Addie. This is about the fact that you don't want me to go.*

Fine! I don't want you to go!

I'd never said it out loud. But there it was, hanging in the air between us.

Fiona stared. *So the thing that's mattered most to me my whole life, the thing I want most in the world, just means absolutely nothing to you?*

Ballet shouldn't be the thing that matters the most to you your whole life. We *should matter the most to you.*

She closed her eyes. It felt like another way to shut me out. *Addie. I've basically been the mom of our family since I was ten. I just can't do it anymore. I need to live my own life. I'm sorry that upsets you. But that's your problem, not mine.*

Then she turned and walked away from me.

So I hurled the worst words I could think of after her, and then I never spoke to her again.

And I've hated myself for it ever since.

"I didn't see anything weird," I tell Seth. "People were looking at us, but that's because I was shouting."

"So after that, you went and got in your fight with Jeremy?"

I was startled. "How do you know about that?"

"You told me about it. That night. Right here." He taps the rock we're sitting on.

I don't remember telling him about my fight with Jeremy. I don't remember telling him much of anything, once we started on the cider. "What else do you remember?"

I brace myself for some embarrassing comment, but instead Seth looks thoughtful. "You said you felt bad for wishing Fiona never got the scholarship she needed. You were afraid she'd join some traveling dance company and you'd never see her again. You were also . . . a little jealous, I think. That Fiona had dance. That Jeremy had football. And you didn't have anything. You said, 'Why don't I know what I love yet?'"

I can't remember telling him that. But I can remember feeling it. Because I *still* feel it.

"I've always remembered that," he says, half to himself. "'Why don't I know what I love yet?'"

"You love old rocks," I point out. "And falling-down castles. Anything buried in the ground you can uncover."

Seth smiles. "I *like* those things. I don't know if I love them." Then he switches back into interrogation mode. "So you told me you fought with Jeremy, but you didn't go into much detail. What did he say to you?"

"Why do you need to know that?" Seth never wanted to talk about Jeremy before, so it's weird he wants to now.

A funny look goes over his face, but then it's gone. "I don't know. Could be relevant. Sometimes when we go over old memories, we remember new things."

I think back. At the edge of the downtown, in front of the old theater, Jeremy's face in front of me. I told him about the fight with Fiona—and he sided with her. Said she was right about me, that I couldn't understand because I didn't have anything I loved the way she had dance. I guessed my family didn't count. So I lost it on him, too.

"I told Jeremy how I didn't really like going to his games, that I just did it for him, and he never even noticed or cared," I tell Seth now. "And it just turned into this whole downward spiral of things I'd never told him.

Like how I hated the way people looked at us, like he was too good to be with me."

Seth frowns. "You actually thought that?"

"You didn't go to our school. You don't know. Everyone loves Jeremy and I'm just—" I wave my hand in the air.

"Addie—"

"It's not important." I don't want Seth feeling sorry for me. "Then he accused me of making all of it up just to pick a fight, and I said I didn't need to pick a fight, since we were already in one. And then . . ." I hesitate. I remember this part clearly. "I said, 'I can't just be your girlfriend, Jeremy, I have to be *me*. And I don't even know who that is anymore.' That finally did it. I ran away and he didn't follow me."

Running through the crowd, eyes blurring with tears. Tripping on someone's foot, almost falling—and then a hand catching me, hauling me to my feet. Seth.

"And then I ran into you," I finish.

If Seth hadn't been there—maybe I would have seen Fiona again, made up with her. Maybe if I hadn't been so stupid and selfish that night, if I'd just looked out for my sister instead of doing what *I* wanted—

But no. I'd run into Seth. Told him to leave me alone and tried to keep running. But there were too many people in my way. He took my arm and guided me to the side of the crowd, asked if I wanted to talk about it. I said no. But then I asked him if he had anything to drink.

We walked away from town, down his street, to this very spot. He handed me a can of semi-warm hard cider. The taste of it on my tongue, fizzy, sweet and sour, like an apple that was about to go bad but hadn't yet. Another sip, the stars starting to wheel overhead. It was a hot night, like this one, the crickets chirping. Little snippets of our conversation still float in my head.

He looks at you like you're something he owns, like you're his. He's always looked at you like that. Since way before you started going out.

So you don't think he really loves me?

I don't think he really knows you. He never did.

What, and you think you do?

We were lying side by side on this rock, looking up at the sky. Seth had turned his head to look at me. *Yeah. I do.*

I'd only had half a can of cider when he asked if he could kiss me. I said yes. The next thing I remember is Seth's hand in my hair, the sweet, stale taste of his tongue.

Heat comes into my face, and I push my memories away.

Seth kicks my leg. I realize I missed something he said. "What?"

"I said, who would have wanted to kill Fiona?"

"I already told you. There's no one. I asked around. At her ballet school, at our actual school. There were no jealous ballerinas, no stalkers. She wasn't dating anyone."

Seth drums his fingers on the rock. "Are you sure?"

"Yes. She'd have told me." I ignore the little voice in my head that adds, *Wouldn't she have?*

He taps out another note on his phone, then looks at me. "I'll share this with you. So we can both have it."

"Thanks."

Then he looks at me. "There's another possibility."

By the look on his face, I'm sure that I don't want to hear it. But I ask, "What?"

He scratches that scar over his eyebrow. I wonder again where he got it. "Did anyone ever look into . . . your mom?"

I stare. "How would that have anything to do with this?"

"Just walk me through it. You've told me your mom was . . . complicated. Like Jekyll and Hyde, you said once."

I was nine when my mom left. I remember her as two people: bright and fun and laughing one day, sullen and moody and slamming her door on us the next, *Mommy needs to be left alone,* my dad looking worried as he shepherded us to the dinner table to eat cereal for the second night in a row.

"Yeah. The summer she left was a Hyde summer. She wasn't around a lot, and when she was, she didn't want to be. And then she was just gone." I hesitate. "I guess you've heard the rumors."

"That she was cheating on your dad?"

"Yeah."

"What does your dad say about it?"

"Nothing."

"Nothing at all? You've asked him?"

I glare. "I can't exactly go up to my dad and ask, 'Hey, did Mom cheat on you a whole bunch? Did she run out of guys around here to sleep with, so that's why she left, to find more? Is that what happened to her?'"

"You could," Seth says after a moment. "What if— I'm not saying it's all true, but what if your mom was having an affair with someone, and their wife found out, and they decided to . . . get revenge?"

"So, what—they killed my mom and came back eight years later to kill my sister?"

He considers this. "Yeah, I guess that doesn't really make sense. But the cops must have looked into your mom last summer, even just to rule it out."

My eyes widen. "You think my *mom* killed Fiona?"

"No," Seth says hastily. "Just, if you can, maybe see what your dad has to say."

I think about it. I don't talk to Dad about Mom. Ever since I could recognize the sadness that would settle in his eyes anytime one of us brought her up, I've avoided the topic.

If it *was* someone after my mom, they picked a stupid way to do it. Hurting the kids she gave so few shits about she'd just up and left them.

Unless she hadn't.

Unless something happened to her, too.

There's nothing I want to do less than talk to my dad about my mom.

But if Seth is right, the cops are right now trying to assemble evidence against him, or me, or us both. And meanwhile, whoever killed Fiona— and Thatcher—is still out there.

They probably spent the past year laughing as I went around telling everyone my theory.

The thought makes my fists clench again.

I need to find this asshole, whoever they are.

Whatever it takes.

"I'll talk to my dad," I tell Seth. "It might just take me a minute to work up to it."

Then I stifle a yawn. I didn't realize how tired I am.

Seth notices. "We don't have to do all this tonight."

I immediately shake my head. "I'm fine—"

"You need some sleep. And so do I."

He's right. I'm exhausted. "Okay."

We slide off the rock and onto the grass, wet with nighttime dew. The temperature's dropped. An owl hoots nearby, making me shiver. The woods are alive around us, fluttering with things our human eyes can't see, and I find myself keeping close to Seth's side as we make our way back past the Montgomery house.

When we come to the place where the path splits off toward the street, we stop and look at each other.

"I'll walk you home," Seth says unexpectedly.

I'm taken aback. "You will?"

"You really want to walk home alone in the dark?"

"I do that all the time. I go running in the dark."

Seth looks like he's about to argue, then sighs. "Just—let me walk you home, Addie."

I want to tell him this is stupid, I'm not some damsel who needs to be escorted back to my house. But I'm too tired to argue. "Whatever."

He gestures to the path. "After you."

I turn, and Seth falls into step beside me.

We reach the road, deserted and dark except for the small yellow pools of streetlight intermittent on the sidewalk.

There's a noise ahead of us. A car, turning onto Bier's End.

Seth and I freeze.

But it's too late to hide anywhere. It's coming toward us, and we're directly in its headlights.

I can't see anything in the bright light shining directly at me. *Let it be just a neighbor,* I silently pray.

The car comes to a halt not ten feet from us. The headlights turn off, and a figure emerges from the driver's seat. Walks into the streetlight so I can see who it is.

It's Kendall Montgomery.

And she doesn't look happy.

9

KENDALL IS DRESSED in black pants, a white sleeveless blouse, and heels. Her dark brown hair is curled to perfection, and she's wearing the same artfully applied makeup she had on at the wake. But she's not quite the polished, put-together Kendall I'm used to. She looks thinner than I remember, and there are dark shadows under her eyes.

Eyes that are narrowed, looking at us. "What are you doing?"

I'm not sure if she's addressing Seth or me, but he answers for us. "Just talking, Ken." He sounds tired.

Her lips press into a tight line. "We're not supposed to be talking to them."

The way she says that—*them*, like my family and I are some inferior species—makes my blood simmer. So I hadn't imagined it, she and Marion running away from Davy and me at the wake.

"So sorry to infringe on your territory. I'll be going now." I start to walk back toward my house, but Seth stops me.

"I don't respond well to being told what to do," he says to Kendall. "Same as you."

Her eyes go to his hand on my arm, and then she looks from him to me. Judging.

Kendall has never been my favorite person. When we were little, she was always excluding me, pulling Fiona giggling to her side, whispering some secret in her ear, and when I asked what they were saying, she'd say it was for "big kids," not for me. I hated that.

She and Fiona didn't have much in common as they got older, but they'd stayed friends. I'd know summer had officially started the day I'd walk into my house and hear Kendall's voice coming from Fiona's room, loud and bright, like someone pulling up the shade and the sun smacking you in the eyes before you're even fully awake. She talked too much, and too fast, about things that didn't interest me.

Kendall goes to UPenn now, I know from her socials. A couple of years ago, her accounts were all these super-staged photos and videos: Kendall at brunch, Kendall on a beach, Kendall at some park in Manhattan, posing on a picnic blanket in some trendy outfit with a drink in her hand. She has something like ten thousand followers and was clearly trying to parlay that into more. But when she began college last year, she deleted most of her posts. Now the only things she posts show her in glasses, smiling over a stack of books, or sitting on the grass, reading, back up against a tree. I don't know if it's part of the same act, Kendall the Serious Student, or if she really doesn't care anymore about being some kind of rich-girl influencer. To be honest, I haven't thought about it, or her, very much at all.

Now, with her standing here in front of me, that judgment in her eyes, I can't help but wonder if she actually has changed or if she's just pretended she has.

"I hate to be the one to tell you this, Seth," Kendall says, "but those accusations all last year about Thatcher? The reason the cops kept calling?" She nods her head at me. "Guess where they came from."

"He already knows," I say, which makes Kendall blink.

She glares at Seth. "So what are you doing with her?"

But he's glaring right back. "If you knew it was her, why didn't you tell me?"

"My father was trying to contain it, Seth, not spread it around. It wasn't even a credible accusation—but it was enough to make this past year the worst Thatcher's ever had." She looks pointedly at me, and again I feel the shame rising up.

"I'm sorry," I say. "I was wrong. Obviously."

"She's here to help," Seth says.

"Help with *what*?" Kendall's eyes go from Seth to me. "You have one of the most expensive lawyers in New York City, and you think Addie's going to be the one to get you off?" She snorts. "You're not exactly thinking with your brain here."

Seth flushes. "She wants to find out who did this as much as I do," he snaps. "And I know for a fact she didn't do it. I was with her both nights."

"I'm not stupid. You worshipped the ground your sister walked on," she says to me. "And I've known you my whole life," she says to Seth. "I think I would have figured out if either of you was a murderer by now."

"So what *do* you think?" I can't help but ask. As Thatcher's sister, maybe she knows something Seth doesn't.

"I don't know. I barely talked to Thatcher this past year, since he was at Oxford and I was at UPenn. I hadn't even seen him since they flew him home when the whole Caleb thing happened. And after that, we didn't talk about it. I had the distinct impression he was avoiding the subject, so I didn't push it."

"What Caleb thing?" Seth asks.

Kendall sounds surprised. "You know. Thatcher's alibi?"

Seth looks as confused as I am. "What alibi?" I ask.

She frowns. "Sorry. I thought you already knew." She shifts from one foot to the other. "At first, Thatcher said he just came home after the parade. But then, later, Caleb Jones went to the police and swore he was with Thatcher during the entire window of time when Fiona could have been killed."

I blink. Caleb Jones was Thatcher's best friend when we were little. He was a quiet, skinny Black kid whose family lives a few streets down from mine. He's the same age as Thatcher, which would make him twenty-one now. He went away to college, I can't remember which one. I haven't seen him in a few years.

"Was Caleb telling the truth?" I ask.

"That's what I asked Thatcher. He told me he was. But then—why wouldn't he have said that before?"

"Caleb had a . . . thing for Thatcher," Seth says. "I don't know if he still does—did—but I know he said something to Thatcher about it a few years back."

I look up at him. "Really? What did Thatcher say?"

"He told him the truth. He didn't see Caleb that way. He was straight, and anyway . . ." He trails off.

"He was in love with Fiona," I finish.

We're all quiet a long moment.

"I kind of thought it sus," Kendall says, "that the night the girl Thatcher was in love with is killed, the person who was always jealous of her gives Thatcher an alibi—and gives himself one as well."

I look at her dubiously. "You actually think *Caleb Jones* killed my sister? He was so nice to us."

She lifts her shoulders. "Or he pretended to be nice."

Seth's shaking his head. "That doesn't make sense. If he was in love with Thatcher—why would he *kill* Thatcher?"

"Maybe Thatcher found out Caleb killed Fiona and was about to turn him in."

"Did you see Caleb that night?" Seth asks her.

She shakes her head. "But I'd had some vodka with my friend Shira, who was visiting from the city. We left the parade early and passed out around eleven. I don't remember Thatcher being home before that, and I wouldn't have heard him if he came in after."

"Where's Caleb now?" I ask.

"No idea," Kendall says.

But Seth is already pulling up his phone. "Philadelphia," he reports after a moment. "Or at least he was a couple of days ago, according to his Instagram."

Philadelphia is only a couple of hours away. I look back at the trees, feel that shiver go down my spine again.

"Oh, right," Kendall says. "I forgot. He actually goes to UPenn, too."

"Did you see him at all this past year?" I ask.

She shakes her head. "UPenn's huge. Even if I were trying to run into him, it would be hard to do. Why, what are you thinking?"

"We could pay him a visit," Seth says. "Ask him if he actually saw Thatcher that night."

"And what, you think he'll confess to making up a fake alibi for Thatcher, just because you say 'pretty please'?" She shakes her head. "Not sure that'll work, Sethy. Especially if he's a secret murderer."

"I really don't think Caleb is a secret murderer," Seth says. "I think, if anything, he was just trying to help Thatcher out. Besides, do you have any better ideas?"

Her snarky facade drops, and I see a hint of grief poking through. "No," she admits. "I've been going over and over it in my head and I just— I can't figure out what happened."

Then she looks between Seth and me, and a speculative look comes onto her face.

"What?" I ask, a little too forcefully.

"Were you guys really doing it the night Fiona died?" she blurts out.

Heat floods my face. Seth, next to me, is rigid. "How did you know about that?"

Kendall looks at her nails. "My father knows everything the cops know. I may have eavesdropped a bit this past year."

I feel a bolt of rage. Of course the Montgomerys have an in with the cops. That's why they're taking Thatcher's death seriously. Way more seriously than they ever took Fiona's. Maybe if they hadn't dismissed my sister as just some dead girl, if they'd done their jobs this past year, Thatcher would still be alive.

I can't believe Caleb Jones—sweet, quiet Caleb Jones—would be capable of anything like this. But the truth is, I never knew him very well. And the theory fits. If Thatcher knew who killed Fiona and didn't tell anyone . . . Seth thought it was because he was afraid. But what if it was because he was conflicted? If the person who killed her was someone he wanted to protect?

Like his best friend?

Kendall's looking at us, eyebrows raised. "Just remember, if my father—or your father—catches you with her, they'll flip their shit." She nods at me.

"So don't go tattling and we'll be fine," Seth says, an edge to his voice.

"What'll you give me to keep my mouth shut?"

She was always like this. There are reasons I never liked her, and I never understood why Fiona did.

"What do you want?" he asks.

Something moves in the shadows—a deer, maybe. I catch Kendall's eyes the second before she turns back to us, and I see a flash of fear.

She may want to hide underneath arrogance and snobbery, but in that moment, I see it clear as day—she's not only mourning for Thatcher. She's afraid.

Of what? Does she think there's some serial killer out here? There are people speculating about that on Citizen Sleuths, too, but I didn't even read through all their threads, it feels so implausible. No. Whatever happened to Fiona and Thatcher, it feels personal.

"I want you to keep me informed," Kendall says. "If you're trying to figure out who did this—I want to know, too. Maybe I can even help."

"Aren't you busy this summer?" Seth asks. "Playing daddy's favorite intern?"

Kendall glares. "I'm only working part-time. And it's not like my dad and I are in the same department. I'm interning in wealth management. He works in private equities."

"Like night and day."

"I also started my own small business on the side, so I'm actually an entrepreneur, too?"

"I just don't understand why you're so invested in this when you're busy riding the reliable tide of nepotism—"

"Oh, don't pretend like you don't do the same," she snaps. "We all do. That's how the world works."

"For you," I mutter.

"I don't work for my dad," Seth counters.

"You don't *work*," she retorts. "And I actually *like* finance, Seth, it's what I'm majoring in. Working for my dad doesn't make me some kind of spoiled brat. It makes me someone willing to work hard for what I want and, yes, taking advantage of what life has given me to help me get there." She looks from me to Seth. "But I'll be out here often enough. I have to keep an eye on Marion. So I want you to keep me in the loop. I want to know who did this." She looks behind her again, into the darkness of the trees.

Despite myself, I look over my shoulder, too. There's nothing there but the trees and the bushes, waving in a night breeze. But I remember that feeling of eyes on the back of my neck. For the first time, I wonder how close *I* came to dying that night, or Seth, or both of us. The person who pushed Thatcher must have still been nearby.

Was it safety in numbers? If it had been only me, or only Seth, would they have hesitated to attack us, too?

Or are we safe—because one of us is meant to take the fall?

That pit in my stomach—the guilt of lying to my dad again, of think-ing about how he would feel if he knew where I really was right now—gets bigger.

"Fair enough," Seth says finally. He looks at her car. "I'm going to walk Addie home. You're okay getting back?"

She rolls her eyes. "The house is right there and I have my car. And I don't think anyone's waiting to murder me in the garage."

So we say our goodbyes after Kendall makes us promise to let her know if we find anything out, and Seth makes her promise the same in return. Then she disappears into her car, leaving Seth and me out in the darkness, alone.

10

SETH AND I don't say anything as we make our way down the moonlight-spotted sidewalk. I'm still worried about Davy, worried about me, angry at the cops and at whoever else is out there trying to hurt us. But I also feel like the burden I was carrying has just gotten a little lighter. I look over at Seth. It's this: for the first time in a long while, having another person by my side.

This past year, I tried to not let myself feel the loneliness. I ran; I tutored strangers on the internet; I recited prime numbers; I googled facts about Stanford, my someday dream grad school. But right now I let the loneliness in, just a little bit, and am surprised to find that with Seth next to me, it doesn't hurt as much.

As we start toward the main road, Seth clears his throat.

"I think we should head to UPenn," he says. "Philly's not that far."

I side-eye him. "You think we can just drive to Pennsylvania, walk up to Caleb Jones, and say, 'Hey, Caleb, did you lie about where Thatcher was the night of Fiona's murder?'"

"No. We walk up to him and just ask what he knows. Maybe Thatcher told him about the fight you saw. Or . . . maybe Thatcher told him who did it."

"I really don't think Caleb did it," I say.

Seth shakes his head. "Me neither. But I think it's very possible he lied about Thatcher's alibi. And I want to know why." Then he looks at me. "But we have to approach him like we're not suspicious of him. Which means you can't be all ragey at him."

"I'm not *ragey*—"

"You're always ragey. And you can leave the talking up to me, if you think it'll be too hard."

I tamp down the retort that springs to my lips. "How are we going to get around not being seen together?"

"I'll pick you up somewhere outside of town. No one will have to know. We can get to Philly and back in a day. I drive fast."

"Comforting."

When I still hesitate, he nudges me with his arm. "Come on. It'll be good to get out of here for a bit, anyway."

I sigh. "We're going to get sick of each other."

He lifts his mouth at one corner in a little half smile. "A risk I'm willing to take."

I meet his eyes, and a zip goes down my spine.

I can't start thinking about *that* again. Yes, I'm attracted to Seth, maybe I always have been, maybe I always will be. But the last time I let myself wander down that path, my sister died. Seth and I are childhood frenemies turned one-night stand turned co-investigators. Nothing more.

We walk the remaining blocks to my house in silence. When we get there, we stop and look at each other.

"Are you going to be okay?" I ask. Then I hastily add, "Not *okay*, I know nothing's okay right now, but if you need to talk . . ." I pull out my burner phone.

He looks surprised. Runs a hand over his face. "I'll be okay." Then: "Thanks, Addie."

He doesn't leave yet. That grief is back on his face, and I know what he's thinking. That I was a good distraction, for a time. But now he has to go home alone, to his room, and think about what he's lost.

We don't speak. It's suddenly awkward. Seth's looking at me and for a moment I think he's going to reach out and hug me. All at once I find myself wanting that: the feel of his arms around me, being engulfed in the scent of him, expensive shampoo and grass and night air and boy. It's been so long since anyone's hugged me.

But instead of stepping toward me, he stays where he is and lifts his hand to his head in a weird little salute. "Sweet dreams, Addie."

"Yeah. You too. Um, thanks for the escort."

"Anytime."

He turns to go, and I have a sudden moment of panic that he won't make it home, that he, too, is heading out to get swallowed by the darkness of Bier's End. "Be careful!"

Seth stops, turns, tilts his head at me. "I'll be all right."

"Just—text me when you get home."

He has a bemused look on his face. "Will do."

Once I'm back inside, I lock the door behind me, then stand, touching Fiona's necklace, and stare out at the still, moonlit night.

I've always painted Seth Montgomery as my enemy. The rich summer kid who once a year deigned to come down from his fancy Manhattan apartment, take time off from his trips to Europe, to tumble around the wilds of Bier's End with the locals. Now I wonder if all that was my way of holding him at arm's length, making sure he never got close enough for me to really look at him. It's so much easier to deal with people when we can stuff them into little boxes.

But now, like on that night last summer, he's forcing me to look at him as something more. A boy with doubts and fears and things he loves and wants to keep safe. Not unlike me.

I don't remember confiding in him my fears about not knowing who I am yet. But he remembers it well enough to be able to quote what I said that night. Why do we remember some things and not others? What else have I forgotten—about Seth, about last summer, about my own past self?

My secret phone buzzes in my pocket.

Seth, of course. **Home safe, though that 5-minute walk was fraught with peril**

I exhale. **Glad you made it**

Seth: **I think that's the nicest thing you've ever said to me**

Then he writes: **Thanks**

Anytime. Good night Seth

Sweet dreams, Addie

I go through my nighttime routine, then double-check that all the doors and windows in the house are locked. I look in on Davy—already asleep—then go to bed, my mind whirling with Seth, his theories, his eyes, and fall asleep with them bleeding into my dreams.

11

THE NEXT MORNING, as I'm coming back from a run, I get a text from Seth.

I found the dorm where Caleb lives. Head out tomorrow?

I exhale. I really don't want to leave Davy alone. And what am I going to tell my dad?

There's also the idea of spending a long car ride alone with Seth. It feels fraught with the potential for uncomfortable conversations, the kind I've always tried to avoid.

But Caleb is the only lead we have so far.

Davy's home when I get there, sitting at the kitchen counter shoveling Cheerios into his mouth while staring at his phone. I'm startled. "I thought you were at soccer camp."

"It's Saturday."

"Oh." I'm losing track of what day it is. "Where's Dad?"

"Grocery shopping."

"He grocery shops on Sundays."

"Yeah, but he has that golf thing tomorrow, remember?"

I forgot about that, too. That's lucky. So Dad, at least, won't even know I'm not here all day.

Davy chews, swallows, raises an eyebrow. "I *am* capable of being home alone."

I try and smile. "I know, just . . . with everything going on, it might be best if none of us were alone right now."

"You went on a run last night by yourself."

"That's different," I say automatically. I don't like lying to Davy, but it can't be helped. "I don't go near the ravine."

"Addie, I wasn't near the ravine. I'm home. I'm not the one you need to worry about."

His tone is patient, like he's talking to a child. I'm not entirely sure when this newer, attempting-to-be-a-grown-up Davy emerged. Last summer? This past year?

That year after Mom left and Dad was gone all the time, when it was just the three of us home alone with our grandpa, who was asleep more often than he was awake, Davy listened to everything Fiona and I said. We packed his lunches, we helped him with his homework, we kicked the soccer ball around with him until bedtime. We weren't parents, exactly, especially not when Dad started spending more time with us again. But we were more than big sisters. And that's what I've remained, even with Fiona gone.

At least that's what I thought.

Davy puts down his phone. "Ethan thinks it's a serial killer," he says abruptly. "He thinks someone else is gonna be next."

I silently curse Davy's annoying little soccer friend. "That's stupid. Serial killers are rare."

"Ethan says they're more common than people think."

"Ethan doesn't know everything."

Davy's face is serious. "Addie, were you really just on a run last night?"

I hesitate a moment too long.

Something falls in his face. "Did you go see Seth again?"

"Yeah," I admit. "I just had to talk to him."

"How is you going to meet up with Seth okay, but me going *anywhere* not okay?"

"It was important that I talk to him about some stuff."

"What stuff?"

"I just wanted to know what the police said to him."

Not totally a lie.

Davy narrows his eyes. "Do they think you did it?"

"No," I say quickly.

"Do they think Seth did it?"

"No. They just were asking us questions because we were there."

"So who do they think did it?"

"I don't know." Also not technically a lie.

Sadie wanders in then, sniffs at my hand, then heads over to eat the Cheerio Davy dropped on the floor.

Davy doesn't pay her any attention. "What made you think it was a good idea to go back there and talk to Seth again? What if it *was* him, and he was just . . . luring you over there to kill you?"

I let out a laugh, but it sounds fake. "Who are you, Dad?" I try and make it sound lighthearted, but it doesn't come out that way.

Davy's frown deepens. "I'm serious."

I turn away from him and start rummaging through the fridge, even though I'm not really hungry. "Seth couldn't have done it because we were together when it happened. I went to talk to him because I wanted to know what's going on."

"So is there something to worry about or not?"

I pull out the cheese, turn to face him. "No."

"Are you lying to me?"

I give him my sternest angry-Fiona look. "Why are you question-ing me?"

"Because I know you're not telling me the truth!"

For a moment, I can't speak. Davy's almost never raised his voice to me.

"What's wrong with you?" I ask finally.

He stands up, faces me. "Oh, I don't know, Addie. Maybe it's that I'm living in a town where people keep getting killed and my sister is just wandering around at night like it doesn't matter?"

I grip the counter behind me. "Davy. Nothing's going to happen to me."

"Just like nothing happened to Mom, and nothing happened to Fiona?"

"Mom left," I say. "You're letting your friend's serial killer theories go to your head."

"So what do *you* think happened to Thatcher, Addie?"

I hesitate. I don't want to scare him. And I definitely don't want him to start playing detective, either. I want him far away from all of this. "Seth said Thatcher was acting weird this past year," I say carefully. "So maybe he did have something to do with last summer. Maybe he didn't even hurt Fiona on purpose. Maybe he ran into her. And she fell. And he never told anyone. And the guilt got to be too much."

Davy's staring at me. "So—he jumped?"

"I think that makes the most sense."

It does make the most sense.

If we hadn't heard him yell.

"It has nothing to do with Mom," I say. "And I really don't think it's a serial killer. But we don't know for sure. So don't go wandering around in the woods by yourself after dark, okay?"

Davy grunts. I let out a silent sigh of relief. He believes me. At least for now.

"Hey, do you want to do something tonight?" I ask abruptly. I need to get some normalcy in his life.

He tilts his head. "Do something?"

"Yeah. Just you and me. Go get some ice cream?"

He looks down at his phone. "Actually . . . I was thinking of seeing the movie in the park."

I'm surprised. During the summer, the old theater does this weekly movie on a projector in the park. Fiona and I used to go, sometimes with Gen or Jeremy or Kendall in tow. I haven't been since she stopped hanging out with me. As far as I know, Davy's never been.

"What movie are they playing?"

"Um. *Vertigo*, I think?"

I frown. Then it comes to me. "Is that Marion's favorite movie?"

"Maybe?"

"It doesn't mean she'll be there."

"I know, I just— You said you wanted to do something. It's something we could do."

I do want to spend time with him. Especially since I'll be gone all day tomorrow. I still need to come up with an excuse for where I'll be—but maybe if I spend the rest of today with him, he won't even notice I'm gone.

"Okay," I say finally, and give him a smile. "Let's do it."

12

DAD AGREES TO us going to movie night, so long as we go there and come straight back, staying away from the woods.

Davy and I walk the four blocks to the park. It's a warm night, mosquitoes in the air. I slap at one that lands on my arm. There are crowds of people here, their blankets already set up, leaning into each other, drinking out of thermoses and SOLO cups, munching on grocery store cookies.

I walk quickly along the side of the park, as far from the crowds as I can get, staring straight ahead of me, willing the sun to go down faster. Davy, in contrast, walks slowly, peering at every brown-haired white girl we pass.

"Slow down, Addie," he says at one point.

"I just want to find a good spot."

He sighs. "No one's looking at you."

I pause. And for the first time, I look out at the crowd. Davy's right.

"Addie," comes a voice behind me.

I turn.

It's Gen.

She's in shorts and a crop top, her black hair pulled back into a braid. I look around but don't see Jeremy anywhere.

Gen hasn't spoken to me directly since our fight junior year. Although she did reach out to me once to see how I was doing after Fiona died. I left her on read.

Sometimes I wonder if I shouldn't have.

"Um—hi," I stammer.

"I heard you were there when they found Thatcher's body," she says abruptly.

Anger rises up inside of me. That's what she wants. Gossip. "Yeah, and?"

Her eyes widen and she takes a step back, holding up her hands. "I was just going to ask if you were okay."

"I'm fine," I snap.

"Do they think, like . . ." She trails off.

But I'm not in the mood to stand here and discuss murderer theories with my ex–best friend.

"Gen?"

And all of a sudden, Jeremy appears through a crowd of people.

Especially not with my ex-boyfriend here, too.

Jeremy's eyes go straight to me. "Oh. Hey." He takes his hat off, runs a hand through his hair, puts it back on—a nervous habit he's had for as long as I can remember.

No one says anything for a long moment. I don't like being stared at like a circus attraction, so I mutter, "I gotta find Davy," and take off through the crowd without looking back.

I managed to avoid them both the whole school year. Why am I suddenly running into them everywhere now?

Why are they suddenly together all the time?

It's my fault. I know that. I cheated on Jeremy. I made him leave me. I know he has the right to do what he wants now.

But I can't help but wonder how long it took Gen to move in once she heard Jeremy and I were broken up.

My brother is standing just five feet away, frowning back at where I left Gen and Jeremy. "Are they dating?" he asks me abruptly.

"I don't know. I don't care." I try and make it sound true.

I start walking again, not slowing. We head to the far back of the local park, which adjoins with the state park. Davy and I set up our blanket at the edge of the trees. I know Davy chose the spot because if Marion comes, she'll likely cut through the woods behind the Montgomery property, which lets out not far from here. I'm not sure if he really believes she'd come to something like this after her brother's funeral, but I don't know enough about Marion and her ways of processing grief to say for sure he'd be wrong.

Davy and I actually manage some normal conversation before night falls and the movie starts rolling on the big screen. I brought a backpack with soda and some cookies, and offer them to my brother, who takes a sleeve and inhales it. He's not watching the movie, though. Just scanning the figures around us, even though it's dark.

Then, about fifteen minutes in, two people pass by on the path from the state park. I look up and stiffen. It's Kendall and Seth.

Next to me, Davy is rigid. He looks back the way they came, but there's no one else.

Just when I think they're about to move on without seeing us, Seth's head turns. I can't see his face in the dark, but a moment later he says something to Kendall, then breaks away from her and walks toward us. Kendall doesn't look back. Which doesn't bother me; there was a fifty-fifty chance she wouldn't have said hi to me before all this went down, either.

Seth slides onto the blanket next to me, his eyes fixed on the screen. "Hey."

"I thought you weren't supposed to be seen with me," I say under my breath.

"It's dark. You're practically in the trees. We're fine."

Davy glances over from my other side. Seth nods at him. "Davy, man, how you doing?" He reaches across me, and the two of them do that boy hand-slapping thing.

Davy hesitates. "I'm really sorry about Thatcher."

"Thanks." The grief in Seth's eyes is still there, of course. But he looks more put together than he did yesterday.

"What are you doing here?" I ask.

"Needed to get out of the house."

"Where's Marion?" Davy asks him.

"She didn't come with us," Seth says, and Davy deflates.

I eye Seth, but he doesn't say anything else. The three of us watch the movie in silence for a few minutes.

Then Davy stands. "I'll be right back."

I blink up at him. "Where are you going?"

"I have to pee."

I look uncertainly toward the trees. "Maybe Seth should go with—"

"Addie." It's his exasperated grown-up voice again. "I'll be fine."

As I watch him move through the darkness, I have to resist the urge to go after him. I guess he did buy my Thatcher-accidentally-killed-Fiona theory and decided there's nothing to worry about. Maybe I shouldn't have been so convincing.

I feel Seth's eyes on me. "He'll be fine."

I'm still watching my brother's back, white in the darkness. He reaches the trees, slips into the woods, and is gone.

My unease grows.

"Drink?" Seth picks up his backpack. "I've got cider."

"A world of no."

A look comes into his eyes I'm not sure I like.

"What?" I can't help but ask.

"It's just cider. Doesn't mean anything has to happen."

I roll my eyes. "I don't make the same mistake twice."

That look drops. Seth turns away from me, opens his cider. He sips, and I sit in silence for a while, my eyes on the movie screen, even though I couldn't even tell you the name of the main character at this point.

"Is that really what you think?" Seth asks.

"Is what really what I think?"

"I'm a mistake?"

But I can't care about whatever he's mad at now. Davy's been gone way longer than it takes to pee.

I look in the direction of the trees, but there's no tall blond boy walking back toward us. I get to my feet. "Where's Davy?"

Seth gets up beside me. "I'm sure he's just—"

But I'm already running in the direction of the woods. "Davy?"

When I reach the trees, I throw myself into them, not caring whether or not Davy is mid-pee and I'll be embarrassing him. "Davy!"

Footsteps behind me. I turn to see Seth.

I peer back into the trees. But there's no one there.

Davy's gone.

13

"DAVY!"

The movie is a distant thrum. All I hear are my own harsh breaths as I run through the trees. It's even darker under the tree cover, but Davy was wearing a white shirt, his hair is blond; I should be able to see him—

A light from somewhere behind me, illuminating a tree trunk—I whip around to see Seth shining the flashlight from his phone in front of us.

Cursing myself for being stupid while I panicked, I forge on, now with Seth's light to guide me. "Davy!"

"Davy!" Seth's voice joins mine.

Then there's a rustling somewhere nearby.

The phone light bounces off the tree trunks. I dart around a big tree—and let out a sigh of relief.

There are two people standing very close together. One of them is Davy.

The other is Marion.

They blink at the light.

"Davy," I finally manage. I don't know whether to scream at him or hug him.

He shields his eyes from the phone light, at which point Seth directs it to a point above their heads so they can see. Neither of them looks guilty. In fact, once Seth stops shining the light in their faces, they go back to looking at each other.

"Davy," I say, louder.

"We're just catching up." There's a note of desperation in his voice, like he's about to be torn away from Marion, like they only have so much time.

Seth's hand is on my arm. "Does anyone know you're here?" That, he addresses to Marion.

The guilty look on her face makes the answer clear. "I just wanted to watch the movie."

Her voice is as soft as it's always been. She's wearing jean shorts and a black crop top, her dark brown hair pulled back in a ponytail. She looks younger than she did at the wake, without the curls and thick eyeliner. She's gotten taller since last summer but is still almost a foot shorter than Davy.

"You don't have to lie to me," Seth says. "I'm not Kendall."

Marion's face gets even guiltier, and she cranes her neck to look past us. "Where is she?"

"In the park somewhere."

"We just wanted to talk." Davy looks defiant now, almost angry. "Is that a crime?"

"No," I say, more gently this time. "But you could have texted me or something. You can't just go disappearing into the woods right now, Davy, you know that."

I expect Davy to look ashamed, immediately apologize. Instead, his frown deepens. "You're the one who told me there was nothing to worry about."

I falter. "I said I *thought* there was nothing to worry about."

He straightens up, takes Marion's hand. "We need to talk."

"Where are you—"

"We'll go back to the park. To the blanket. Could you leave us alone for a little while, please?"

I can only watch as my brother walks off through the trees, Marion at his side. When they disappear, I make a motion to follow them, but Seth's hand on my arm holds me back.

"I think you need to give them a minute," he says.

I shake his hand off. "Don't tell me how to deal with my own brother—"

"I'm not. I'm just saying, if you don't want to push him away further, you should give him some space."

I look into Seth's face. "Push him away? I'm not . . . He's never *talked* to me like that."

"He just wants you to stop treating him like a little kid, Addie. You do that, you know."

It's on the tip of my tongue to tell him Davy *is* a kid, that if I'm not looking out for him, no one is. But there's a lump in my throat that makes it difficult to speak.

"This is your fault," I manage.

Seth's eyes widen. "How do you figure that?"

"If none of you had come back here, none of this would be happening!"

His brows come together. "I'm really sorry that Thatcher being murdered has been so inconvenient for you—"

"That's not what I mean, and you know it. You could have had your grandma's funeral in the city, but no, your family has to be here, fighting over her will—"

"We were always going to come back here, Addie. Fiona's murder didn't just happen to you. It happened to all of us. What happened to Thatcher—it was always going to happen, so long as whoever did this is still out there. Did you suddenly forget about that?"

"I don't forget about anything."

"Could have fooled me."

I stare. "What's that supposed to mean?"

Seth's eyes are on me, dark and serious. I have the feeling I don't want to hear what he's about to say.

"Do you ever even think about that night?" he asks.

I look away from him, then back again. "I try not to."

A flash of something in his eyes. It comes and goes so fast I can't be sure, but if I had to guess, I would have called it *pain*.

"Is that really your biggest regret?" he asks. "Spending the night with me?"

He's seriously asking me this. "I was cheating on my boyfriend while my sister was being killed. I'd say that falls into the category of life regrets, don't you?"

His mouth twists, and for a moment, he looks like Kendall. "Good to know."

"Seth, it's not about you." I can't believe I have to explain this to him.

"I get that, but you could at least acknowledge that night happened. You wouldn't even message me back! I wanted to talk to you, I was trying to"—he runs his hands over his hair—"be there for you or something—but you blocked me and never spoke to me again."

He's waiting for me to respond, but I have no idea what to say. When I don't speak, he turns away. "I think we've given them enough catch-up time, don't you?" His voice is gruff.

Without waiting for my answer, he takes off through the trees. After a moment, I follow.

Was he saying he . . . *liked* our night together? I mean, of course a teenage boy is going to like having sex. But I thought that was all it was to him. Sex. I didn't even know if it was good sex.

For just a moment, moving through those dark trees, I let myself remember it. The stone against my back, still warm from the sun. Seth's curls falling down, tickling my cheek. The grin on his face right before he kissed me.

I had no idea he'd thought about me that much. When I let myself think of that night, I felt angry. I figured he saw me as a one-night stand, no different from any others he'd had. Or maybe a little different. Because we'd been frenemies our whole lives. I thought he must have seen it as some sort of twisted conquest, getting me to cheat on Jeremy with him.

It's strange to think that maybe I was wrong about all of that. I never once considered that in addition to everything else I did that night—I hurt Seth in some way, too.

I push it out of my head. I don't know how to fix whatever it is Seth is mad about.

All I can do is try and find out what happened to my sister and Thatcher.

I owe them that, at least.

14

THE NEXT MORNING, I meet Seth on a quiet corner where no one will see us. Dad's already at his golf thing, and Davy actually left before me to go hang out with Marion. It's a gray day, with the possibility of rain, according to my weather app. When I get in his car, he just grunts at me. After a coffee and pork roll, egg, and cheese stop at a QuickChek near the highway, we're on our way. It's two and a half hours from here to Caleb's dorm, so we'll have a few hours to locate Caleb and get him to talk to us before we'll need to be on our way home for dinner.

We drive in an uncomfortable silence, filled with everything we said—and didn't say—last night.

"So are you going to major in math?" Seth asks after about half an hour.

I blink. I was caught up in a daydream where Fiona is still alive, and I've gone to the city to meet her, and we're having the kind of sisterly day we haven't had in . . . ever.

"What?" I ask.

"At Rutgers. You're majoring in math?"

"Um—yeah. If they don't kick me out for being a murder suspect first."

Rutgers isn't exactly my dream school, but it ticks all the boxes: nearby, affordable, decent. Stanford is the dream. California, a world away. I can't go there for undergrad, not without a significant scholarship, and my grades took a nosedive at the start of last year. And I didn't want to be too far from Davy. But Stanford has a grad school. My plan is to work hard at Rutgers, straight As. Someday, if I can talk Davy into a West Coast school, too—maybe I'll make it out there.

"They won't," Seth says, but he doesn't sound super confident. "So, like, what do you want to be? Do you want to work on Wall Street, or be an accountant . . ."

I snort. "No to both of those. Why do you want to know?"

"Just making conversation."

I look over at him, but I don't see anything teasing on his face. So I answer, "I kind of want to go into academia."

"So head to grad school after?"

"Yeah. I'd love to go to Stanford for that." A pause. "There's just the matter of money."

He gets quiet then, which is weird. Seth never shied away from talking about money before.

"So what would you do at Stanford?" he asks a moment later.

Then we go on to have an actual conversation about something other than murder for a good half hour.

But of course that can't last.

Somewhere along the way, we hit traffic. There's nothing, and suddenly it's bumper-to-bumper.

Seth beeps at someone who tries to cut us off, mutters a curse under his breath. Then he looks at me. "I saw Ramsay at the movie last night," he says out of the blue.

A shiver goes down my spine. "Gross."

"Do you really think he doesn't like you?"

"Does he talk to you the same way he talks to me?" I demand. "Half the time like you're a kid wasting his energy, the other half like you're a suspect?"

Seth shakes his head. "He's always been polite to me."

"Of course he has."

"Addie, why would he have a reason to hate you specifically?"

"Because his niece hates me? I don't know."

"He's a cop," Seth points out. "You think he's going to be concerned about girl drama?"

I exhale. "Way to trivialize me losing my best friend."

"I'm sorry," he says after a beat. "What exactly happened there?"

I put my head back against the headrest. Ahead of us, traffic is still crawling. I don't necessarily want to get into all of this, but Seth is glancing at me curiously and it's not like we have anything better to do right now. So I tell him.

"When Jeremy and I started dating, Gen saw it as, like, a betrayal of our friendship. I mean, I understand that she was upset. I suspected that she might like him, too. And I know she was worried about what it would do to our dynamic—the three of us were best friends, and if two of us got together, things would inevitably change. But—"

I don't want to get into all my reasons for saying yes to Jeremy with Seth. I can't exactly say, *He's the opposite of you, so I decided to give it a shot*.

Instead I say, "He liked me. I liked him. What were we supposed to do?"

"You can't put your own happiness on hold for other people," Seth says. "You didn't do anything wrong."

I'm surprised. He sees my face and snorts. "I mean, I can criticize your *taste*. You could always do better than Jeremy fucking Reagan." His fingers tighten on the steering wheel. Jeremy and Gen used to tag along sometimes when we went to the Montgomerys', before football and cheerleading preseason got in the way. Seth and Jeremy never especially liked each other—they were both super competitive in whatever game we were playing, but so was I. I didn't think Seth actively hated him or anything.

"Jeremy's a good guy," I say. "You knew him, too."

"Like you said, people change." Before I can ask what he means by that, he says, "So Gen got pissed you were dating and you guys stopped talking and that was it?"

"That wasn't all. We got into this big fight and she said . . . She said, 'I knew you were like this. No different from your mom.'"

I can still feel the pain of those words. Like a slap in the face. By then, I'd heard the rumors about my mom that missed me when I was nine. That she'd been sleeping with half the unmarried men in town, and some of the married men, too. That she'd run off with one of them. I just didn't know Gen was one of the people repeating those stories.

"Damn," Seth says.

"Yeah."

I missed Gen. Especially after everything else I'd lost. It was hard walking through school and seeing her face impassive, her blank eyes staring through me. And I can't help but think about the way she talked to me, actually said something to me, in the park the other night. That text she sent me right after Fiona died. But no. She was just fishing for gossip. Both times, probably. If she couldn't forgive me for going out with Jeremy, I definitely can't forgive her for what she said about my mom.

Seth looks over at me. "So, did you ever think . . . that Gen might have something to do with all this?"

I blink. "What?"

"You said she hates you."

"So, what, she killed my sister to get back at me for dating Jeremy?" I shake my head. "That doesn't make sense. And anyway, she'd never do something like that."

"That's not what I'm saying." He pauses. "I'm not saying this to freak you out or anything, it's just a theory—"

"Just say it."

Another pause. In the distance, someone leans on their horn. "What if it wasn't supposed to be Fiona that night?" Seth asks finally.

I stare. "What?"

"You and Fiona used to look a lot alike. Before you dyed your hair. What if—what if someone saw her in the woods that night and thought it was you?"

I shake my head. "Fiona's shorter than me—"

"By, like, two inches."

"And our faces are shaped differently—"

"From behind," Seth interrupts, "in the dark, late at night. Whoever did it could have been drinking or on something. It's possible."

A chill goes through me. "So you think—someone was trying to kill *me*?"

"I'm not saying that for sure," he says hastily. "I'm just saying, you said Fiona had no enemies. But what about you?"

I take a deep breath. "You really think Gen hated me enough to try and kill me?"

"Psychopathy is more common than people realize," Seth says. "Around one percent of the general population. And some are very good at hiding it."

I look at him sideways. "You get this from all your time on the true crime boards?"

"That's not the point." Then he pauses. "Or what if it was her, and she did mean to kill Fiona and frame you for it?"

I frown. "Why would she—or anyone—do that?"

"Well, if she's smart—and if she pulled this off without being caught, she's smart—then she would have thought it through. If the goal was to get Reagan to break up with you, killing you might not work."

Seth's always called Jeremy by his last name, *Reagan*. I stare at him. "You are making no sense."

"I mean, with how obsessed that kid was with you, if you died, he'd probably build some kind of shrine to you and worship at it the rest of his life." Before I can object to that, he goes on, "But turning you into a person he didn't recognize? That might do it."

I shake my head. "Yeah, Gen said some shitty stuff to me, but she'd never try and kill me over Jeremy. Besides, she didn't need to turn me into a murder suspect to make me look bad." I stare straight ahead of me. "I did that just fine all by myself."

A touch on my arm. I look over at Seth.

"How long are you going to punish yourself?" he asks. "Just an estimate."

I ignore that. "Besides, if Gen—or anyone else—was trying to frame me, like you said, they did a shitty job. Didn't drop anything that belonged to me near the ravine or anything like that."

"She could have messed it up," he offers. "And now she's trying again. And there's the missing journal. Did she have a key to your house?"

I go still. "No—but she knows where we keep our spare key. Under the rock by the maple tree in the backyard."

"Who else knows about that key?"

"Just her and Jeremy, but . . . I've never actually understood that whole thing. Why would anyone have risked coming into our house that night to take Fiona's journal?"

Suddenly the GPS starts talking to us. Seth looks at it. "It wants me to get off the highway."

I gesture at the traffic. "Big surprise."

We stop talking theories then as Seth takes the next exit. It spits us out onto a smaller road somewhere in rural Pennsylvania. But the traffic isn't great here, either. And the sky overhead has turned a deep, ominous gray.

I'm glad for the distraction, honestly. My first reaction to Gen possibly being the killer is how ridiculous it is. But Seth's right. People change.

Could Gen have changed that much? So much that she'd try and *kill* me?

The thought makes me feel ill. I've always wondered if I made the right choice. Choosing Jeremy over Gen. When he asked me out, I could have said no. Things could have gone on the way they had been. The three of us best friends.

But he was *Jeremy Reagan*, the boy everyone wanted, the earnest, wholesome quarterback—it was like just by being with him, it made all my own flaws feel lesser. Made me feel like I was a better person, just because he'd chosen me. My mom left me, Fiona was getting ready to leave me, and I'd wondered, more than once, if there was just something fundamentally unlovable about me. Being with Seth, the way we only kissed when no one was around, the way I was sure he wanted to keep me a secret—that didn't make me feel great. But every time I looked over at Jeremy and he squeezed my hand or gave me that smile of his—it made me feel like he could see past everything that was wrong with me and love me anyway.

But Gen—Gen was with me through all of that, too. And she wasn't perfect like Jeremy. She was flawed. She was terrible at school, she had a bad temper that landed her in detention every month, she had acne, and she and her mom never got along. She didn't know what she wanted to be, either. We understood each other.

Sometimes I wonder if I picked Jeremy over her because I was afraid of how much alike we really were.

Sometimes I wonder how far I would go to get what I want, too.

Who I would be willing to hurt.

"There's something wrong," Seth says, interrupting my spiraling thoughts.

"With Gen?" I shake my head. "I just can't see—"

"No, I mean with the car. It's making a weird noise. Listen, can you hear that?"

I try. But I don't even have a car of my own and know next to nothing about them. "Um, no?"

Seth curses. Traffic's eased slightly, but we're still on a two-lane back road going past fields and the occasional horse farm. The sky ahead is getting darker. We're somewhere outside of Allentown, Pennsylvania, according to the map, when the skies open up.

Soon it's raining so hard we can barely see five feet ahead. Seth has his windshield wipers on high, his lights on. "Shit," he mutters as the rain starts to come down harder. It's black as night outside, even though it's only two thirty in the afternoon.

"Stop!" I exclaim when a truck's taillights appear in front of us. Seth slams on the brakes, sending the back of the car skidding. One of my hands grips the door and the other clutches Fiona's necklace as we jack-knife across the road, finally coming to rest partly on the shoulder, partly sticking out into the right lane.

There's a honk somewhere behind us as a car goes by, barely missing us, but the rain is coming down so hard it won't be long until we have another near miss.

I catch my breath. Next to me, Seth looks dazed. "Are you okay?" I ask.

He blinks. "Are *you* okay?"

"I'm fine. We're fine." My voice sounds mechanical. My heart is still racing in my chest.

Seth looks down at his foot, then eases it up off the brake and onto the gas. The car lurches forward a foot or two and then stops.

"Shit." He presses his foot on the gas. Another lurch, another stop. "SHIT."

"What is it?"

"I don't know." His mouth is set in a grim line.

Another car passes by. "Seth, could we at least get off the road—"

"I'm *trying*."

He steps on the gas. Another lurch. Then we stop.

He turns the car off, curses again, looks down at his phone. "I'll call Triple A."

Two hours and a tow truck later, we find ourselves at a garage in Bethlehem, Pennsylvania, as a mechanic tells us there's something wrong with . . . some part of the car that I don't quite understand. The bottom line is, it's almost five in the afternoon and the mechanic is going to have to keep the car overnight.

I'm hungry, tired, and dazed from being stuck in that dark car as the rain poured down and cars rushed past and I wondered each time if this one was going to be the one to crash into us and kill us. Seth nods as the guy talks, and then he pulls out his phone. "I'll find us a place to stay."

I'm startled. "We can't just . . . uber home?"

"And what, uber back tomorrow? I need my car. Besides, we're closer to Philly than we are to home."

"We're in the middle of nowhere, Pennsylvania, I didn't exactly pack an overnight bag—" He just looks at me. I sigh. I know he's right. But: "What am I going to tell my dad?"

Seth's phone buzzes. He looks down. "It's Kendall. She wants to know if we found Caleb."

He starts to tap something out, then instead presses the phone to his ear. "Hey."

While he tells her about our car, I rack my brain for something to tell Dad.

I can't do it alone. I'm going to have to get Davy to help me.

But I don't want to tell Davy where I really am, either.

And then I get an idea.

"Can I talk to Kendall?" I blurt out to Seth.

He looks surprised but says into his phone, "Addie wants to talk to you," and hands the phone to me.

"Hello?"

"Hey. I need your help."

"What can I do for you?"

She doesn't sound sarcastic, at least, so I say, "Can you be my alibi tonight? In case anyone asks? I'll tell Davy I'm staying over. We're . . . bonding over our shared grief or something."

"Sure," she says after a moment. "Actually, I'm supposed to be hanging out with Gen tonight."

I startle. "Gen? Why?"

Kendall knows Gen because I used to bring her over with me sometimes when we were younger. But they'd never been friends.

"I ran into her at the movie in the park. We ended up chatting and making plans to catch up. Seth told me about his theory, so I thought I'd ply her with booze, see what shakes out. I told you, I want to find out who did this as much as you do."

I feel a little spasm of anger that Seth told Kendall about his Gen theory before me. But I need to focus. "Um. Okay. So I'll say I'm with you?"

"Yup, and if anyone asks, I'll say the same."

She's being surprisingly helpful. I guess she wasn't kidding about wanting to be useful. "Okay, thanks. And did you happen to see Davy today?"

Kendall exhales. "Yeah. They were here earlier, holding hands by the pool."

"You sound about as happy about that as I am."

"It's not that I'm not happy for them, they're so *in love*, it's just . . . Marion was really upset last summer when she broke things off. I don't want to see her like that again."

"Yeah, tell me about it."

"She's my sister. I'm just trying to look out for her."

"I know."

And I do.

"Thanks," I tell Kendall. "Seriously."

"No problem."

I hand the phone back to Seth, then call my brother.

Davy's on his way home, planning on eating dinner with Dad. I tell him I'm staying over at Kendall's but that I don't want Dad to know, so I ask him to do the pillows-under-the-covers thing. Dad leaves for work before I wake up most mornings, so I think it'll work. I hope. Davy agrees and doesn't even ask any questions, which is weird, but at least that's taken care of.

"All settled?" Seth asks when I hang up the phone. I nod. "There's an Airbnb ten minutes away."

"Great." I look at the mechanic. "Sir, is there a Target or something around here?"

"Or a deli?" Seth asks.

"Walmart five minutes that way," the man says. "Food's in the town center, though, and you can't get there without a car."

"We'll figure it out." I pull on Seth's arm. No way am I spending a whole night with him—again—without a toothbrush. "Let's go."

Half an hour, two toothbrushes, and two sets of cheap clothes later—it's surreal, wandering the fluorescent-bulbed aisles of a Walmart, picking up a three-pack of cotton underwear with Seth by my side—we're in the parking lot, Seth once again on his phone. "The Airbnb lady can come pick us up. And we can stop at a deli she knows."

Twenty minutes later, Tess, a thirty-something blond white lady who isn't at all fazed by needing to pick two teenagers up at a Walmart on a Tuesday night, arrives. She takes us to get sandwiches, then drives us back to our Airbnb, a three-story house on a quiet suburban block. It's bigger than my house but nowhere near the size of the Montgomery mansion, old-fashioned and cute, hedges out front, a fireplace and built-in bookshelves inside, pictures of Tess and someone I assume is her wife on the walls. The guest suite is on the third floor, she explains, bedroom, bathroom, amenities provided, feel free to help yourselves to whatever you need.

It's only eight when we're done eating our sandwiches, but I'm exhausted and just slightly alarmed at the fact Tess said bed*room*, not bed-*rooms*. After cleaning up after ourselves, we ascend two sets of stairs, me in the lead. There's a hallway that leads to a small bedroom with slanted ceilings and a window unit air conditioner humming away in the corner.

"Seth," I say.

He comes up behind me. "What?"

"There's only one bed."

"Is there?"

But there's no surprise in his voice.

I glare. "What were you—"

He sighs. "We're not exactly in a metropolis. It was the only room nearby that didn't look sketchy. I didn't think it was that big a deal."

"Hope you like sleeping in the bathtub."

"There is no bathtub—"

"Enjoy the hardwood floor, then." I stomp—quietly—out of the room and down to the tiny bathroom, where I find that he's right: no bathtub, just a small stall shower.

I shower quickly, change into my Walmart underwear and PJs—cheap shorts and a black T-shirt—and brush my teeth, my mind going the whole time. The bed in that room isn't a twin, at least, but it doesn't look that big. Probably not even a queen. Maybe we could take the comforter off and make some kind of makeshift bed on the floor.

When I come back to the room, Seth's changed into his own Walmart PJs: mesh shorts and a white T-shirt. He's looking at a framed photograph on the wall. He turns, takes in my damp hair, bare feet. It feels weird and intimate, being in this little room together at the top of a stranger's house in the middle of Pennsylvania, going through my bedtime routine with him here.

"Have you ever been to Ireland?" he asks.

I blink. "I've never been anywhere."

He nods at the photograph. I come stand beside him. It's of a curving gray wall, some kind of ruins, set on a cliff over the ocean. The inscription on the bottom reads: *Dún Aonghasa, Inishmore, County Galway, Ireland.*

"There's this little group of islands off the west coast of Ireland called the Aran Islands." Seth's voice is low, quiet, soothing. "They're covered in stuff like this. This one's an ancient fort, built in 1100 BC, but there are also castle remains, old cottages and churches, and this amazing thing they call the Wormhole."

He points across the room to another framed photo of what looks like a rectangular swimming pool cut into gray rock, a spray of salt water rising out of it.

"How'd they cut it into the rock so perfectly?" I want to know.

He shakes his head. "They didn't. It's naturally like that. Isn't it cool?"

But instead of looking at the photo, I'm looking at him. His brown eyes are lit up, a lock of hair falling over that new scar above his eyebrow. He has this soft smile on his face that sends a shiver through me. Then I realize why: It's the same look he had on his face when he was about to kiss me.

I push that thought aside. "Cool," I echo. I grasp at Fiona's necklace.

"Thatcher did a genealogy project once and traced one of our great-great-something-grandfathers to this island." His voice is quiet. "We were supposed to go there together someday."

There's an ache in his voice that breaks my heart. Because I know it so well. You build this whole future with someone, and even when things aren't perfect between you, you think you still have time to fix it. To do the things you always wanted to do. You keep your plans safe inside your heart, hold on to them when things get hard.

But then that person dies. And that pretty future inside of you, that dies, too. And you learn that nothing is safe, nothing is guaranteed, there's nothing to stop everyone you love from leaving you, in one way or another, nothing to stop everything you want from just withering away. That it's very possible you'll end up alone.

I'm searching for the words to say to Seth and coming up empty when he clears his throat. "I'll sleep on the floor." He gestures down, and I see the pillow and comforter already there. "I didn't mean to make you uncomfortable. I'm sorry."

It's strange, hearing him apologize. I remember the time we jumped the wall to the Bier property on one of our treasure hunts. We must've been about eight. We'd started digging around the ancient oak tree, like we always did. Seth and I were bickering about getting in each other's way, and at the end he finally got fed up and pushed me into our hole. It was deep enough at that point that it was a real fall. At the bottom, I twisted my ankle, and it took all of us to get me back out. He refused to apologize, even when Thatcher tried to make him.

That's the boy I remember. When did he turn into this other boy, one who apologized, who looked at me the same way he looked at the things he cared about?

He's looking at me that way now. His eyes are deep and dark in the low lamplight. I think he's about to say something. But then he walks out the bedroom door without another word.

Once he's gone, I sigh, then pick up the comforter and pillow and put them back on the bed.

15

I CLIMB INTO the right side of the bed. The ceiling slopes down to the headboard, so when I sit up straight, it's not very high above my head. Seth will have to be careful. The sheets are white, and cool from the air conditioner, and I shiver a little as I slip between them. I lie on my side, facing away from where he'll be.

I spent the past year trying not to think about that night with Seth, trying not to think about Seth at all. I didn't let myself feel anything other than guilt over what I'd done. Didn't let myself think about how, if it weren't for everything, I might look back on that night—the rock pressing against my back, the Milky Way glittering overhead, the look in Seth's eyes like I was the only thing he could see—as something good that happened to me. Not something bad I'd done.

There are footsteps, then the door creaking open. Footsteps stopping.

"I'm okay sleeping next to you," I say without looking at him. "If you are."

A long silence. Then another footstep, then the bed depressing as he sits. "I'm not gonna argue with you."

I listen to him crawl into bed, feel the covers pull, the mattress bounce. I keep my eyes on the air conditioner.

"Lights out?" he asks.

I nod.

He switches off the lamp, and then it's dark in the room except for a little street light coming in through the blinds. Seth shifts in bed, and so do I.

Maybe it's the darkness that makes me bold, but I say, "That night was my first time."

I feel him grow still behind me. "What?"

"That night. With you. It was my first time."

A long silence. "You and Reagan never—"

"No."

"Why not?"

Why not? It's something even I have never fully understood. Jeremy wanted to, obviously. He brought it up a month after we started going out. He'd never had a serious girlfriend, despite all the attention he got, and he'd never done it, either. I told him I wasn't ready. And he never pushed me. Last summer, before everything went so wrong, there was one night when we came close. But I stopped it, saying I wasn't ready yet. And again, he didn't push. He'd waited for me. And I never said yes.

"I just . . . didn't think I was ready."

The bed frame creaks as Seth shifts again. "Were you . . . I didn't mean to, like, pressure you, or—"

I shake my head. "You didn't." With Seth, there wasn't even much of a conversation. We were kissing, and then his hands were in places only Jeremy's had been, and then I was pulling his shirt off, and he was tugging at mine. His voice in my ear: *Do you want to . . .* Me nodding, pushing all my doubts to one side, Seth's hand fumbling in the pocket of his backpack, our breaths hitched in the air, every nerve of my body thrumming—

I squeeze my eyes shut, even though it's dark, even though he can't see my face. "You didn't," I say again. "I wanted to."

After a long while, he says, "It was my first time, too."

I freeze. "What?"

I turn in bed to face him. I can see the outline of his features in the dim light. His eyes are wide open, and he's looking at me, his mouth quirked up on one side. "Is that so hard to believe?"

"Yes."

"Why?"

"You're . . ." I gesture toward him.

"I'm what?"

"I don't know. I guess I just figured you always had some Manhattan prep school girl back home or something."

He shifts, props his head up on one elbow. "And what gave you that impression?"

"You know."

"I don't. Tell me."

"I mean, you're . . . not bad to look at. You sometimes have interesting things to say."

An exhale that might be a laugh. "Don't flatter me, Addie."

"And . . . I don't know. All those times we made out before, and then we'd never talk about it . . . It felt like you were ashamed of me."

He snorts. "I thought *you* were ashamed of *me*. That's why I never talked about it."

Oh. That never even occurred to me.

We don't say anything for a long moment, just breathe next to each other in the dark.

"So why me?" I ask finally.

"Why me?" he counters.

I think about it.

"I just remember . . . I was so mad, so pissed at everyone, and then we were talking, and—it seemed like you were the only one to understand."

"Understand what?"

"Me? When my sister didn't? When my boyfriend didn't?"

"He never understood you," Seth says unexpectedly. "That was always his problem. He wanted you to be perfect. If he really loved you, he would have seen that you weren't and not cared. That's what love is. Or at least that's what I've always thought. The kind I've always wanted."

I rest my head in my hand, too, so we're lying face-to-face. I don't know if he can see me or not. "So you've never had a girlfriend?"

A shake of his head. "I had the kind you have when you're thirteen and it lasts a week. But not since then. Not a real one. No."

One of his curls is resting at an odd angle across his forehead. I have to resist the urge to brush it away. Something is blooming up from deep inside of me, something I thought had gone back to sleep forever. I remember all too well why I kissed him.

"You didn't answer my question," I say.

"Which one?"

"Why me?"

He lifts his hand in the air, hesitates. Then slowly, slowly, he reaches out, touches a lock of my damp hair. "Because I wanted to," he says simply. "I wanted you."

He still wants me. I see it in his eyes, even in the near darkness. I wonder how long I've known.

It would be so easy. Reaching across those inches between us, wrapping a curl around my finger, the way I did that night. Pulling his face to mine, getting lost in the feel of his hands, the taste of his tongue, the weight of his body. Falling asleep with his arms around me. Feeling safe. Against all odds, feeling safe.

But the last time I did that, my sister had been falling through space.

Her neck had snapped at the bottom of the ravine. While I was feeling safe, she never would be again.

Seth's hand moves higher, his fingers pushing my hair back from my face. I close my eyes.

His hand freezes.

"What's wrong?"

"I can't," I whisper.

His hand disentangles from my hair. I open my eyes. But all I see is a sadness in his eyes I don't fully understand.

"Seth." I swallow. "It's not . . . I mean, if it hadn't been for everything else that night—maybe it wouldn't have been something I regretted."

He's still looking at me. "It's never been something I regretted. Even with"—he lifts a hand in the air—"everything. I guess that's the difference between you and me."

I don't know what to say to that.

He exhales.

We lie there silently, breathing in the darkness. I turn on my other side again, facing away from him. In the corner, the air conditioner hums. I shiver.

"Seth?" I whisper, wiping away a tear.

"Yeah?"

"Do you remember after . . . when we put our clothes back on, and you laid your blanket down on the grass, and we just . . . slept?"

His voice is soft. "Yeah."

"Can we do that part again?"

I know I don't deserve it. I drove my mom away, and I drove Gen away, I drove Fiona away, I broke the heart of the only person who was ever stupid enough to love me while my sister was dying, I didn't save Thatcher, and somehow, in this whole process, I hurt Seth, who is good to me, is still being good to me. I don't deserve it.

But I want it.

Seth stirs. The bed frame creaks. And then he's right behind me, his chest pressing up against my back. His arm goes around me, holding me securely to him.

"Like this?"

I exhale. "Like that."

Even though it's cold, not hot, and even though we're tucked up in an attic bedroom in Pennsylvania and not lying on a blanket under the stars of Bier's End, I close my eyes and feel transported back to that night. Lying in Seth's arms, sore and throbbing and warm and guilty and happy, a tangle of things I couldn't even begin to unravel. I know I shouldn't be feeling like everything is going to be okay. There's a whole world waiting outside this attic bedroom, a world with Fiona and Thatcher's killer in it, with truths we haven't yet blown apart, and I don't know how damaged I'll be, we'll all be, in the blast. I know I shouldn't be feeling safe. But I am.

Just in this moment, I am.

16

I WAKE UP when the sunlight filtering through the blinds over the air conditioner hits me. Seth's arm is warm around me, which feels good in the cold room. I don't want to move, to wake him; I want to stay in this weird alternate reality in this attic in Pennsylvania where I can sleep in a bed with the one boy in the world who knows the worst thing about me and doesn't care.

I lie there, listening to his breathing behind me, watching the sun get brighter behind the blinds. I don't want to get up, deal with all the things we're dealing with.

But I need to find out who killed Fiona and Thatcher. Because I don't trust the police to do it, because I don't want to get kicked out of college before it even starts for being a murder suspect, and most of all, because I want this person to pay.

I turn in bed just as Seth stirs. His breaths turn into grunts, his arm lifts as he stretches, and the night is officially over.

His eyes open, fall on me. "Morning."

"Morning."

I can't read the expression on his face. After a moment, he scratches his head. "I'm gonna shower."

"Okay."

While he's in the bathroom, I get dressed in a new black T-shirt and underwear and the same jean shorts I wore yesterday. The mirror over the dresser shows my hair's gotten frizzy overnight from sleeping on it wet, and I have mascara under my eyes. I run my hand through my hair, rub at the mascara and apply a fresh coat, all before Seth reappears in the doorway in nothing but a towel.

I haven't seen him without a shirt on since that night, and it had been dark then. Now, in the filtered daylight, I can see the muscles of his chest and shoulders clearly. He looks like he's gotten bigger, and he has more hair on his body than before, I'm pretty sure. Little black curly hairs across his chest, forming a trail downward, disappearing into the towel—

"Um." He averts his eyes from mine. "I left my clothes—"

"I'll go brush my teeth." I hurriedly slip past him into the hallway.

I brush so hard I make my gums bleed. When I come back, Seth is fully clothed, thank God. We head down to the kitchen, where Tess and her wife are leaving for work, but they tell us to stay and eat from the plate of pastries they've left out, and to drop the keys in the box outside when we're ready to go.

Once they're gone, Seth clears his throat. "So—"

Just then his phone rings.

He picks it up while I text my brother. **Dad didn't notice anything?**

Davy's message back: **No. He's at his golf thing. When are you home?**

Prob around lunchtime, I write back, hoping it's true.

"The car's ready," Seth says. "We can get an Uber to pick it up."

But he's frowning down at his phone.

"What?" I want to know.

"The mechanic's not positive, but he thinks someone might have messed with my car."

"What? How?"

Seth launches into some technical explanation I don't understand, but the bottom line is that the car seems to have been scuttled deliberately.

"Someone didn't want us to make it to Philly." Seth looks grim.

"But who even knew we were going?" I ask.

"Kendall," he answers. "But she wasn't home last night; she went back to the city, and when I drove my car yesterday, it was fine. Besides, she was the one who told us about Caleb. My mom and dad knew I was coming to Philly, but not why. Oh, and Marion knew."

I frown. "Did you tell her why we were coming here?" I don't want Marion telling Davy where I am, or that I wasn't with Kendall.

"No, just that I was meeting up with a friend."

I try and process all this. "I mean—it could have been just a problem with the car, right?"

Seth nods, but he looks unsure. "Or—" He hesitates.

"What?"

"Maybe someone was following us that night. Heard us say we were coming here."

A shiver goes down my spine, even though it's broad daylight. "You really think that?"

"I don't know." Then he frowns. "Or it could have been someone just trying to mess with me, not even knowing where I was headed."

"Who? Has anyone given you weird looks when you're out and about? Like they suspect you of something?"

He shakes his head. "Do people do that to you?"

"I assume they are, so I just don't look at anybody."

An exhale that may be the start of a laugh. "I still think you're letting those posts from that one guy get in your head."

I shake my head. "Whatever. Now that the car is fixed, let's just go."

To Philly. To our only lead so far.

———

Skies are clear today, and there's hardly any traffic on the hour-and-change ride to Philadelphia. Seth keeps his eyes straight ahead of him. There's no trace of what happened last night on his face, and I wonder if he decided to leave whatever he felt for me behind in that little attic bedroom when I told him no.

Caleb lives in a dorm in the city center. Seth's big plan is to follow someone in, walk around looking like we belong there, and if we don't see him, ask someone which room is his.

It works. We're about five feet behind a redhead, and when she swipes a key fob to the door, Seth steps forward and catches it before it closes. He holds it open for me, and we walk through another doorway and into a two-story lounge with long windows and tables and chairs and couches.

We search but don't see Caleb anywhere. After a few minutes, I finally go up to a guy and ask if he knows which room is Caleb Jones's, making up some story about needing to borrow notes. He directs me to a room on the third floor.

As we make our way down the hallway, a knot forms in my stomach. It gets bigger when we reach his door. Was someone really trying to stop us from talking to him?

What could he possibly have to say that's so important?

I touch Fiona's necklace, take a deep breath, and knock.

No answer.

I knock again. Nothing.

I hold my ear to the door, but it doesn't sound like anyone is inside, hiding from us. Seth and I look at each other.

He pulls out his phone. "That post I saw from a few days ago, he was at some diner."

I look over his shoulder as he scrolls. There are a lot of photos, though hardly any with Caleb in it. A stack of books. A stack of pancakes. Sunset over the city.

He enlarges the pancake photo. "The Blue Heron. He was there last Sunday. We could try that."

It seems like a long shot, but I don't want to face the idea that we've come all this way for nothing.

I nod.

Seth shrugs. "If nothing else, I could use some pancakes."

———

The Blue Heron is farther into the west side of the city, where things are decidedly less modern and shiny. The diner is silver and blue, with a little parking lot attached. We park and cautiously approach the door.

A bell jangles when we walk in. There are tables in the center of the room, booths along the side, in the same blue and silver colors as the outside. I scan the room as the hostess leads us toward the back, my hopes not very high—

When a movement in one corner catches my eye.

Tall Black guy with close-cropped black hair. Glasses. His back is to us. The hostess sits us at the booth in front of him, and he's facing away from us. I'm flipping through our options—walk by like I'm going to the bathroom, happen to glance down? Just walk right up to the table?—when the guy turns around and looks straight at us.

It's Caleb Jones.

17

AT THE SIGHT of us, Caleb freezes.

Seth glances at me and then swiftly slides out of our booth and into Caleb's. A moment later, I follow.

Caleb's paused with his coffee halfway to his lips. Now he sets it down, eyes flickering around the diner, then back to Seth and me.

"I can guess why you're here." Caleb's voice is soft, the way I remember it, his wrists thin. He wears a button-down short-sleeved shirt with a checkered print on it. His dark eyes are huge behind his glasses.

"We just want to talk," Seth says.

Caleb's eyes dart to the exit. "I don't have anything to say." He starts to rise.

"Thatcher's dead," Seth says bluntly. "The cops might think Addie and I are to blame. We're not. But we need to find out who is. So if you know anything that could help us—please."

Caleb's eyes are wide. He doesn't look guilty, as far as I can tell—just scared.

"You joining him?" A server appears at our table, a twenty-something person with orange hair and a pierced lip.

"We need a minute," Seth says. Then he looks at Caleb. "Please. Just a minute."

The server shrugs and walks away.

Once they're gone, Caleb uncertainly eases himself back down.

"Is it true you were with Thatcher the night my sister died?" I ask.

Caleb still looks nervous. "You're not recording this, are you?"

"No." Seth places his phone on the table in front of us, and after a moment, I do the same.

"We won't tell anyone anything you tell us," I say, not knowing whether I'm lying. "We just want to know who did this. Up until recently, I thought Thatcher killed my sister."

At this, Caleb comes alive. "He didn't." His voice is quiet but forceful.

"But you weren't actually with him that night. Were you?"

His eyes go from me to Seth again, and then he exhales. "No," he says. "No. I told the police I was because . . . they were asking him questions, and I had some gallant notion of saving him, I suppose." His mouth twists briefly into an imitation of a smile. "Not that it mattered, in the end."

"Can you start at the beginning?" Seth asks.

Caleb grips his coffee cup in both hands. "There is no beginning. I did meet up with Thatcher that night, at the parade. But we both went home around eleven. I told the police I went to Thatcher's house instead of saying I went back to my own." He looks at me. "He didn't ask me to do that. It was my idea."

"Why did you feel like you had to lie?" I ask.

"I thought it might look bad. We saw Fiona that night, before we went home, and she and Thatcher were fighting again."

I go still. "Fighting *again*? About what?"

"I didn't hear. We saw her across the green, looking upset. Thatcher ran ahead of me to talk to her. Whatever he said seemed to upset her more, and she ran away. I just assumed it was more about the ballet school money, but when Thatcher came back to me, looking angry, he said he didn't want to talk about it. So I didn't push it."

I blink. "What do you mean, the ballet school money?"

Caleb's eyebrows go up. "When Fiona went to Thatcher about ballet school." I must look totally clueless, because Caleb goes on, "They only gave her partial financial aid. She wanted Thatcher to lend her the money for the rest of her tuition."

Beside me, Seth sucks in a breath. But I frown. "No. She got a scholarship for the rest of it."

"That's not what she told him. She came to him sometime in the spring, asking for money. He said no. And she got . . . upset with him."

I sit back, processing this. "But—she was *going* to the American Ballet Academy. She was leaving in a week. She was practicing extra and everything."

"Did you tell the police this?" Seth asks Caleb. "Did Thatcher tell the police this?"

Caleb shakes his head. "Maybe I should have, but I didn't want them to have any more reasons to look at Thatcher. I don't know if he told them. He stopped talking to me after that week."

"How much money did Fiona ask Thatcher for?" I ask.

"Forty-two thousand dollars and change."

I let this sink in. Then I ask Seth, "Did Thatcher have that much money?"

Seth nods shortly.

"That doesn't mean he had to give it to her," Caleb says. "You know how Thatcher felt about Fiona, I presume?" He directs the question at Seth, but I nod. "She knew, too. She told him a few years back that she was sorry, but she just didn't feel that way about him. Then one day last spring she showed up at his place in the city, asked him if they could talk. And she just flat out asked him for money." He shrugs. "It bothered him. And

I don't blame him. He told her she didn't get to use him like that, and she got upset. Then he got upset with her for being upset, and . . . it affected their friendship, to say the least."

My mind is going furiously. I wonder how upset Thatcher really was. I catch Seth's eyes on me and feel like he's reading my mind.

"He did feel bad about it," Caleb adds. "It wasn't even that much to him, and she needed it so badly, but he didn't like feeling used. I told him it was the right thing to do. But then again, I'm biased." His mouth twists again, and it's then I see it: the deep sadness in Caleb's eyes.

I want to leave Caleb alone, to his grief. But there's no helping it. We need to know everything we can. I lean forward. "But why were they fighting that night? And why did he show up at our house looking mad last July? He'd already said no. She had the scholarship, she didn't need his money. It was over."

He lifts his shoulders. "I don't know. All I know is what Thatcher told me."

"Why do you think Thatcher stopped talking to you?" Seth asks then.

"I don't know."

"Did he seem scared of someone to you?" Seth presses.

"I don't know," Caleb repeats. "There's not much you can guess from one text message."

"What text message? What did it say?"

"*Thanks for everything, C. It means a lot. Need some time to process all of this. Be in touch when I can,*" Caleb quotes.

"And you never heard from him again?"

Caleb shakes his head. "I gave him a week, then just texted him to check up on him. He was at Oxford by then. But he didn't answer me. He never answered me. Not my texts or my emails. I sent a card when I heard about your grandma. And then when I heard about—" He chokes on the words, and I feel awful again for being here, for making him talk through all of this.

"I couldn't go," he near whispers. "I couldn't see him—not like that."

The pain on Caleb's face. His soft voice. I believe him.

I never really believed that Caleb was the killer. But now I'm sure. It wasn't him.

Which means it was someone else.

And I have no idea who.

Caleb's hands go to the table in front of him, rest in front of his coffee cup.

"I'm sorry." I rise abruptly. "We didn't mean to bring it all up, we just—"

"We're desperate," Seth says quietly.

"And this helped. A lot." I don't know if it's true. But I say it anyway.

Caleb gives us a stiff nod. "I know how close you and Thatcher were." This to Seth. Then his eyes go to me. "And how close you and Fiona were. I don't believe it was you. If I did, I wouldn't be talking to you."

"Thanks," I say, even though it seems like a weird thing to say.

Caleb's eyes flicker from me to Seth again. "That means there's someone else out there who . . . hurt them." He grips his coffee cup tightly. "Be careful."

Seth and I exchange a glance. "We will," I say.

Then Seth and I go without eating, leaving Caleb in the Blue Heron Diner, bent over his cup of cold coffee, alone.

18

SETH IS SILENT as he drives. Before long, we're in New Jersey again. I'm quiet, too, going over everything we just learned.

Fiona found out she made it into the American Ballet Academy one day mid-spring last year. We got home from school and her phone buzzed. She pulled it out and froze. *The academy,* she whispered.

I stood there, my traitorous heart in my throat. I didn't want her to go. I knew how intense that school was. She used to say she never wanted to actually go away to a ballet school. Didn't want it stealing her childhood. But all that changed after Mom left. At first, she'd say she wasn't good enough for ABA. It wasn't until high school that she seriously started thinking of applying, and even then it was always *They hardly ever take anyone as old as me. It's just a dream.* But then she was practicing more, and that dream was becoming a reality.

It wasn't like she wasn't there for us after Mom. She was home at dinner every night, she and I preparing it together, a nine- and ten-year-old doing our best to cobble together sandwiches, salads, even getting brave enough to boil water for pasta. But when Grandpa died and Dad was back in the picture, that was apparently the permission she needed to throw herself back into dance. She never missed a lesson, even practicing on her days off.

I daydreamed about what our future would be like without ballet. Maybe we'd go to the same college, be roommates, take some of the same classes. Maybe she'd even find something she wanted to do at Stanford and we could move out there together. Get some cute little apartment near a coffee shop or a park. We'd decorate it together, come home late from our respective classes or jobs, catch each other up on our days. Normal sisters with a normal life.

I didn't want her to get into the American Ballet Academy. I wanted it to be a rejection.

But it wasn't. Fiona's hand went to her mouth, tears in her eyes. My heart sank. *I got in,* she said, over and over. *I got in.*

She told Dad and Davy over dinner. My dad asked to see the email. And then when he read it, a frown appeared on his face. He took her into the other room to tell her he couldn't afford it, not with only partial financial aid. She emerged, face tear-streaked, and locked herself in her room, refusing to let even me in.

The next few months, Fiona was . . . off. I gave her space. She was gone even more, practicing, always practicing. I thought it was some form of denial. She took a job cleaning at her ballet studio, so she was there more often than she was home. And it wasn't just her physical absence; she was distant, too. She didn't have time to help me with my homework. She barely listened when I went to her to talk about Jeremy. She came to prom, but her heart was somewhere else, eyes gazing into the distance. I thought she was mourning her dreams and eventually she'd come around, realize that there's more than one way to live a life.

Then, in July, Fiona hovering in the doorway to the kitchen. *I got the money for school.*

I was shocked. I didn't even know there was another way. It took me a moment to compose my face, to jump up to hug her, even as my heart was breaking. This little smile on her face through it all—

That was weird, now that I think about it. She wasn't jumping up and down, smiling ear to ear. Just a little half smile, her eyes downcast. This quiet certainty. And that wording: *I got the money.*

I *assumed* she meant a scholarship. But what if it was something else?

"What are you thinking?" Seth asks.

I tell him. He listens, a frown on his face. "So—you think her scholarship didn't exist?"

"I mean, I don't know for sure. But if there was no scholarship—where would she have gotten the money? I don't think she was lying about leaving for school. I mean, why would she?" I frown. "So maybe when Thatcher said no, she went to someone else."

"Or . . . she did something not so great for it."

I stare. "Like what?"

"Like drugs?"

"You think Fiona was dealing drugs?"

"I don't know a ton of jobs that pay that much in a short amount of time."

I shake my head. "Fiona never broke any rules in her entire life. And you think in a few months she learned how to be a drug dealer?"

"Just throwing it out there."

I think about my sister. The school of her dreams was just within reach—and suddenly it was gone again because she didn't have enough money. And down the road, a boy she'd known her whole life held the solution.

And he said no. It must have burned her up inside when he said that.

"What if she stole the money from Thatcher?" I look at Seth. "Caleb could be lying."

Seth doesn't blink. "I believed him. And even if she'd stolen it—this is going to sound obnoxious, but forty-two thousand dollars isn't that much money for Thatcher. His trust fund had . . . a lot more. He wouldn't have killed her over that. No one in my family would have."

I close my eyes. "That *is* really obnoxious."

"I know. That's why I said it."

"You're all part of the problem, you know. You could use that money to house people who need homes, or help people with their medical debt, or—"

"I know, Addie. We've been over this, like, a thousand times? I donate to charity."

"How much?"

"None of your business." He shoots me a look.

But I'm not embarrassed. "Someday, we're gonna eat the rich. And don't count on me to save you."

He sighs. "Yes, you've said as much before. Can we get back on topic, please? And can you take notes, since I'm driving?"

I'm tempted to keep railing on the rich, but instead I open the Notes app on my phone and write down our latest theories.

"You said Fiona was gone a lot last summer," Seth says. "More than usual."

"She was practicing, and she also got a job at the dance studio. Cleaning it after hours."

"Are you sure that's where she really was?"

"You think she was lying about that? That instead of working and practicing, she spent all that time dealing drugs?"

"It's just a theory."

I rub one eye. "We could be wrong about all of this, Seth. She might have gotten the scholarship; maybe it just took a while to come through and she panicked and went to Thatcher. We should make sure before we start assuming my sister was a drug dealer or a thief. I'll call the American Ballet Academy and ask." I add that to our list.

Seth flicks on his turn signal, and we ease off the highway. I realize we're at our exit. The drive home flew by.

"And I can check Fiona's room again," I add. "Maybe there's something in there somewhere about ballet school."

He nods. "Good idea. But if we find out there wasn't a scholarship— we need to figure out where she got that money."

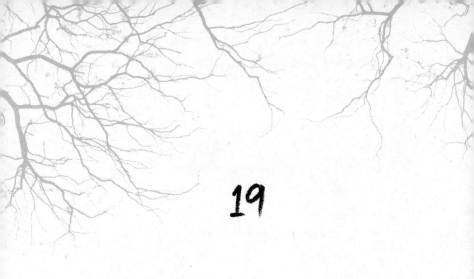

19

SETH DROPS ME off on a dead end a few blocks from my house. There's an awkward moment when we say goodbye where I'm not sure if he's about to hug me, but he just gives me a wave and I hop out of his car without looking back.

It's afternoon and the house is empty. Dad's at work, but Davy should be home. I'm about to call him when I realize I should take advantage of the empty house while I can.

No one goes into Fiona's room. It's an unspoken rule. I definitely don't want to do it while my dad or Davy are home to ask questions.

The top stair creaks when I step on it. The upstairs hallway is shadowy and silent. Fiona has a desk in her room I'll check first. There's also her closet. I made myself go in there last fall to search for clues, for anything pointing to Thatcher or to anyone else who might have killed her, and found nothing. But that time I had no idea what I was looking for.

I'm halfway down the hallway when I hear a creak.

I freeze.

There's someone inside my sister's room.

My hand flies to my pocket, but I left both phones downstairs. And why wouldn't I? I'm alone in my own house in the middle of the day.

I have a brief war with myself. To run down there now and get a phone, then come back? To run out of the house and call the police? To fling open the door and surprise whoever's in there?

Another noise—a door creaking open. Her closet.

I touch Fiona's necklace. Then I make a split-second decision, close the three feet to her door in two strides, and fling it open.

To find my brother standing in front of the closet, eyes wide.

"Davy." I'm so relieved, I can't think. "What are you doing in here?"

"Um." My brother shifts. The look on his face can only be described as guilt. "I was searching for something."

"What?"

"I thought . . . Dad might have stored some of my stuff back here," he mumbles.

Davy is a terrible liar. I frown. "Davy. What are you doing in here?"

His eyes go from me to the window and back again. "I was looking for Fiona's journal."

I blink. "What? Why?"

Ramsay was the first one to tell me about my sister's missing journal. *Your father says Fiona kept a journal. When we searched her room, we couldn't find it. Where do you think it could be? There was no sign of a break-in. The doors were all locked. So if someone stole it—it would have to be someone with access to your house.*

The implication was clear. He thought I took it. I told him I had no idea where Fiona's journal was. Because I don't.

"Um, so you know how the police asked us where it was after Fiona died?" Davy asks. I nod. "They asked Marion, too."

I narrow my eyes. "Why would they ask *Marion* if she knew where Fiona's journal is?"

"Well, the thing is—Marion was here that night."

"What?"

"The night of the parade last year. She spent the night here. With me." The expression on his face is a mix of embarrassment and guilt. "We're not little kids, Addie, we're sixteen years old—"

"You were fifteen last summer."

"Yeah, well, we didn't do anything—or that much." He averts his eyes. "So she was here that night, and she told the police that because it's the truth, and then they started asking questions about the journal and if she went into Fiona's room, but she didn't, I know she didn't, I would've woken up if she did, you know what a light sleeper I am, and anyway, Marion didn't *do* anything."

"Okay." I put a hand on his arm. "I believe you." But my mind is racing. Marion, here with Davy the whole night, the night Fiona died. "That still doesn't explain why you're looking for her journal now."

He lifts his shoulders. "I thought maybe if I could find it, it would prove to them that Marion didn't take it. They called her to the police station again yesterday to ask her questions. Her dad had to have her lawyer come out from the city."

My heart skips a beat. Why do they think Marion, tiny little mouse Marion, has anything to do with all of this?

"What else did they ask her?" I ask Davy.

"Just about what she did when she was here that night, and then about what she was doing the night her brother died. She told them she was just at home, but she doesn't think they believe her. They even—they even asked about our relationship." Davy looks mad now. "Like they thought it wasn't real or something."

My mind is racing. I don't know what to think. "Did you really think you'd be able to find Fiona's journal when the police couldn't?"

"I thought I'd at least *try*." He frowns. "But all I found was this box of paper." He picks up a shoe box off the floor with what indeed looks like paper in it. "No journal."

I walk forward. "Let me see that."

I riffle through the shoe box, thinking maybe the scholarship info came in snail mail form, but there's nothing in there from the American Ballet Academy, just old receipts, mostly for leotards and tights. Next to me, Davy's moved on to her desk.

"Did you find anything else in here?" I ask. "Anything from the American Ballet Academy?"

Davy shakes his head. I set the box down and frown.

Just because there's no proof of any scholarship doesn't mean it didn't exist. I'll just call them and find out.

I go over to Fiona's desk. Her pink music box with the pop-up pink ballerina sits on top, the one I took her necklace from the day after she died. It's been a long time since I've heard that tinkling tune, but I remember it like it was yesterday. *Dunn-dun-dunn-dun-dunn-dun-dun-dun-dunn* . . . "Greensleeves," it's called. It's sad and haunting, and I have no idea why anyone ever thought it would be a good song for a little girl's jewelry box.

That song's creepy, I told her once.

I like creepy music, she replied. *Someday I'm going to star in* Giselle, *which is, like, the creepiest ballet ever.*

You're weird.

You love me.

When I was searching her room last fall, I didn't open the jewelry box. I didn't want to hear that tune again. It would have made me too sad. But maybe she kept something from ABA in here—something I might have missed the day I took the necklace out. I was in too much of a daze then, my eyes puffy from crying. I open it now.

There's a second where I hear only silence, and I have a moment of panic, thinking it's stopped working. But no—there are the notes that will always remind me of Fiona.

Dunn-dun-dunn-dun-dunn-dun-dun-dun-dunn . . .

There's no letter in here. But I do notice a little scrap of paper curled around the tiny ballerina. I pick it up. It's a torn bit of paper with a series of numbers on it: *073114*.

I frown. It doesn't mean anything to me. Probably Fiona's locker combination at her studio or something. I pocket it just in case.

I listen to "Greensleeves" one whole way through while Davy rummages through the lower desk drawer. It's a mess of random things: old cards, a stuffed animal, a tangle of ribbons. The top drawer is no better: pens, paper clips, hair ties.

Davy sits back with a frown. "There's nothing here." He sounds frustrated.

"I didn't think there would be." I rise. "Clean up before you go," I tell him. "And, Davy?"

"Yeah?"

"Just tell me if you find anything from the American Ballet Academy, will you?"

"Sure," he says, but his head is bent over the bottom drawer, moving things around, and I'm not even sure he heard me.

20

THE NEXT DAY, I call the American Ballet Academy to ask about Fiona's scholarship, but the lady on the phone is distinctly unhelpful, refusing to disclose any information on the grounds of privacy.

I'm filled with pent-up anger when I hang up the phone. If it were any closer than the city, I'd march over there right now and demand to—I don't know, speak to the manager or something. But I can't do that from here.

So I throw on my sneakers and head out on a run.

Running's like math. Predictable. Uncomplicated. One foot in front of the other, over and over again. Put two and two together and get four. No interpretation, no nuance. When I was little, whenever things would start to veer off course for me, I would retreat into numbers. Multiplication tables. Prime numbers. The digits of pi. This past year, I ramped up my running, added it to my list of coping mechanisms, chanting my prime numbers along with my steps.

Forty-one, forty-three, forty-seven, fifty-three, fifty-nine—

Jeremy used to come with me on my runs, jogging along next to me and calling it his "pre-workout" before the more intense ones he did for football.

Not Gen, though. Gen hated running.

I don't want to think about Seth's theory. How Gen might have been there that night.

Gen has no money, at least. So there'd be no way that part of the puzzle could be connected to her.

But what if it's not about the money, and Seth's theory that someone was trying to kill *me* is the right one?

Could Gen really hate me that much?

Jeremy and Gen. Her hand on his arm at the wake. Him looking for her at at the movie night in the park.

What are they doing together?

Seventy-three, seventy-nine, eighty-three—

A car flies by, going too fast, making me jump.

I don't really think someone's about to come along and hit me with their car. But I miss the days when I used to run along the trails in the woods. The path I liked best goes along the border between the Montgomery property and the state park, past the abandoned tree house Fiona and I used to play in with the Montgomerys, then winds out to the park before you hit the Bier property. It's grassy, but the middle is worn down enough that it's mostly dirt, easy to run on.

I told Dad and Davy I wouldn't go there anymore.

But it's broad daylight. And suddenly, that's where I want to be. It was my place to run with only the trees watching me. I want it back.

One fifty-seven, one sixty-three, one sixty-seven—

I look over my shoulder. No one on the road. Then I stop midstride, turn, and head back toward the woods.

There's no one around when I slip in between the trees. Soon they're all around me, reaching into the sky, reducing it to little spots of blue between leaves. The dirt path is more overgrown than the last time I was here, over a year ago. I wonder, with a pang, if the old tree house is even still there or if it's collapsed, swallowed up by the woods.

My eyes flicker downward when I pass the log with Jeremy's and my initials on it. He carved them there last summer, before everything fell apart.

Why are you doing that?

I want to immortalize us in a place we like to go.

I push the memory away. I don't need to be thinking about Jeremy right now.

Four forty-three, four forty-nine, four fifty-seven—

It can get so green back here in the summer, it hurts your eyes. It's like that now, every shade crowding around me, blotting out the still-blue sky. Crickets and birds chirp; the wind blows through the trees. The day is starting to take on that golden syrupy quality I love. Maybe it's the way it makes everything softer and prettier; maybe it's how this time of day makes me feel like I'm a little kid again, before everything went so horribly wrong.

Jeremy likes this time of day, too. Not like Seth, who always comes out at twilight. I remember one day with the light like this, lying in the grass in my backyard, Jeremy talking about our future . . . *And we're gonna have this big farmhouse with a huge yard, and we'll have chickens and goats and maybe a horse—*

Me, laughing at him. *Do you know how much work it is to have a horse?*

I don't care. I want space. A big house. Land. So I can feel like even the sky is mine.

Jeremy. His face crumpling when the truth of Seth and me finally got through to him. When he realized I was telling him about Seth not to ask for forgiveness, but because I wanted him and me to be over. Sometimes I wonder what would have happened if I'd asked Jeremy to stay. But I didn't. I didn't want him to. I knew I didn't deserve him.

Five oh three, five oh nine, five twenty-one—

And now he's back to hanging out with Gen.

Is it possible that what I did changed him, changed Gen, in some fundamental way? That the best friends I had are gone, just like that, and new people have taken their place? That I really, truly don't know either of them anymore? Do people change that fast, that drastically?

I did, when Fiona died. That knock on my door, my dad's face ashen, the officer behind him. The moment his words sank into my brain. There was before-Addie and there's after-Addie. The one who had hope that she and her sister would become close again, and the one who knows that hope is dead forever. They're two different people. I know that.

But Gen losing me, Jeremy losing me, wasn't the same as me losing Fiona. Wasn't as final.

Unless they didn't see it that way.

The day is still hot, but the sweat on my neck feels clammy. There's a break in the foliage ahead. When I reach the tree house, I stop.

It was built far up in a hulking old maple, only accessible because of the little wooden boards nailed into the trunk decades before we were born. Most of it was too unstable to play in, rotting and cracked wood, but that never stopped us. Fiona and I found it first and used to leave messages for each other here. Then one day we arrived to find the Montgomerys here, playing pirate ship. That was our first turf war with them. It would not be our last. Fiona and I always lost because they were bigger and there were more of them. But we never went down without a fight.

During the school year, we brought our other friends here, too. The day after Jeremy's dad died, Jeremy and Gen and I spent an entire afternoon up on the lower platform, the only solid one, having a long conversation about life and death and God and heaven and hell. I remember concluding that none of us believed in the "cloud castles with angels playing harps" version of heaven we were taught, but all of us hoped that there was some version that existed somewhere.

As I got older, I effectively rejected even that. Then when Fiona died, I started praying again. *Please be somewhere. Please don't be gone. Please.*

I gaze up at the tree house now, wondering if that lower platform would even hold us now.

I grab on to Fiona's necklace. I don't want to be here anymore. I take off running.

If you go far enough, the trail eventually links up with the state park and, from there, the Appalachian Trail. You could get on it and head to Maine or Georgia, depending on which way you turn, run and run until your legs gave out, until you've left Bier's End far behind.

I've been pounding along for less than five minutes when I round a sharp bend—and almost run smack into someone coming the other way.

"Whoa!"

I dodge to avoid them, then promptly trip on a tree root and fall, hard, onto the ground. My palms are stinging, and my elbow's hit the edge of a log. I brush off the bits of dirt and wood. It's bleeding but not that bad.

A hand on my shoulder. "Addie."

My heart drops.

Because I'd know that voice anywhere.

It's Jeremy.

21

"ARE YOU OKAY?"

I turn slowly, to give Jeremy time to run away if that's what he wants to do. But he doesn't. Here he is, all six-foot-one of him, white T-shirt, mesh shorts, backward cap over his brown hair, standing in front of me, breathing hard. His hand's dropped, but he's still looking down at me.

"Fine." I hope he doesn't hear the tremor in my voice.

His brows come together. "You're bleeding."

His hand hovers in the air, unsure. I get to my feet on my own, brushing my palms together. "I'm fine," I say again.

A flash of his smile, so quick I might have imagined it, and then he averts his eyes, pulls one arm into a stretch. "Didn't know you ran this way anymore."

"I don't usually. Just decided to today for whatever reason."

It's strange, standing here in this place I used to stand in, talking to the person I used to stand here with, but with the gulf of a year and everything that happened between then and now. Jeremy looks like he's gotten bigger in the time we've been apart, his muscles straining through the thin fabric of his T-shirt.

"Yeah. Me too."

I look down at my right hand. Little beads of blood bloom alongside the bits of dirt wedged there.

"So, are you okay?" His brows are drawn in that concerned-Jeremy way. "I don't just mean your hands. I mean—are *you* okay?"

I know I don't deserve this. Him standing here, acting like he still cares. But I miss it. And not just because he was my boyfriend. Because before that, he was one of my best friends.

"I'm fine. Thanks."

A moment of quiet then, us pausing there in the gold-edged leaf shadow, looking at each other. Birds chirping, the scamper of a small animal in the undergrowth. Jeremy's eyes go over me, taking in my black hair, black running clothes. I wonder what he thinks about them, about how thin I've gotten. He used to tell me he loved my curves, my plain dirty-blond hair.

I don't want to bring up anything to ruin this strange trucelike space we're in. But maybe he knows where Gen was the night Fiona died. If she has a valid alibi, then I can stop torturing myself with the theory that my former best friend tried to kill me.

"Jeremy, can I ask you something?"

A slight paling of his skin. His green eyes shift from right to left. "Sure."

His casual tone is forced. He's nervous.

I frown but forge on. "Um . . . so I noticed you've been hanging out with Gen."

His eyebrows go up. That wasn't what he was expecting me to ask. "It's not what you think."

"I mean, it's not my business, but—" I hesitate.

We look at each other.

"We're not together," he says at the same time I ask, "Are you together?"

I exhale, and so does he.

"So do you know what—"

And suddenly—footsteps along the trail, from the direction of the Montgomerys'. Both Jeremy and I turn to look.

The figure who appears around the bend makes my heart drop.

Seth.

"What are you doing here?" Jeremy and I say at the same time.

Seth looks from him to me, his face unreadable. "Just going for a stroll."

My eyes go down to his feet. Flip-flops, not loafers, at least, but still. There's no way on earth Seth is out here *going for a stroll*.

"Bullshit," I say.

Seth looks like he's about to argue, but then he jerks his head at Jeremy. "Fine. I followed him."

"Why?" Jeremy's voice is flat, and his hands are in fists at his sides.

Seth's arms are crossed. A mistake; if someone swung at him, he'd be late in trying to block it. I wonder if he's ever been in a fight in his life. "Wanted to know what you were doing, running past my property."

"What's it to you, Seth?" Jeremy's voice is tight.

Seth's eyes flicker to me. A muscle in Jeremy's jaw twitches. The woods around us have stilled, the birdsong ceased.

"So you guys are hanging out again?" Jeremy asks.

"No," I say quickly.

"What's it to you?" Seth asks.

Jeremy shifts to his other foot, looks at me. "He told you what I did."

I'm startled. "What are you talking about?"

"I didn't tell her, actually," Seth says.

I look from Seth to Jeremy. "Tell me *what?*"

Seth's hand goes up to touch the scar over his eyebrow.

The scar that wasn't there last year.

"What happened?" I ask.

When Jeremy doesn't say anything, Seth, not taking his eyes off him, says, "Your boy paid me a visit last year."

"What? When? Where?"

"At Columbia. Beginning of September." After I told Jeremy about me and Seth. My heart is sinking. "I was walking through campus with a buddy, minding my own business, when all of a sudden Captain America's standing in front of me, all riled up. Before I could say a word, I was on the ground."

"If I'd known you had no idea how to block a punch, maybe I wouldn't have swung so hard," Jeremy says.

Despite himself, Seth's mouth quirks up in a half smile. "This kid fucking *laid* into me, Addie. He broke my nose. Gave me this scar. Almost broke my arm."

A lift of Jeremy's shoulders as he gazes at Seth. He doesn't look at all sorry. "I didn't know it was going to go like that. I thought you'd be able to hold your own."

"Kind of hard to hold your own when a fist comes at you out of nowhere."

Jeremy lets out a short laugh. I've never heard him laugh that way before. "Keep telling yourself that, man." His fists clench and unclench again. He's barely holding himself back, I realize. I've never seen him like this. Even the night I told him about me and Seth, he was just . . . blank. Not angry.

Then Jeremy turns to me. "What is it, Addie? His money?"

I stare. "What?"

"'Cause it's not like I don't know what not having money's like. But is it really worth it, being his . . ." He stumbles over his words.

A flash of rage goes through me, so strong it temporarily blinds me.

"Watch your words, Reagan." Seth's tone is mild, but he moves a step closer to me, and his fists are at his sides now.

I look at the boy I used to love. His green eyes are flat and he's breathing hard, even though he stopped running what feels like ages ago.

For the first time ever, he looks like a stranger.

Jeremy breaks my gaze, sets his jaw. "Just stay away from me. Both of you."

Then he turns and sprints down the path, back the way I came, putting as much distance as possible between himself and Seth, between himself and me, as fast as he can.

I don't stick around to hear what Seth has to say.

A moment later, I'm running in the same direction as Jeremy, counting on two things: that I'm not fast enough to catch up to him, and that Seth isn't fast enough, especially in his flip-flops, to catch up to me. I'm right on both counts. I need to put some space between myself and whatever alpha male bullshit all that was.

I arrive home breathless and with a lump in my throat that makes me angrier than anything else. As I shower, the thing simmering inside me only gets hotter.

Seth. What was he doing? Why did he follow Jeremy? What was he trying to prove?

And Jeremy. What was he thinking? Going into the city, tracking down Seth at school, walking up and hitting him in exactly the right way to damage him the best way he knew how?

What happened to him? Did I really mess him up that much?

Why didn't Seth tell me?

Davy's not home. I text him and find out he's on another bike ride with Marion. After walking Sadie, I flop down on my bed and squeeze my eyes shut. And there Jeremy is, his twitching jaw muscle, his eyes flat and angry.

And across from him, Seth.

I'm not a napper. But somehow, maybe because of everything swirling around in my head, I fall asleep. And I dream.

We're in the woods behind the Bier mansion, all of us: Thatcher and Seth, Kendall and Fiona, me and Jeremy and Gen, Davy and Marion. The sky is an oddly bright blue. I hear someone call my name, so I push through the leaves to see Fiona in the stone circle near the ravine, dancing. But she doesn't see me, dances away from me, twirling so fast I can't catch her. A rope hangs from a tree branch, and I'm afraid to go near it. Someone laughs behind me, a deep, loud laugh that makes the hairs on my arms stand up, and I run, away from Fiona, away from the rope. There's a boy in front of me, catching me, and I look up at his face but I can't tell whether it's Jeremy or Seth. Then the boy changes into Thatcher. I scream, but no sound comes out. Then Kendall is behind me, reaching out her hand, whispering to me to follow her, Davy and Marion huddled behind her, but I don't know who to trust or who to follow, so I run off into the woods, the leaves a whirl of black and green, pressing in on me, making it hard to breathe.

I wake up sweating. And that night, it takes me a long time to fall asleep.

22

THE NEXT MORNING, I wake up to a text from Seth.

Can we talk about what happened yesterday?

I don't answer.

I know that isn't fair. Seth was the one who was assaulted. By my ex-boyfriend. Because of me. It wasn't his fault.

But he could have told me.

There's a small, uncomfortable voice in my head asking me if I would have believed him. Would I have thought it was that bad? If he had no scar? If Jeremy hadn't been there yesterday , if I hadn't seen the truth written on his face?

Addie? We ok?

I can't talk right now. Heading to Fiona's studio

I didn't get the chance to ask Jeremy if he saw Gen the night Fiona died. And now I don't know when or even if I will. So maybe Fiona's old dance teacher knows something about her scholarship. It's the only lead I have right now.

I visited the dance studio last year, when I was doing my own investigation into any stalkers or jealous ballerina friends Fiona might have had. But I never asked about her scholarship.

Another buzz. Seth: **I'd come with if I could**

I'll be fine

The sky is gray, but my weather app says no rain until later, so I hop on my bike and ride to The Studio, on the outskirts of downtown, alone.

I lock my bike on a rack a block away. The Studio is a small local space, clean white front, picture windows stenciled with the outlines of dancers. I took ballet for two years here when I was little, in an effort to be more like Fiona, before it became clear I sucked at it. There are two actual studios plus a changing room and bathroom. Nothing fancy. Most of the kids who go here never have a shot at anything like the American Ballet Academy.

A tinkling bell announces my arrival. The only person in the small lobby is the woman behind the desk, gray-haired and spectacled. She looks up, sees me, and visibly sighs. "Madame LeGrand is with a class right now, Ms. Blackwood."

I fix her with my I'm-not-going-anywhere expression. "That's okay. I'll wait."

I sit down on one of the chairs in the lobby, directly across from a professional portrait of my sister. It's from the winter performance of *The Nutcracker* her junior year. She was Clara, of course. She was always the lead. She smiles at me, her white dress immaculate, her blond bun impeccable. I feel a deep sadness go through me. Sometimes I think about what loss must have been like in the days before photographs. I wonder if it was worse, never being able to see their face again except in your memories. Or better, because you weren't constantly reminded of how alive they used to be.

The sound of a door opening makes me look up.

A flurry of chattering ten-year-olds in leotards pours out of the nearest studio, heading for the changing room. Madame LeGrand is just behind them. She's a tall woman in her forties, made entirely of muscle, dressed in a black leotard and skirt, with white skin, dark hair, and hooded dark eyes. Her eyes flicker to me as she walks by—and then she stops.

"Miss Blackwood." Madame LeGrand gives me a nod.

"Hi. I'm sorry to bother you again, but I have another question, if you have a minute."

She nods. She's always been exceedingly nice to me. "Come with me."

I rise and follow her through a door to the left. Inside is a small office, one window, a chipped wooden desk. Framed pictures of dancers adorn the walls. I don't know if they're past students or just dancers she admires. Fiona's picture isn't in here.

Madame LeGrand sits down behind her desk and gestures to the chairs across from her. "How may I help you today?"

I sit down. "Do you know anything about Fiona's scholarship to the American Ballet Academy?" I blurt out.

Madame LeGrand frowns. "You mean her financial aid?"

"Not that. I mean the scholarship she got to pay for what the financial aid couldn't cover."

Her perfect black eyebrows rise. "She never told me about this scholarship. From what I understood, your father was paying for the rest of it."

I blink. "I— He was?"

Madame LeGrand sits back. "Your sister came to me in tears when your father told her he couldn't afford the American Ballet Academy with only partial financial aid. I offered to start some sort of fundraiser for her; she was so talented, it would have been such a waste for her not to go . . . but she didn't believe the town could raise that kind of money in a few short months. I was afraid she was right. But I was willing to try."

"And then what happened?"

"She came in a few weeks later, said she'd sorted it out with your father." She looks at me shrewdly. "I'm guessing from your expression that this is news to you."

I don't want to tell her that Fiona lied to her. "Maybe they just didn't tell me because they . . . thought I'd be jealous or something." I realize as I say it that it could be true. But I don't think so. Where would my dad have gotten forty-two thousand dollars on that short of a notice? And why would they both have lied to me about it?

I only have one more question. "What about— How much did you pay her for her cleaning job?"

Madame LeGrand frowns. "Cleaning job?"

I'm still. "That's what she told me. She was gone so much last summer. She was here practicing, and then she took a job cleaning to make some extra money."

But the dance instructor is shaking her head. "No. We have a woman cleaning now, the same one we had last summer and all through the year. Fiona never asked me for a job. And she was not here practicing much, either. Last summer, she was here even less than usual. I was worried; she needed to keep up with her practice for school. It was so rare for them to accept a student at eighteen, and she was already going to be behind as it was. She told me she was spending extra time with her family before school started." Her brows have come so sharply together, they're a black V. "But I take it from your questions that this is not true, either."

"No." I don't see the point in keeping Madame LeGrand in the dark. This woman saw my sister even more than I did over the years. If anyone deserves to know what happened to Fiona besides me and my family, it's her.

"Where do you think she was?" I ask.

She taps her chin. "I don't know." She hesitates. "But—and I didn't tell you this last fall, as I wasn't sure it was relevant—but there was something off with her last summer."

My heart skips a beat. "Off how?"

She waves her hand in the air. "Her heart, it was . . . somewhere else. It was disturbing her, whatever it was. Taking her away from her practice— from her family, too, apparently."

"What? Why didn't you tell me this before?"

She looks at me with sympathy. "I thought—because of the way she was acting then—I thought it was possible she'd taken her own life. And I know that was something you didn't want to hear. But now, with the news of this Montgomery boy . . ." Her voice trails off.

There's a knock at the door. "Come in," Madame LeGrand says, and the front desk lady pokes her gray head in.

"Sorry to disturb you, Madame—"

"But I have a class," Madame LeGrand finishes. "Thank you, Sandra."

The woman nods and closes the door.

"I'm afraid I need to take my leave of you," Madame LeGrand says. "But please do let me know if there's anything else I can help with." Her face softens. "I miss your sister dearly. She was a serious dancer. The passion in her, that fire . . . it is something you so rarely see in a town of this size. She could have gotten to where I only ever hoped to be someday." A sad smile crosses her face. "If only."

"Thank you again for your time," I manage before Madame LeGrand is gone with a swish of her skirt.

I follow a moment later, nearly bumping into the doorframe on my way out of the office. I have to grab on to it to steady myself.

Fiona not only lied to me, my dad, and Davy, but she lied to Madame LeGrand, too.

Was there anyone she didn't lie to?

Was the American Ballet Academy really worth all of that?

The lobby is empty now; even the receptionist is gone. I open the door and am about to step outside when I nearly run into someone coming the other way.

"Sorry—"

And then I look up to see Mrs. Rodriguez staring at me.

Gen's mother. Who never liked me. Gen always said it wasn't me, she was like that to everyone, and had been ever since Gen's dad ran out on them. But I was never sure that was true. She was never hostile to Jeremy, only to me.

I haven't spoken to her in almost two years. She looks the same: pale skin, bleached-blond hair, thickly applied makeup, short skirt.

What is she doing here?

"Hi, Mrs. Rodriguez," I say uncertainly. "Um. How are you?"

She stares. "Why are you here?" She's not even trying to be polite. Her voice is raspy, a smoker's voice.

"I, um, just had to talk to Madame LeGrand about something."

Her frown deepens. "Little whore. Just like your mother and sister."

Then she practically shoves me aside to get in the door.

I can't move. Can't see anything. Can't hear anything but a strange rushing noise in my ears.

Slowly, I come back to myself. The blurry form of Mrs. Rodriguez is still in the corner of my eye, her back to me. I want to ask her what she means. How she can dare say that about my family. About me.

But when I turn around to confront her, she's gone.

23

I HURRY DOWN the street, trying to ignore the tightness in my throat. The sky above is now a dark gray, clouds rolling in from the west.

I turn the corner and the bike rack comes into view. I stop short.

And stare at the spot where my bicycle used to be.

Now it's just a wheel.

My throat gets tighter. Not because of the bike, even though I've had it since I was twelve and now it's gone, just like that. It's Mrs. Rodriguez.

Little whore. Just like your mother and sister.

Was she just trying to hurt me? Gen and her mom are close, since they only have each other. Gen obviously told her the details of why we weren't friends anymore. I picture her coming home to their trailer after our big fight, the day she insulted my mom and I screamed at her never to speak to me again. Mrs. Rodriguez seeing Gen all upset, dropping whatever she was doing. *What's wrong, what happened, talk to me,* and Gen spilling out how I'd stolen Jeremy away and she'd lost both of us. I can see why she'd hate me.

But there are other ways to hurt me besides insulting my family.

Why did she say that?

I've been putting off talking to my dad about my mom and any potential connection between her disappearance and Fiona's murder. It always seemed like the most far-fetched of our theories, and I don't want to hurt him if I don't have to.

But maybe it's time to pull that Band-Aid off.

I blink again. Swallow. Turn on my heel and start toward the road.

The sky is getting darker by the minute. The wind is picking up. All signs of an imminent summer thunderstorm. Stupid lying weather app.

I'm only a block away from the studio when the skies open up.

I wrap my arms around myself, but there's no point. I'm soaked through in moments. At least on my bike I would've been home in ten minutes. On foot, it will take at least thirty. And in this rain—

Thunder booms overhead. I start to jog. My Converses are soaked. My bare legs are freezing. I notice a car out of the corner of my eye and keep going.

The car pulls up beside me and honks.

I look over to see Seth in his black BMW, gesturing for me to get in.

I don't hesitate. I fling open the passenger-side door and throw myself into his car.

Inside, the rain is instantly muffled, pounding on the roof. Seth has the heat on, thank God. I hold my hands up to it, shivering, as he pulls off his hoodie and hands it to me.

"Th-thanks." I wrap it around me. It's big and warm and smells like him. "How did you—"

"Saw the storm coming. Know you have no car." Seth pulls out from the curb and drives slowly down the empty street through the pounding rain. "Why didn't you at least ride your bike?"

"I d-did. Someone stole it." I tell him about locking it to the bike rack and coming back and finding just the wheel.

"Didn't anyone ever tell you not to lock your bike by the wheel?"

I pull his hoodie more tightly around myself and glare. "Most of the time I don't even lock my bike up at all."

"Well, you should have."

"Thanks so much." I stare out the window at the blurry houses going past. Maybe I should be acting more grateful for the ride, but my mind is still on Mrs. Rodriguez.

We're on my street. But then Seth drives right past my house.

"What are you—"

"I want to talk to you," he says, glancing at me. "My house is empty. No one'll be home for hours."

"I'm f-freezing," I object.

"I have clothes." He turns onto Bier's End. "Come inside."

24

WE RUN THROUGH the rain from the Montgomerys' oversized detached garage—it was once a stable, for actual horses—to a side door. In the mudroom, I shed my soaking Converses and pad on wet feet to the kitchen.

I've been inside the Montgomery mansion before, just not in a long time. When we were little, we'd dart in to grab snacks in between our treasure hunts, pretzel sticks dipped in Nutella or butter cookies in tiny paper wrappers from those big blue tins Seth's grandma used to have. The kitchen is enormous, taking up the whole of the back of the house. Unlike the rest of the mansion, it was actually renovated in the past hundred years, and has this solid nineties vibe. In the past I had glimpses of the dining room (huge, with a table that could seat twelve people), and the living room beyond that (all mahogany and velvet furniture and mirrors, like something out of a castle). But I've never gone farther, never even gone up the stairs.

The kitchen is dark, as is the rest of the house. "Where's your family?" My hair drips on the tile floor.

"In the city. My mom had some meetings, my aunt was taking Marion shopping, my dad and uncle are at work, obviously, and Kendall said something about her 'side business.' Which is probably just posing for Instagram photos."

We pass through the kitchen—I'm sad to see no blue tin of cookies on the counter—to a small, spiraling stairway on the opposite side of the room.

"The servant staircase," Seth says.

I roll my eyes.

"We don't actually *have* servants," he clarifies. "That's just what it used to be for."

I'm still shivering as I follow him up two flights of stairs and down a narrow, shadowy hallway with half a dozen closed doors. He opens one to reveal a small, gray-lit room, with only two windows looking out onto the backyard, where the rain is still coming down in buckets. It patters overhead, louder than downstairs. A full-size bed sits beneath one window, neatly made with a blue bedspread. There's also an antique-looking dresser, nightstand, and desk, along with an incongruous modern desk chair. A book sits on the nightstand; a closed laptop is on the desk alongside a set of binoculars. Framed art hangs on the walls, mainly sketches and paintings of old castles. Of course.

There's also a photograph of Seth and Thatcher. In it, they're both a few years younger. They're somewhere tropical—some rich-people resort, probably—look tanned, and have their arms around each other, laughing. They look so carefree, so happy.

"That was in St. John," Seth says from behind me. I turn to see him holding a folded set of clothes. "Thatcher loved it there."

"You didn't?"

He shrugs. "I like . . . rockier places. Old castles and stuff like that. But that was a really great trip, actually." He's gazing at the picture with such sadness.

"I'm sorry," I say again. "I'm sorry I made this past year so hard on him."

Seth meets my eyes. "I've already forgiven you for that."

"Still. It was the last year of his life, and I spent so much time accusing him—"

"There you go again."

"What?"

"Blaming yourself. The person who killed him—who killed both of them—is to blame. Not *you*, Addie." I open my mouth to argue, but Seth asks, "Do you want these dry clothes or do you want to sit around in those wet ones?"

I realize how cold I am and hold my arms out. He throws me the clothes, and I reluctantly pull his hoodie away from my body. Seth's eyes move down to my T-shirt, which I suddenly realize is now transparent. Heat floods my face, and I see Seth's cheeks flush before he leaves the room.

I quickly change into the plain white T-shirt and navy sweatpants he gave me. Both are way too big, but they're clean and dry and that's all that matters.

I'm shaking out my hair when Seth knocks on the door. "Come in."

He enters, in a fresh hoodie. His hair is still wet, black curls shining in the light from the lamp he switched on. He gives me a look I can't read when he sees me in his clothes. "Better?"

"Yeah. Thanks."

Outside, thunder rumbles, and a moment later, another crack of lightning lights up the sky. I perch on the foot of his bed, pull my legs up, and wrap my arms around them. I suddenly feel acutely awkward.

Seth sits across from me, in his desk chair. I look at him.

"I'm not going to apologize for following Jeremy," he says abruptly.

I shift. "I didn't ask you to." Then I can't help but add, "But you being there definitely didn't help. We were having an actual conversation, which we haven't done in a year. I was about to ask him if he knew what Gen was doing the night Fiona died, and then you showed up and—" I make a gesture with my hands coming apart.

"Yeah, well. I'm not sorry."

My eyes go to the scar above his eyebrow. I reach up, let my hand hover in the air, then drop it. "Why didn't you tell me?"

The anger falls from his face. "Pride or some shit. I don't know." He looks away, and a muscle in his jaw tenses. "Now you know."

"I'm sorry."

Seth's voice is gruff. "Not your fault."

Then whose? I want to ask but don't.

"Tell me what happened at the studio," he says then.

I tell him everything—including what Mrs. Rodriguez said to me.

He stares. "What the *fuck*."

I look over to where the rain is dripping down the windowpane. "Basically."

"Are you okay?"

"I'm fine." I try to sound like I mean it. "I always knew she didn't like me."

He scratches his scar. "What was she doing there?"

I didn't even think of that. "She—"

Out of the corner of my eye, Mrs. Rodriguez, standing in front of a closet. Holding—

A mop.

"She works there," I realize. "She was taking out a mop. I wonder how long—" Then I remember what Madame LeGrand said about them having the same cleaning person for a year. I tell Seth that.

"What if—" Seth sits up suddenly. "What if Fiona stole the money from *her* and that's why she's working at the ballet studio?"

"No," I say. "Why would she and Gen still be living in a trailer if they had forty-two thousand dollars just sitting around for someone to steal?"

"Because she was saving it for Gen's college fund?"

I shake my head. "Fiona wouldn't do that. It's one thing asking

Thatcher for money. But stealing Gen's college fund? She would *never* do that."

Seth's look says he isn't sure he believes me. He pulls out his phone. "I'm just gonna write it down. As a theory." He taps something out, then looks back up at me. "And why do you think . . ." He trails off, but I know he's thinking of what she said.

Little whore. Just like your mother and sister.

Mom. The rumors surrounding her disappearance. The guys she'd been sleeping with.

And something clicks.

Gen's dad left just a few months after my mom was gone.

I never connected the two before. But now . . .

Seth comes to sit next to me on the bed. "You never asked your dad about . . . the rumors."

I shake my head.

"Maybe . . ."

He's walking on eggshells. It's annoying. Does he really think I'm that fragile?

"I'll talk to my dad about it."

Seth hesitates. "Can you?"

"Yes," I say irritably. "If I can handle everything I've already handled, I can handle this."

"You're right," he says after a moment. "I've always liked that about you."

I'm startled. "Liked what?"

He looks down at his hands, then back up at me. "How you handle shit. You've had more happen to you than anyone I know, and you just keep going like it's nothing."

I look out at the rain. "It's not nothing. If I could trade with someone with a boring life, I would."

His laugh is a little husky. "Yeah, I get that."

His eyes flicker to mine again. I can't think. I put my head in my hands.

"Addie." Seth's hand is on my arm. "It's okay. We'll figure it out."

Suddenly, I don't want to think about any of this. It's all too much. Mom, Gen's mom, Fiona—

And Seth sitting here, looking at me the way he did in the Airbnb. It's dim in here with just the light from the desk lamp. The rain is still falling on the roof.

"Why did you pick this room?" I'm afraid of what might happen if we don't keep talking. "There have to be bigger ones."

He breaks my gaze and looks up at the slanted ceiling. "That's why I picked it. My room in the city is big for the city, but that just means it's about this size. And the ones downstairs are, like, five times this. Sleeping in a giant room, you feel so . . . exposed. There was a reason the old kings had beds with drapes around them. Castle bedrooms are too big." A pause. "Also, I like the sound of the rain on the roof."

"I do, too."

There's something charged in the air between us. Seth looks warm and soft, sweatpants and T-shirt and drying curls. Our hands are inches apart, splayed on his navy bedspread. I don't know what's coming over me. Only that I want to touch him so badly it hurts.

And so I do.

I lift my hand and run a finger up his arm, on the underside where the skin is soft and the hair not as thick. Seth looks down, startled; then his eyes move from my hand to my face. "Addie?"

"I just want . . ." I swallow. It's all the questions swirling in my brain—I want to wipe them from my mind, close my eyes and feel Seth's hands on me. Suddenly I want that more than anything in the world. I burn with it.

My finger is still trailing up his arm. His body is half-turned toward me. His hand moves up and touches my face. I see the decision in his eyes solidify. He leans forward and presses his mouth to mine.

Darkness, then an explosion of color behind my eyelids. Seth's lips are soft, the stubble around them rough, making me shiver. And I remember it. I remember exactly what this feels like. How good it is.

His hand moves to the side of my face, then the back of my head, holding me firmly to him, his fingers threading through my still-wet hair. I twist my body so it's facing his, and a moment later he gathers me onto his lap, my legs straddling him. He pulls back for a second, questions in his eyes; my breath is ragged in the second it takes me to press my lips to his again.

And then we're falling onto the bed, rolling to the side, his hand still in my hair, kissing like the world is ending. Each kiss is like a spark going through my body, each touch a thunderbolt, and oh, why didn't I let myself do this before? There is nothing this good, nothing in the world—

Suddenly there's a creak somewhere in the hallway. In a flash, Seth is moving away from me, off the bed, and to the door.

He opens it and goes still. I compose myself, then peer around him. I'm startled to see his father, Harold Montgomery, standing in the doorway.

The hairs on the back of my neck stand up, and suddenly I'm freezing.

Seth's dad looks from his son to me, a deep frown on his face. "Seth? What's this?"

"What are you doing here?" Seth's breathing hard.

"That's not your concern." His frown deepens. "Who gave you permission to have girls over, up in your room, with no one home?"

I expect Seth to snap back that he's nineteen, he doesn't need permission, but he keeps his mouth shut. "She got caught in the rain, and—"

"I don't want to hear excuses." Harold looks at me. "Adelaide, I think you should go home."

"I'll walk you—" Seth starts.

"You will do no such thing," Harold Montgomery says. "You and I need to have a chat."

I hop off the bed, my face burning. Seth's father steps to the side to let me pass, but he doesn't leave me much space. After grabbing my still-wet clothes, I turn sideways, intending to just slip out of the room, but I make the mistake of looking into his face. Again I'm struck by how little he and Seth look alike.

"I'm sorry," I manage. "We were just talking, and—"

"Olivia, just—"

He stops. His eyes flicker downward and meet mine. A muscle in his jaw twitches. "Adelaide," he says. "I meant Adelaide. Just go, please."

I hurry away, leaving Seth and his dad behind, as a chill goes down my spine that is deeper than the wet, the cold.

25

I JOG THE four blocks from Seth's house to my own as fast as I can.

Once home, I take a hot shower, as if I could wash off everything that just happened. I look at myself in the mirror once the steam's cleared, the way I did that morning, trying to see if I looked different. White skin, blue eyes, black hair with roots that are growing back in pale. Fiona's gold ballerina settles against my collarbone. I look a little alien. A little older than before.

My secret phone buzzes, making me jump out of my skin. I pick it up off my bathroom sink.

Sorry about that

Typing, then deleting. Typing, then deleting.

You okay?

Fine. You?

Fine

I'm suddenly gripped with the certainty that I shouldn't have left Seth alone with his dad.

I knew Seth and his dad never really got along. But I wonder now if there's more than that, more than he's ever told me.

My dad gets home at six, just as I'm finishing throwing vegetables into the soup pot. Davy messages he's having dinner at Ethan's. I hope that kid isn't spouting off more conspiracy theories. Though, without Davy here, there's something I can now do.

"Dad?" I ask cautiously as I pass him the bread. "Can I ask you something?"

He blinks at me through his glasses. "Of course."

"Were you going to pay for the American Ballet Academy, even though you said we couldn't afford it?"

His eyebrows rise. "We didn't have the money for it. I told your sister that. That's why she applied for that scholarship."

I have to be careful. I don't want him to think I'm running my own investigation. He would not be happy about that.

Inspiration strikes. "What kind of scholarship was it? Like, is it something I could apply for, too, or was it . . . dance school specific?"

My dad frowns. "I think it was for ballet only. I don't know all the details. Madame LeGrand, your sister's teacher—she helped her with it."

That proves it, then. My sister lied to everyone.

Dad is dipping his bread into his soup. I decide to wait until he's finished eating to ask him about Mom. I don't want to ruin his appetite.

Once Dad's bowl is almost empty, I say, "Can I ask you something else?"

He nods.

"Did you ever look for Mom?"

When I look at photos of my mom—bright swinging hair; wide laughing mouth; always looking slightly off to one side, like she had a secret you couldn't see—the differences between my parents are even more pronounced. My dad is ten years older than her, and he looks every day of his fifty-four years. Mom was thirty-five when she disappeared, but even in the last photo we have of her, she looks much younger.

I know very little about her past. Mom was from Nebraska. She was an only child who ran away from home when she was eighteen and spent four years wandering around various parts of the US before landing in New York City, where she met my dad. She didn't talk to her parents or talk about them. I don't know who my grandparents on that side even are, or what went wrong between them. Before becoming a stay-at-home mom, she was a waitress, a retail worker, a receptionist. She never went to college, never held a job for very long.

We asked about her a lot right after she disappeared. Dad would say things like *I don't know when she'll be back, but she'll be back,* and later, *She loves you. But she just can't be with you right now,* and later than that, just *I don't know. But I still love you. Never forget that.*

And I haven't. My dad may not be the most exciting guy around, he may not be the best cook, but if love means showing up, I've never doubted his love for us. He comes home for dinner, attends all our things: soccer games, track meets, dance rehearsals, graduations. He's reliable. In a world where people regularly disappear, there's something to that.

My father blinks. Sets down his piece of bread. He's looking at me like he's not sure who I am. I feel a sudden absurd urge to remind him.

"Yes," he says. "That's why I was gone so much the year after she left. I was looking for her."

I'm startled. I wasn't actually expecting him to say that.

"Where did you go?" I ask. "What did you find? Why didn't you tell us?"

He runs a hand over his face. "I didn't want to get your hopes up. I talked to the people in her past. Those I knew about. Wrote her emails. Called. I knew she'd left *me*—not any of you—and I knew she wouldn't want to hear from me. But I just wanted to know she was okay. That she hadn't . . ." An exhale. "But I never got answers. I tried again, after Fiona died. I thought she'd at least want to know. But again, I had no luck."

"So what do you think happened?"

Dad lifts his shoulders. "Your mother was good at disappearing. When we were younger, when we'd fight—she'd leave for days, sometimes a week. I could never find her. She turned back up when she wanted to. Not before."

"So—you don't think something happened to her. You think she just left. And doesn't want to be found."

"That's what I hope, at least." He's quiet a long moment. "I knew it was a waste of time. Looking for her. But I couldn't not try."

His mouth is turned down, and for a moment he looks so much like Davy I want to hug him. But Dad isn't a hugger. It would be weird.

"Whatever happened—I believe it was her choice." He meets my eyes. "She was always a little wild, your mother. She burned too bright for . . . all of this." He gestures to the space between us, then out, to include the house, the town. "I think it was an experiment for her. See if she could be a wife, a mother, live in a suburb. And in the end, she couldn't."

He looks at me again. "I don't want you to hold that against her. She was who she was. She had a hard life, from very early on, and all she knew was running. It's how she survived. And once you get into that habit, I think it's hard to stop."

It's too much. I want to retreat to my room, dive into my bed, hold Sadie close, forget I ever heard all of this. All this time, deep down, I've held on to this hope that it wasn't her choice. That she was gone because something happened to her. I thought maybe that's what my dad thought, too, that that was why he didn't talk about it.

I don't know what it says about me. That I would rather think that something bad happened to my mother than that she's out there some-where happily living her life without us.

But I have to stop being soft. Have to stop being the sad, unwanted, abandoned daughter and sister. Have to stop turning my head from what I don't want to see.

"What kind of a hard life?" I ask. "Was she running because someone was after her?"

I can feel Dad judging me, trying to decide if I'm old enough to know whatever it is he's about to say. "She didn't tell me everything. But I do know she . . . had a traumatic childhood. She didn't talk to her parents. I believe she was abused, though I don't know if it was her father or someone else, and they just . . . let it happen."

"Was there anyone else who might have wanted to . . . hurt her? Or hurt her family?"

Dad looks startled. "No. No, Addie. I don't want you thinking like that." He shakes his head. "What happened to Fiona had nothing to do with your mother."

That's what he believes. I can tell by his face. But that doesn't necessarily mean it's true.

There's one more thing I have to ask.

"I ran into Mrs. Rodriguez today." I hesitate. "And she said something . . . about Mom."

Like someone letting down a curtain, all the little parts of my father's face—his eyes, the corners of his mouth, the skin around his hairline—fall. And that's when I know.

"What did she say?" he asks quietly.

"She said Mom was a . . . whore." I can't look at my dad when I say that. "And I know there were rumors, when she disappeared. That maybe she was"—I almost choke on the words, but I get them out—"cheating on you. So I can't help but wonder if there's any truth to that."

My dad's face is pale.

He clears his throat. "I suppose I should . . . You're old enough to . . ." He clears it again. "Mrs. Rodriguez said that because—your mother and Mr. Rodriguez had an affair."

I let out a breath. "When?"

"I didn't find out about it until after they were both gone. It was Gail—Mrs. Rodriguez—who told me. Apparently, it had been going on the year prior."

"Do you think they ran away *together* that summer?"

Dad looks so tired. And so old. "I don't know."

"What does Mrs. Rodriguez think?"

"We haven't discussed it in a very long time. But that was her theory."

I'm still for a long moment.

It was all true. Mom cheating. I wonder if something like that is hereditary. If that's what led me to Seth that night.

Then Dad goes on: "When your mother and I were dating, she would . . . do things like that. Ed was the first one since we were married that I—" He stops himself. But I'm almost certain he was about to say *that I knew about.*

That omission makes me bold. "Was there anyone else?"

My father looks down at his plate. "Not that I was aware of."

But I have the sudden sense he's lying to me.

I don't know *why* my dad would lie. If he'd tell me about Gen's dad, why not tell me about any others?

All I know is I'm pretty sure he did.

———————

That night, alone in my room, after Davy gets home, I think about everything I've learned.

What if my mom didn't just run away?

What if Mrs. Rodriguez killed her?

Or—what if it was one of the other men my dad didn't tell me about?

And then, what if one of them came after Fiona, too?

I think about Ramsay and Carter again. I don't want to go to the cops. But as far as I know, they're still looking in all the wrong places.

I look down at my secret phone. Before even fully deciding to, I'm calling Seth.

He picks up on the first ring. "Hi."

"Hi."

A silence. I realize we have never in our lives talked on the phone.

"I'm sorry about my dad," he says.

"It's not your fault."

"He's just . . . been under a lot of stress at work. And sometimes he takes it out on me. Also, he's worried for me. Not taking my lawyer's advice and all."

It sounds like an excuse. But I let him have it. We can't control what our parents do. I know that better than anyone.

"Um, so I talked to my dad," I say.

"Yeah?"

I tell him what my dad said about the scholarship, then pause. "And— my mom had an affair. With Gen's dad."

Seth sucks in a breath. "Well. That explains why her mom never liked you."

"Yeah." It should make me feel better, knowing Gen's mom not liking me isn't my fault. But it doesn't.

"Do you think Gen's *mom* killed your sister in some kind of warped revenge scenario?"

"I don't know," I say. "I was actually wondering if the cops knew about this."

"Do you want to go talk to them?"

I bite my lip. "What do you think?"

That's why I called him. Because I can't decide this by myself. I've come to rely on him. My partner in all of this. For better or worse.

"I don't know," Seth says. "Maybe we should try and get something more concrete before going to them. So they don't think we're just making up stories."

"How?"

"Try asking Gen about it?"

I start to shake my head, then pause.

We don't have any other leads right now.

I exhale. "Let me think about it."

"Okay." A pause. "We'll figure this out, Addie. I promise you."

I suddenly wish I wasn't here alone, but in Seth's little attic room, curled up on his bed under the picture of an old castle, with the rain falling outside, his arms around me, holding me tight. Falling asleep to the sound of him breathing.

"Addie?"

I blink. "Sorry. Yeah?"

"I said, sweet dreams."

"You too, Seth."

I hang up the phone, wishing more than ever that Seth and I had been born into a simpler world, one where we weren't separated by our families and their drama, where we could just fall asleep next to each other without worrying what people would think.

Where we could just be us, and that would be enough.

26

I WAKE TO a knock on my door.

It was a restless night, and I'm disoriented, unsure if the reality in which Fiona and Thatcher are dead is the dream, or if what I was just dreaming is. Sadie lifts her head, alert, nose pointed toward the door.

The knock comes again, louder. "Addie? You awake?"

My dad's voice.

He doesn't wake me up, ever.

I grab both my phones, shove them in the pockets of my pajama pants, and stumble to my door.

My dad is on the other side, looking tense—Detective Ramsay behind him.

Sadie barks.

I feel a flash of fear, followed by rage.

They've come to arrest me. They couldn't figure out who the killer is, so they're going for the easy target. The girl who comes from nothing.

I look wildly down at my pajama pants, wondering if I'm allowed to go back and change or if they'll make me go like this, when Ramsay clears his throat.

"Good morning, Miss Blackwood." His tone is a lot more polite with my dad standing right there. "We have a warrant to search your room. Would you please step aside?"

A warrant.

Not an arrest.

But still: a warrant.

"Why do you think I had anything to do with this?" I blurt out. "Seth told you we were together the whole time."

"We can't discuss that right now," Ramsay says, in that same weirdly polite tone.

My hand goes straight to my pocket.

Ramsay notices. "And yes, we'll need to borrow your phone as well as your laptop."

Behind Ramsay are two more police officers, a younger Latina woman and a freckly-faced blond guy I might have seen at the police station before. The woman gives me a curt nod while the man steps toward us.

Sadie barks again, louder this time. Her ears flatten back, and she emits a growl.

"Sadie, down." I put a hand on her neck, calming her, even as my own heart races. The blond officer steps around me and into my bedroom.

My dad puts his hand on my shoulder. I clutch Fiona's necklace as the officer starts through my room, picking up things, putting them back down. He has gloves on. Ramsay also goes past me, calling out behind him, "You don't have to stay and watch. Please hand your phone over to Officer Cortez before you go."

I blink up at the woman officer. "Um. Sure."

I hand her my real phone, praying she won't notice the sag in my pocket on the other side of my pants. She takes it from me with gloved hands and immediately places it in a plastic bag, then gives me another curt nod before following the others into my bedroom.

"Is this really necessary?" my dad asks.

"Just exploring all angles," Ramsay says, not even looking back.

I want to scream at him that he's wasting time. But I don't.

"It's fine, Dad." I tug Sadie past him toward the kitchen. "Let's just . . . go have breakfast."

Breakfast is tense, to say the least. Davy is already at the table, mussy-haired and wide-eyed. I switch on the coffeemaker and get out the bowls and cereal and milk, but no one's eating.

I itch to take out my secret phone and tell Seth what's happening, but no way am I risking getting that taken away, too. Instead, I pull a long zip-up on over my PJs, hiding my pajama pants pockets more.

"Why are they doing this?" Davy blurts out at one point.

"I don't know." I try and sound like I don't care, but from the look on Davy's face, I don't think I succeed.

"Probably just covering all their bases," Dad says. But the worried look hasn't left his face, either.

We sit there in silence. I tell Dad he can leave for work, but he insists on staying.

"Davy, why don't you go get ready for soccer?" Dad suggests.

Davy looks about to protest but then slinks away from the table, head bent over his phone, leaving me and Dad alone.

"Addie." Dad's keeping his voice low. "If there's anything you want to tell me—anything at all—you know I'm always on your side. No matter what."

I look at him warily. "Thanks?"

He waits. I don't speak.

"You were so certain it was Thatcher last summer." Another pause.

"Yeah, and obviously I don't think that anymore."

Dad lowers his voice. "If you saw him that night—if you had an argument, or an accident happened—just tell me, Addie. Tell me why they're searching your room."

I stare.

Does my own father really think I killed Thatcher? For revenge?

Suddenly, those threads on Citizen Sleuths about me feel much more real.

Who's going to believe I'm not a murderer when my own *dad* isn't even sure?

"I didn't see Thatcher that night." I try to tamp down the anger rising in me. "Not until after he was already dead. Seth and I were together the whole time. I have no idea why they're searching my room."

I want to leave. Run out the door and not come back. But that probably wouldn't look good in front of the cops. Dad doesn't say anything else, and neither do I. I sit there with my hands balled into fists, cereal getting soggy, until Ramsay comes into the kitchen five minutes later, announcing they're finished, they've put everything away "as best we could," and telling me I'll have my things back "most likely by the end of the week."

"Thank you for your cooperation," he adds. "We'll let you know if we need to speak with you about any of our findings."

I don't like that look in his eye. He's *happy* doing this to me.

I want to yell at Ramsay that he's looking in all the wrong places. But I hold my tongue.

I could go to Carter. But they're partners. And it's like Seth said—I have no proof that Mrs. Rodriguez or my mom were involved at all.

So I let Ramsay leave without saying anything, still wondering if it's a huge mistake.

27

I MESSAGE SETH the moment the cops leave. He tells me not to worry, he wouldn't be surprised if he's next. But it doesn't escape me that both of us were in that clearing yet *I'm* the one whose room is being searched. Of fucking course it's me.

I then go onto Citizen Sleuths to see if there's anything new.

There are a few more posts from that same user, RdHerrng41. It feels like they have some kind of personal vendetta against me. They continue to maintain I killed my sister out of jealousy, then killed Thatcher because he figured it out. Other people think the same thing my dad does: that I killed Thatcher for revenge.

And somehow, it's gotten out that Seth and I slept together and that he's my alibi. **He's probably just covering for his gf**, one user posits. **Or maybe they did it together** is another sentiment I see.

I read each and every message, the ball in my stomach getting bigger by the moment.

I didn't *really* think I was going to end up in jail for something I didn't do. People staring at you at school, a few random posts on the internet— those aren't things that put you behind bars.

But a warrant to search my room? That has to mean they're truly considering whether I did this.

There's no evidence. Nothing to put me at the ravine at the time Thatcher was murdered.

But the only thing that puts me anywhere else during that time is Seth's word.

The cops must not believe him. I don't know *why* they wouldn't. But if they did, they wouldn't have come here.

Later that night, Seth texts me to meet him and Kendall in the clearing tomorrow. She has something to tell us, he says, and wants to do it in person. I just hope it's good news.

The next afternoon, I tell Davy I'm going for a run and leave my house before I need to, to make sure I reach the clearing first. I need to prepare myself for seeing Seth again.

At least Kendall will be there, a buffer. Something to stop me from losing my mind and just reaching for him mid-sentence. I don't know what came over me the other day. I can't remember ever wanting Jeremy in that way—so badly I could only focus on how much I wanted to kiss him.

Where did that come from? Was it all of a sudden, sitting on his bed, the rain pattering on the roof, looking into his eyes? Or had it been building up since Pennsylvania, since the moment I walked into the clearing at the start of the summer, since last summer, for years?

I climb onto the star-watching rock and wait, look at the sun sinking into the trees. The shadows across the clearing are long, the air cooling, the mosquitoes coming out. I slap at one on my knee.

A rustling noise: Seth and Kendall emerging through the bushes. I try to ignore the flutter in my stomach at the sight of him, the burst of heat in my face. I hope they'll take my flush for sunburn.

Seth nods at me as Kendall chirps hello. Nothing on his face betrays anything, but his eyes might linger on mine just a moment longer than normal.

They climb up onto the rock, and we face each other.

Kendall tucks her legs up under her. She's dressed in this long, flowy flowered dress with a little jacket over it. "So I wanted to tell you what I found out the night I hung out with Gen. God, that girl can *talk* when she drinks."

I feel a swift stab of envy. Gen is an emotional drunk; all it takes is a few hard seltzers and she's crying into your shoulder, telling you how much she loves you. It's one of the things I miss about her, and the idea that she's going around doing that with Kendall, of all people, makes me want to throw something.

Kendall looks at me. "She was talking about how she and your boy have started—"

"Jeremy's not my boy," I interrupt. "And I don't really want to hear about that."

"It could be relevant," Seth says.

"Oh, I'm getting there," Kendall says. "So, Gen's had a thing for Jeremy, like, pretty much her whole life. And she told me about how she, like, tried to time her move real well. Like she was all *there* for him in the aftermath of your breakup, gave him a shoulder to cry on when he needed it. Then one night, they were drunk and ended up hooking up—"

I feel ill. "How is this relevant?" I feel Seth's eyes on me but refuse to look at him.

"I'm getting there. They've had this on-again, off-again hookup thing for months, but he won't commit to more than that. Basically, Gen thinks he's not over you." She looks directly at me when she says this.

I'm startled. "Really?"

She nods. "So that's put a bit of a damper on things for her."

"Where was Gen the night Fiona was killed?" Seth asks.

"Oh, I'm getting there." Kendall pauses—for dramatic effect, I'm sure. "The night Fiona died, Gen was with Jeremy."

I blink. "What?"

"Apparently, Jeremy was all upset after his fight with you. And he ran straight into Gen's open arms. He got home and confessed everything to her. The whole fight you had about football, all your problems . . ."

I feel a jolt of anger. That Jeremy would tell *her* all of that, stuff that should never have left that space between us two—

And then I realize I did the same. I confessed it all to Seth. I did worse than confess. I have no business being mad about this.

But I'm still mad about it.

"And I'm saving the best part for last." Kendall flips her hair over her shoulder. "So according to her, he ended up passing out at her place. But I kind of got the impression she was lying."

I frown. "How do you know?"

"She's not a good liar. With my father, it was a skill I needed to master pretty quickly. Trust me, I can spot a bad one."

"So you think she was lying about Jeremy being there all night?" Seth asks.

Kendall nods. "So then you have to wonder—why would she do that? If she had nothing to hide?"

I take this in silently. Is Kendall right? I don't know anything about spotting a liar. But that's obvious, isn't it? If Gen spent years lying about being my friend, and Fiona spent all last summer lying to our whole family about what she was doing, and I never had a clue—

Maybe Gen's been secretly plotting to drive me and Jeremy apart ever since we got together. And that night, she saw her opportunity. Jeremy ran into her after our fight, spilled everything. He'd been drinking. He went home and passed out. Gen decided, for whatever reason, that it was a good time to confront me. She went through the woods to get to my house. Saw me, or who she thought was me, in the dark. Decided to take care of her problems with one push. Or, like Seth theorized, she knew it was Fiona and decided to try and frame me. And then, when I was never arrested, she offed Thatcher. Thatcher, who somehow knew it was her and never told anyone.

Could all of that be true?

But I'm shaking my head before anyone even speaks. "No. Gen's said some stuff to me—but I *know* her. She was my best friend. She's not capable of killing anybody."

"Well, to know for sure," Kendall says, "it would be really helpful if you could find out from Jeremy whether or not she's lying."

"No," Seth says before I can answer.

Kendall and I both look at him. "What do you mean, *no*?" I demand.

Seth hesitates, then seems to decide something. "Did you ever think about Jeremy?"

"Think *what* about Jeremy?" I ask, even though I'm pretty sure I know what he's saying.

"He's got a good reason to hate you," Seth says.

"Seth, he didn't know about you and me until *after* Fiona died."

"So you think."

"So I think because it's *true*."

"Addie. Just consider it. What if he followed you that night? And saw us?"

For a moment, I picture it. Jeremy creeping through the rustling dark, seeing me and Seth on the rock in the middle of the clearing, watching as Seth pulled off my shirt—

I close my eyes against the image.

"That kid was batshit in love with you," Seth goes on. "And you cheated on him. With *me*."

"It— He . . . Even if he *had* seen us that night—in what warped world would Jeremy then decide to get revenge on me by killing Fiona?" I shake my head. "That doesn't make any sense."

"That's not what I'm saying. He used to cut across the Bier property to get to my house from the trailer park. So maybe after he saw us, he used that same route to get back home. He'd been drinking. It was dark. He was beyond upset. He was walking along the ravine and sees blond hair ahead of him. He thinks it's you. He chases after her, she runs, he reaches out to grab her, she falls—"

"And then what?" I demand. "He pretended to be shocked when he found out the next day? Pretended to still be into me for a month afterward, until I told him about you and me? Spent the past year lying to everyone? Jeremy's not that good an actor. And even if he was—no. I know you guys aren't each other's biggest fans, but that's seriously the dumbest thing I've ever heard, Seth."

I can see the storm brewing on Seth's face. "Maybe you don't know him as well as you thought you did."

"I know him better than that, Seth. And so do you, actually. Just—leave Jeremy out of this. There is absolutely no way he killed Fiona. *Or* Thatcher."

"Would you have believed he'd come to my school and assault me? If you didn't hear it from his own lips?"

"I—"

Because it's true. I might not have.

But I shake my head. "It's one thing to lose his temper and hit you, it's another to commit *two* murders and lie about it."

"Addie." Seth's voice is a little softer now. "It was probably an accident—"

"Would Thatcher have been an accident, too?"

Seth hesitates. "Maybe Thatcher was threatening to tell, and he panicked—"

I'm still shaking my head. "No. I'm telling you, you're wrong. It can't have been Gen, and it can't have been Jeremy."

Kendall frowns. "If there was just some way to know for sure—"

"I'll ask Jeremy if he was really with Gen that night," I say.

They both look at me. "And you don't think he'd lie about it?" Kendall asks.

"Jeremy wouldn't lie to me."

Seth barks out a laugh. "If all of this is true, he already *did* lie to you. Over and over again. It's not safe for you to be alone with him."

I glare at him. "Why do you want to make him the bad guy so badly?"

"Why do you want to make him the good guy so badly?" he counters.

"Guys, stop," Kendall breaks in. "This isn't getting us anywhere." She pauses. "Another thing I've been thinking about: What was Thatcher even doing back there? What was *Fiona* doing back there?"

"Maybe Fiona was meeting someone," I say. "Maybe—whoever gave her the money?"

"Or maybe there was no wealthy benefactor, and she finally found old Mr. Bier's treasure," Kendall says. "And *that's* how she was paying for ballet school."

I roll my eyes. "Sure."

She tilts her head at the darkening sky to the north, in the direction of the Bier property. "Just because we never found it doesn't mean it wasn't there." Kendall's phone buzzes. She looks down. "It's my mom. Be right back." She heads off down the path toward the house, pressing her phone to her ear, leaving Seth and me alone.

He looks at me, and I don't know if he's going to go on about Jeremy or bring up our kiss, and I'm not sure which I want less.

"Do you remember how obsessed with that treasure we were?" he asks.

That wasn't the question I was expecting. I shake my head. "We were young and dumb."

He smiles. "You were obsessed. You would get all worked up about how messed up it was that me and Kendall and Thatcher were looking for it, too, because we were already rich."

"It was the principle of it. Not that I thought we were really going to find it."

"Do you remember when we were digging near the ravine and my shovel hit that rock?"

I remember. We couldn't have been more than eight, nine. "We all stopped what we were doing and dug like crazy in the spot you were at."

He nods. "It was you and me and Thatcher and Fiona. We went nuts; dirt everywhere, pebbles flying—"

"The hole we dug was huge," I say. "We could all fit inside it."

"And we just kept digging."

"And the only thing down there was that big rock."

You would think it would've been a disappointment, digging for an entire afternoon and only hitting some long-buried rock at the end of it. But when we were done, sitting in that hole, coated in dirt, panting from the heat and the effort, the sun low in the sky, shadows long—I remember leaning back against the wall of dirt we'd made, closing my eyes, and having one of those moments you're not usually conscious of when you're little: a sudden rush of joy at being alive.

"It might not be a bad idea to take a look," Seth says.

"Look at what?"

"The area around where he—they—died."

"What would we be able to find that the cops didn't?"

"They might not have been looking in the right place." Seth's thoughtful face is on. "What if Fiona actually found something?"

"You really think she found the Bier treasure and that's what she was using to pay for school?" I shake my head. "If there was something back there, wouldn't we have found it already?"

"Things shift," Seth says. "Time has a way of turning things up."

I look to where the sun is in the west. It stays light out late in July. We'll be able to see for two more hours at least.

"I went to the ER after our fight, you know," Seth says suddenly.

I blink. "What?"

"When your boy paid me a visit at Columbia." His hand hovers near his pocket. "I can show you what he did. If you want to see."

I hesitate a moment too long, and Seth is pulling out his phone, scrolling, and handing it to me.

I catch my breath. The face in the picture is barely recognizable. Eye swollen shut, stitches above one eyebrow, nose with a bandage across it, a cut across one cheek, bruise on his chin—

"And that's *with* me fighting back," Seth says, "*with* my buddy and another guy pulling him off me as soon as they realized what was going down. He could have killed me, Addie. He wanted to. I could see it in his eyes."

My voice is caught in my throat. Seth's phone is still in my face, the damage Jeremy did to him all I can see.

I close my eyes, push it away. "Okay. I get it, Seth."

Seth's voice is gruff as he takes his phone back. "You seem to have this idea that Jeremy Reagan is some perfect shining beacon of humanity. I just want you to know the truth."

"I already told you I'm sorry."

"And I already told you. It's not your fault."

"Yeah, nothing's ever my fault," I mutter.

"I mean it. Stop apologizing for shit other people did. You didn't do anything wrong."

I look at him. "I cheated on him. That's what I did wrong."

"And so, what—if he killed Fiona and Thatcher, that makes it your fault, too?"

"He *didn't* kill them."

"You still in love with the kid or something?"

I stare at him, outrage burning through me. "*No.* That's not what it is."

"Then why do you keep defending him?"

"*Because*, Seth." How does he not get this? "Haven't you ever been in love with anyone?"

I realize, as I say it, that I already know the answer.

Seth's eyes slide away from mine. "No," he says shortly.

"Well, it's—"

"I don't need a lecture on the greatness that was your love with Captain America, thanks." He looks even more pissed now.

I take a deep breath. "I'm just saying. You don't know what it's like to hurt someone the way I hurt Jeremy. He's been there for me my whole life, since we were little kids, whenever I needed it. And I took that and I—I smashed it. I hurt him in the worst way you can hurt a person. In a way that only I could." When he doesn't say anything, I go on. "Seth, can you just tell me—how much of you wants to find out who's behind this, and how much of you just wants to get revenge on Jeremy?"

His frown deepens. "I don't need revenge, like that jacked-up small-town fuck—"

"And stop with the asshole big-city-boy act," I interrupt. "It was never your best look."

Seth folds his arms. "Did you ever consider it's not an act? That I am just an asshole big-city boy?"

"I know you're not."

We're sitting facing each other on the rock, the first place we ever kissed, the twilight insects chirping around us. The sunset light washes Seth in gold, glinting in his hair, his eyes, his drawn brows.

"So what am I to you?" he asks.

And here we are again. "What do you mean?"

"I mean, you spend our entire lives telling me how much you hate me, then you give me my first kiss. Last summer you sleep with me—lose your *virginity* to me—then don't talk to me for a year. You argue with me for weeks, then cuddle up next to me. You tell me you 'can't,' then you kiss me. And now you're acting like it never happened."

I close my eyes. "Seth, I'm telling you what I know is true. Jeremy didn't kill anybody. And I'm *not* still in love with him, but I *do* still care about him; I can't just switch that off after all this time. And *you*—" I look into his eyes, glinting gold. "I'm not acting like it never happened. I mean, in front of Kendall I was, because I don't need her opinions on this, but—what do you want me to say?"

"I want you to tell me what that was the other day," he says quietly.

I hold out my hands, palms up. "It was a kiss."

"Why did it happen?"

"Because I wanted it to."

He shifts closer to me. "And now? Do you regret it?"

I force myself to maintain eye contact. "No."

I know I should regret it. I know the last thing I need is to get involved with Seth again. I can't see how this will possibly turn out well, for either of us.

"Do you?" I ask him.

"No." He leans in, grabs me by the arm, and kisses me.

I fall into it like I'm drowning—his lips on mine, his hand hot on my skin. The world is red behind my eyelids.

"Sorry, kids."

At the sound of Kendall's voice, we jump apart, my face burning. But when I turn to look, she hasn't even emerged from behind the trees yet. I let out a breath.

A moment later, there she is, tucking her phone back into her pocket. She looks at us expectantly. "Any progress?"

"We were talking about checking it out." Seth's voice is gruff as he jumps down from the rock. "The ravine. See if there's anything there."

Kendall's eyes widen. "Right now?"

"You got anything better to do?"

For a moment, I hope she'll say she does. I want to be alone with Seth again. Finish that kiss. But then, I'm not sure it would end there.

"No," Kendall says after a moment. "Let's go."

So it's with a small sigh of relief that I jump down from the rock and head off after the two of them into the gathering twilight.

28

WE PUSH ASIDE overgrown bushes and step over fallen branches as we make our way toward the wall that separates the Montgomery and Bier properties. I take a moment to text Dad and Davy that I'm on a long run, will be home later, eat dinner without me. We reach the wall and scramble up. Seth leaps down first. I follow a moment later, the impact of the jump reverberating through my legs and knees. Seth holds a hand up to Kendall, and then the three of us are heading off through the darkening undergrowth.

We don't speak. Just push our way through the bushes, wilder here than on the other side of the wall, the green reaching out to twine against our arms, branches tripping us up, scratching our ankles. I don't remember it taking long that night, but we were running then, and it was much darker. Seth and I have to stop occasionally to wait for Kendall, who is slower. The terrain starts to slope uphill the closer we get, boulders appearing through the brush.

We make our way toward the hill with the circle. It's quieter all of a sudden, just the call of a few stray birds. We're in shadow now, the last trickles of sunlight gone.

I touch Fiona's necklace. We spent so much time searching for the Bier treasure around here because it's the kind of place that looks like it's hiding something. It's a clearing with seven stones, placed at even intervals. They're covered in lichen and ivy, so you might not even see them at first. And they aren't like the boulders that come up naturally out of the landscape here; these stones are smooth, lighter in color than the others. It was Thatcher who first put out the idea that they'd been brought here, Seth the one who had us dig at the base of one of them to determine that, yes, they were loose stones, brought here by who knows who, who knows when. I remember one summer when Seth spent all his free time researching it. He never found anything definitive, though. I wonder sometimes how much of his interest in archaeology started right here in this circle.

Seth is walking around, his eyes on the ground. I do the same, not totally sure what I'm searching for.

After a few minutes, he says, "It doesn't look like anyone's been here. No disturbed branches or footprints. No sign of digging, either."

Something moves through the trees to our left, making me jump. Seth's head whips around, and then his shoulders relax. "Just a deer."

Not just any deer: a stag. It's ten feet from us, big and dark in the shadows, its antlers as still as its head. It pauses just a moment, then takes off through the trees.

There's another behind it, then another. A whole herd of deer racing away from the ravine. "Something spooked them," I say, a pit of unease rising in my stomach.

Kendall frowns after them. "Let's go see what." She nods in the direction of the ravine.

I don't want to follow, but I'm not about to chicken out. It's not the middle of the night, I tell myself, and there are three of us. I follow them through the brush headed west. I hear nothing apart from the crickets and birds; the deer have gone, have fled as fast as they could from whatever scared them.

We emerge from a thicket of evergreen trees. There it is: the ravine. Seth's hand moves to hold me and Kendall back, but there's no need; neither of us moves any closer. The bottom of the ravine is impossibly far down, its sides gray and sharp, the slope steeper than I remember. All I hear now is the running water; even the birdsong has paused, the birds holding their breaths in deference to this death-filled place.

"There's someone over there," Seth says suddenly.

I peer through the trees, but it's all shifting shades of green. "Where?"

"Right—"

A loud noise, like a firecracker, startles me.

It takes me a minute to recognize it for what it is.

A gunshot.

I stare at the nearby tree where the bullet left a hole. My brain feels slow, dreamlike.

And then there's another shot. Crackling past my ear.

I unfreeze, look at Seth for a split second, then grab his arm.

"Run."

29

SETH, KENDALL, AND I run as fast as we can. Something flies past my face, a bullet, a branch, I don't know. Blood pounds in my ears. I look back once and trip, come down hard on my knee. A hand grabs mine; Seth, hauling me to my feet.

"Kendall—"

"She's just ahead. Now *move*."

He practically pulls me along next to him as I struggle to keep up, ignoring the stinging from my knee. I run through branches and undergrowth, no idea which direction we're headed except that it's away from the ravine.

Seth and I round a tangled copse of trees and vines. And there's the wall in front of us. There's no sign of Kendall. We stop, breathing hard, listening, but I don't hear anything else. No gunshots, no sounds of pursuit, no deer. Just the rising insect song. And I can hear the birds again.

"Where's Kendall?" I breathe.

Seth's face is a mask of worry. "I don't know."

He pulls out his phone, holds it to his ear. After a moment I hear, "Seth?" and we both let out a sigh of relief.

"Where are you?"

I can't hear everything she says, she's talking fast on the other end, but some of the tension drains out of Seth's body.

A moment later, he says, "See you there," and hangs up. "She ran toward the house." He nods in the direction of the mansion. "She's fine."

"Good." I nod. "Good."

We scramble over the wall. On the other side, Seth looks down at me, reaches out as if to touch my face. "You're bleeding."

"I'm fine." My voice sounds mechanical.

"Even so. We should take a look at that. Pool house?"

"Will we be safe there?"

"Kendall's calling the cops. Whoever did that—they'll be gone by now."

My knee is still stinging, and I don't exactly want to walk into my house oozing blood. "Okay."

The sun has fully set by the time we reach the pool house. Seth lets us in and switches on one of the old wicker lamps. Then he checks the windows and locks the door behind us.

A musty scent hangs on the air. Nothing's changed from when we were last in here. There are the white wicker couches with their pale blue cushions, the faded framed print on the wall of some New England beach, the pile of pool noodles and deflated rafts in the corner. A bookshelf holds a handful of paperbacks and stacks of board games. There's a kitchenette I can never remember anyone using, and a full bathroom. We head for the bathroom, where the light above the sink is bright enough to examine ourselves.

I look in the mirror. My skin is white everywhere except where branches scratched at it, leaving fine red lines. There are smudges of dirt on my cheek and forehead, scratches across my arms and hands. My knee is bleeding from whatever I scraped it on when I fell.

In contrast, I only see three tiny scrapes on Seth, but I don't have the chance to examine him further before he's out of the bathroom and rummaging around in the main room. He returns a moment later with a dusty box of Band-Aids. "Thought we might still have these."

I look at the box doubtfully. "You sure they haven't all disintegrated by now?"

He ignores me, grabs some toilet paper to wipe the layer of dust off the top of the box. I turn on the tap, letting the water run until it isn't brown, while Seth pulls more toilet paper off the roll and arranges it into make-shift pads. "Sit down," he says, indicating the closed toilet. "I'll help."

He's surprisingly gentle as he presses the toilet paper to my knee. We use the dried-up soap to wash the dirt off our hands and faces, apply Band-Aids where they're needed. Seth presses one over a cut on my ankle, then looks up at me from his position crouching on the floor. "You okay?"

"Fine," I say automatically.

He brushes a lock of hair back from my face. "Good." His voice is low, hoarse.

"Are *you* okay?" I ask.

His eyes are huge, looking up at me. "When you tripped, I thought—I thought they hit you." He swallows. "I thought—" His hand is still hovering near my face. "I've never been so scared in my life."

His face is naked, no armor up, no careful expression to guard his thoughts. He looks the way he did that night almost a year ago. But this time it's not dark, I can see him by more than just starlight, and his expression makes my heart stutter.

"Are you saying you actually care about me?" I try and make it a joke, but my voice comes out in a whisper.

He lifts a corner of his mouth in that little half smile. "What do you think?"

And then his mouth is on mine.

This kiss is different from the others. It's burning, almost desperate, like Seth is trying to assure himself that I'm here, that I'm whole. I respond in kind, my arms circling his neck and pulling him to me. Before I know it, my legs are around his waist and he's rising, taking me with him, out of the bathroom and into the dimness of the main room.

He lays me back against the mildewy-smelling pillows, still kissing me, his hand moving up the side of my body, catching at the spot between my shorts and T-shirt. A flick of fabric, and his hand is on my bare skin. His palm feels hot, like he might be feverish, and I have the sudden urge to put my hand to his forehead to make sure. But then his lips are moving down my neck, and I gasp out loud, tightening my grip on his hair and pulling his mouth back to mine.

He kisses me hungrily, his hand moving up, up, and then he leans away, looks me in the eye. "This okay?" I barely have the time to nod before he's kissing me again. His hand moves over my bra, gently at first, and then more firmly. I lift my arms over my head as Seth pushes my shirt up and off, then I'm tugging at his buttons. I have a moment to admire his bare chest, broad and muscled and covered in little curling black hairs, before he's kissing me again, his body pressed against mine.

It's like that night almost a year ago, and it isn't. There's no stale taste in our mouths from the cider, none of the fumbling awkwardness of that first time. Seth tastes clean, feels warm, his movements sure and practiced, fluid. My shorts are gone, then so are his. He leaps up midway, disappears into the bathroom, and emerges with a condom. I don't even question it. I don't want to think about how this might be a bad idea. I'm ready, and so is he. There's pressure—I gasp out loud—and then Seth is hovering over me, grinning, and I can't help but grin back.

It feels longer this time, or maybe I'm just remembering wrong. When Seth finally collapses on top of me, panting, I look up at the dark ceiling and it feels like we've been in this pool house, on this couch, for hours.

After a moment, he drags himself back up, props himself on one arm next to me. "You okay?" he breathes.

"Yeah." My breaths are shallow. "You?"

"Yeah." He leans in, kisses me again, smiles. There's something a little heartbreaking about that smile—like he thinks all our problems are solved, like we're on our way to a happy ending.

"Be right back." He gives me another kiss and then heads to the bathroom. I try to conjure up the joy Seth seems to be radiating, but I can't. A familiar feeling is wrapping around my heart, the same one I had when I woke up that morning, in the gray light of the clearing, in Seth's arms: guilt.

You didn't do anything wrong, I tell myself. *You have no boyfriend. No one's dying this time.* But no matter what, I can't shake the guilt.

I've put my clothes back on and shoved my phone, which fell onto the floor, into my pocket before Seth emerges from the bathroom.

"Hey." He's put his shorts back on, but not his shirt, and he's running a hand through his hair, like he's nervous. "You want to, um—"

"Yeah." I slip past him to use the bathroom and also to just be alone for a few moments, collect myself.

Sitting on the toilet, clutching Fiona's necklace, I can feel it, in my bones, in my hair, in my skin. The guilt, seeping into every part of me.

I half hope Seth will be gone when I come back out, will have fled over the same feelings; but no, there he is, sitting on the couch, phone in hand. He looks up when I reenter. "Hey."

I want to run out the door, not stop until I reach my bathroom, throw myself under the showerhead, let the hot water wash me clean. But I make myself walk forward, sit gingerly beside him. "Hey."

His brows come together. "You okay?"

"Yeah." My voice sounds artificially bright. I cringe internally, clear my throat. "Yeah," I say again, trying to sound more normal.

But he's still looking at me funny. "No, you're not," he states flatly.

"I just—" I rub one eye, searching to find the right words. "I just wonder if that's the kind of thing we should be doing right now? With everything else going on?"

I'm looking at my feet—my sneakers are dirty—and wait for his response. Finally, I dare to look at him. The line between his eyebrows is gone, and his face is filled with a deep sadness.

"You didn't do anything wrong." His voice is low.

"I didn't say—"

"And honestly, I'm not that convinced you did anything wrong last time. Jeremy wasn't innocent in all of this."

Not this again. "You don't know that."

"Really, Addie. Who do you think was shooting at us?"

I stare at him. "What?"

His face is hard, defiant. "You heard me."

I would laugh if I wasn't so shocked. "You think *Jeremy* was shooting at us?"

"Someone was."

"Seth—people hunt at the state park. Remember the herd of deer we saw running by? Like they were being hunted? Because they were?"

He stares at me. "You seriously think that was some hunter? Hunting season's not until fall!"

I falter. "It could've been someone hunting illegally, or— Seth, no one knew we were going to be back there! Not Jeremy—not anyone! How do you explain that?"

He hesitates, too. "I don't know. Maybe there was someone watching us. It wasn't a coincidence, Addie—between the gunshots and my car, someone doesn't want us looking into this." He runs a hand over his face. "Jeremy could be keeping tabs on you. He could have been listening the night we decided to go to Philly. And tonight, he could have followed you here. We were getting too close to something and—"

"And he just decided to shoot all three of us?" I demand.

"Maybe he didn't mean to kill us just now. Maybe he was just trying to scare us away. Because there really is something to find out there."

"But he—" I stop. I can't give in to Seth and his absurd theories.

"Whoever it was, whether they meant to kill us or scare us, or if there's someone following us—it was not Jeremy."

He glares. "You're so fucking stubborn. Why don't you just admit you're still in love with him?"

I've gotten to my feet now, my fists clenched at my sides. "I am *not* still in love with him. I'm just not blinded by hatred, or jealousy, or— Jeremy doesn't even own a gun!"

He stands, too. "You don't know that."

I exhale. This was a mistake. Maybe *everything* I've done since I walked into the clearing at the beginning of the summer has been a mistake. "This is pointless. I'm going home."

But I've only gone two steps before Seth stops me. "You never answered my question."

I'm so tired. But I force myself to look at him. "You're full of questions, Seth. Which one?"

"What am I to you?"

His brows are drawn, and I can't tell if it's in anger, hurt, or a mixture of both. For a moment, I wish I could just give him what he wants, be the girl he wants me to be. It would be so much simpler if I were someone else.

But I might as well wish for time to reverse itself, for Fiona to come back to life.

"I don't know," I finally tell him. "And I know that doesn't help you, but it's the truth."

He searches my face for another moment. Whatever he was looking for, he must not have found it, because he lets go of my arm.

"Go." His voice is low, quiet.

He doesn't have to tell me twice.

I flee.

30

WHEN I GET back—keeping to the main road—it's past eight. My dad isn't home from work yet, which is weird, but at least I don't have to explain my disheveled appearance. I take a long hot shower, Sadie lying on the bathmat the whole time, head on her paws.

I towel off and go back to my room. I have no idea what's going to happen between me and Seth after this. Will things be awkward from now on? Or will one of us make a joke, the other smile grudgingly, and we'll go back to our pre-kissing normal?

Or is it over? Not just our investigation, but . . . everything else? Have I ruined it? Am I on my own now?

Is that what I want?

Lately Seth's been texting me when I get home, making sure I've gotten in safely. I check my secret phone. Nothing. Something hollow pings in my heart.

I check on Davy—lifting weights in his room, which is new, but he signals at me he doesn't want to talk—then shovel some leftover pasta into my mouth. My dad gets home a little while later, saying something about an urgent deadline. It's just as well. I don't have room in my head to make conversation. There's only space for my own confused thoughts.

Someone was shooting at us.

Someone sabotaged Seth's car when we drove to Philly.

Were either of those things supposed to kill us?

Probably not. But the car trouble did stop us from getting to Philly that day, delayed our meeting with Caleb. So what was it they didn't want us to find?

Caleb was the one who told us about the money Fiona asked Thatcher for.

So that has to be the answer. The money.

But if we go with Seth's stupid theories, that it's Gen or Jeremy, that doesn't make sense. Neither of them has money. Neither does Mrs. Rodriguez.

And whoever was shooting at us at the ravine—what could be out there that they don't want us to find?

I want to go back and look around. But I'm not dumb enough to go on my own after that.

My dad would want to know about this. I'm sure he would. Same with Davy.

But then I'll have to tell them what I've been up to. And they'll put a stop to it. I know they will.

And I won't have gotten anywhere. Fiona's and Thatcher's killer is still out there.

I clean up my dishes. Sadie's whining at the door. I don't really want to go out by myself right now, but I should be okay doing a quick walk around the block.

As I wait for Sadie to do her business, I can't help but check my Seth phone. What's he doing right now? Having a casual dinner after all that? Did he and Kendall tell their parents about the gunshots? Or are the cops Kendall called there now, combing the woods?

Then I wonder if Seth's dad is there tonight. I shiver, thinking of the way he looked at me the last time I saw him.

And then I'm still.

Olivia, just—

Harold Montgomery called me by my mother's name.

I didn't register it at the time. But I remember it now.

I didn't even know he knew my mom.

Was there anyone else?

My dad, looking away. *Not that I was aware of.*

What if my mom didn't just have an affair with Mr. Rodriguez?

What if she slept with Harold Montgomery, too?

And what if, years later, Fiona found out about it? And used the information to blackmail him?

My first instinct is to say there was no way Fiona would have done that. But with the American Ballet Academy hanging in the balance—it's starting to feel like there was nothing she wouldn't do.

I'm suddenly cold all over.

Sadie is waiting patiently for me a few feet away. I quickly pick up after her and head back home.

My house is dark now. I unlock the front door, hang up Sadie's leash, and head to my room.

Maybe *I* should go to the police. Tell them everything from my perspective.

I get a queasy feeling in my stomach thinking of bringing Carter my theory without letting Seth know. But what if I'm right and his dad is involved? Would Harold Montgomery really off his own nephew? I don't know him well enough to be sure.

And what if the police are actually compromised? If the Montgomerys have paid them off?

That's even more likely if one of the adults is involved.

And I have no proof. Only my hunch. Which they'd never take seriously.

I'm lost in thought, fingers tugging on Fiona's necklace, as I open my bedroom door and fumble for the light switch.

But before I can reach it, a hand closes on my arm, drawing me into the darkness of my own room.

31

I START TO scream. But a hand clamps down on my mouth, muffling it. I have a moment of panic—Seth was right, someone *was* following me, they tried to shoot us, and now they've hunted me down, I'm going to die right here in my room, my dad and brother just upstairs, where is Sadie, is Sadie okay—

"Shhhh, shhhh, Addie, it's me!"

I freeze.

And then my eyes adjust to the darkness, and I look into the eyes of my captor.

It's Gen.

She releases me. My heart is still pounding in my chest as she flips on the light.

I take in my ex–best friend. She's dressed in torn jean shorts and a white crop top, her long black hair loose over her thin, tanned shoulders. Her nails have chipped gold polish on them, and there are dark circles under her eyes.

Before, it wouldn't have been uncommon for me to walk into my room and find her or Jeremy here, hanging out. Gen has her own room in her mom's trailer, but it's basically a closet. Sometimes she'd come here just for some extra space. She always knew where we kept the spare key.

But that was before.

"Gen. *What* are you doing?"

She takes a deep breath. "I need to talk to you."

She looks—not pissed, exactly. But not happy with me, either. She's shifting from foot to foot, her eyes darting toward the outside door, which she must have come in through.

"About what?" I demand.

Sadie trots forward, greets her with a nudge to the hand. A faint smile comes over Gen's face, and she scratches Sadie's head. No wonder Sadie didn't bark. She loves Gen.

The way I used to.

All at once, I'm exhausted. I sit down on my bed, run my hands through my hair. It feels like a hundred years since I met up with Kendall and Seth in the clearing, when Kendall told us about Gen saying Jeremy was with her that night. But now it all comes rushing back to me.

Gen hesitates, hovering in the space between the door and my bed. "You can sit," I say impatiently. "So long as you tell me what you're doing here."

She sits gingerly beside me, still stroking Sadie's head, and takes a deep breath. "So I know we're not exactly talking—"

"And whose fault is that?"

Her eyes widen, and some of the nervousness goes out of them. "Um, yours? For hooking up with Jeremy and ruining everything?"

I can't believe her. "Me and Jeremy getting together didn't ruin everything, Gen. You being a bitch to me did."

"Oh, please." She crosses her arms, looks away. "Yeah, I said some shitty things, but I was *hurt*. You were my best friends and you betrayed me."

I stand. "Look, I don't know what you're doing here, but if it's just to have this fight again—"

"It's not." She stands, too. "I'm actually here to help you."

"*How?*"

She hesitates, then blurts out, "I notice you're spending a lot of time with Seth Montgomery."

"Are you following us or something?"

"No," she shoots back. "Jeremy told me."

Of course he did. "Why do you care?"

She pauses. "You know my uncle's the lead detective on the case."

"Yeah, I know that, thanks."

"So—I may have seen something when he was over the other day."

"Seen what?" I demand.

She exhales. "There was this email—just, like, a note from him to his partner. And it said something about how they were close to arresting Thatcher for Fiona's murder when he died."

I stare at her.

Thatcher. My original theory. But I'm already shaking my head. "No—no. It couldn't have been him. We— I was there that night. The night he died. I heard him yell."

She bites her lip. "So maybe whoever killed him was his accomplice, trying to keep him quiet. And who do you think they're looking at?"

It clicks into place, and my heart stops.

"Seth?"

Gen nods.

Then I come to my senses. "That's not possible. Seth and I were together that night. *And* the night Fiona died."

"You were together one hundred percent of the time?"

"*Yes.* We were together when we heard Thatcher yell, and then we were chasing after him." I pause. Seth *did* get ahead of me right before we reached the ravine. But I caught up to him just seconds later. Right? No more than ten seconds—maybe a little more, but definitely not enough time to push someone. "And the night Fiona died, we were together the whole night," I finish.

"But you must have fallen asleep at some point."

"I'd have noticed if he left—"

"Addie, you sleep like a rock. Especially when you've been drinking."

I pause. "I know, but—no. It's not Seth."

It *can't* be Seth.

"What about you?" I ask her. "Were you and Jeremy really together the night Fiona died?"

She hesitates. And in that moment, I see it.

"Yes," she says, but I'm already shaking my head.

"Don't lie to me."

She sighs. "Okay, no."

I stare. "But you told the cops you were."

"Yeah, I did, but it was because Jeremy was a mess that night, after that fight you got in. I'd never seen him like that."

"Were you guys even friends then?"

"No, but he was walking past my house when he came back from the parade and he just looked so . . . lost. So I asked him if he wanted to talk about it. And he did. He sat on my stoop, told me about your fight, and drank until he was incoherent, then—" Another pause.

"Then what?"

"He kept saying he had to go talk to you. I tried to talk him out of it, told him he was in no state to do that, to leave it until tomorrow. But at some point, he stumbled off to go look for you. I didn't see him again until the next day, all hungover at his place. He couldn't remember what happened. At all."

My mouth feels dry. "And you lied because—"

"Because I didn't want anyone suspecting him, obviously. Walking around in the woods the night Fiona died with no memory of what happened? It doesn't look good. But he didn't do it, Addie. He had no reason to kill your sister."

I don't tell her about Seth's theory that it was an accident. That he was looking for me. Because I don't want it to be true.

But if what Gen is saying is true and the cops are seriously considering Seth—he'd have a real good reason to want me looking at someone else.

I hate that I think it.

But I can't help but think it.

"Besides, Jeremy was with me the night Thatcher died," Gen says. "So I know for sure that couldn't have been him."

Outside, the crickets are chirping, reaching a crescendo. Inside my head, my thoughts are all pushed up against each other, making it hard to focus on one.

I look at Gen. "Why are you here?"

"I told you. I saw that email and I thought you should know—"

"No, I mean, why do you *care*? You threw a temper tantrum over Jeremy and didn't speak to me for a year and a half, and *now* you suddenly give a shit?"

Gen's face has gone red. "I did not throw a fucking *temper tantrum*, Addie. I was justifiably pissed off that my two best friends I'd had my whole life started dating behind my back—"

"I told you *the day after* we kissed. I sat you down and talked to you about it because I knew you deserved to hear it from me—"

"And you knew I'd be upset about it!" she whisper-shouts. "You knew you and Jeremy together would ruin everything, and you did it anyway. Which only proves you never cared!"

"I *did* care, I've spent every day since then doing nothing but caring. Caring that you then basically called me and my mom a slut—"

Then I stop.

"You knew," I say.

Gen's silence says it all.

"You *knew* my mom and your dad had an affair, and you never told me?"

"My mom didn't tell me until after you told me about Jeremy."

I consider her. "Where was your mom the night Fiona died?"

Gen blinks. "She was home. I saw her."

I stare at Gen, but there's no indication she's lying now.

Then her face hardens again. "My mom has nothing to do with this. I just saw that thing about Seth and wanted to warn you."

"You obviously don't give a shit about me anymore. So again I ask: Why?"

Her eyes lock with mine. "Maybe because I don't like seeing rich assholes get away with murder. Or maybe because I *do* still give a shit about you, and you're just too stubborn to see it."

Then she spins and walks out into the dark night, leaving me staring after her.

32

I RISE SLOWLY the next day, feeling as though I've been hit by a truck. My legs have scrapes on them. My hair's a tangled mess. I can't stop thinking about what Gen told me. There are still no texts from Seth on my secret phone, and I don't know how to feel about that.

I find Dad at the kitchen table, newspaper in hand. He clears his throat. "How are you?"

"Fine," I say automatically.

Dad and I have barely seen each other since the morning the cops confiscated my stuff.

Since he basically accused me of killing Thatcher.

"You look like . . . you haven't been getting enough sleep."

"Just last night," I say with my back to him. "I think I ate something weird."

Dad doesn't say anything for a long moment, so I think he's bought it.

And then he says, "I called a lawyer."

I turn. "Dad. We can't afford that."

"Don't worry." He's set his newspaper down and is looking at me seriously over his glasses. "I spoke with him at length yesterday, and he thinks it's in your best interests that I employ him immediately."

"Of course he's going to say that. He wants to get paid."

"Addie. They had a warrant to search your room. He told me that even just being caught up in something like this could affect your college acceptance. If you could just talk to him—tell him the truth—"

Part of me wants to yell at him that I'm innocent. That I didn't kill Thatcher. That if my own father doesn't believe me, there's no hope for me anywhere.

But then I think—could a lawyer really help me? If I tell him everything I know? The shooting, the car, my suspicions about Seth's dad, about Mrs. Rodriguez?

Or would he be like the cops—not believing anything I have to say without proof?

The cops are incompetent, I remind myself. That's one of the reasons Seth and I teamed up in the first place. Because they were looking in all the wrong places. He even told me that they were looking at him.

But why didn't they search his room instead of mine?

What did they have on Thatcher?

Why didn't Seth tell me about that? He must know, right?

"He's coming out from the city next week," Dad says, interrupting my thoughts. "I want you to meet with him. And—be honest."

I turn away. I can't take that look in Dad's eyes.

"Okay?" he asks from behind me.

"Okay."

I eat as fast as I can, then toss my bowl in the dishwasher, throw on my running clothes, and take off.

Two, three, five, seven, eleven—

I run straight west along the side of the road, wishing with every thud that Fiona were here.

I wish she could tell me what to do.

I imagine going up to her room. The way we'd talk, curled up on her bed, her dance posters looking down on us. I think of walking into the kitchen, seeing the angle of her shoulders under her pale pink leotard, her leg up on the counter, head bent over it, the tight perfection of her blond bun. The fire in her eyes when she was dancing.

Twenty-nine, thirty-one, thirty-seven, forty-one—

The way her eyes skittered away from mine anytime I walked in last summer. How she was always on her way out the door. *Need to practice* or *have a lesson* or *need to get to work.*

Except there was no work. She was lying. The whole time, she was lying.

I've run toward the center of town for once. I wasn't consciously heading here. But now I know what I want to see.

The memorial bench they dedicated to her in the town square. There are people out and about today; they could be looking at me, whispering about me. But I don't look up. I run to the bench and stop.

In loving memory of Fiona Josephine Blackwood. Sister, daughter, friend.

They put *sister* first. I don't even remember being asked about it. Whoever decided on these words—Dad, I'm sure—knew.

My big sister. My best friend. She let me crawl into bed with her when I was afraid of the monsters in my closet. Held my hand on the first day of kindergarten and offered to fail first grade so I didn't have to be alone. Threatened to beat up Seth when he pushed me off the lower platform of the tree house. She had my back. Always.

And then Mom left us. And suddenly dance got more intense. It was like Mom leaving made her think she couldn't count on anyone. So she attached herself to the one thing she could count on.

But she was still there for me. For us. Patiently helping Davy with his history paper. Opening the jar of tomato sauce when I couldn't manage it. Teasing me when I came home from the clearing after kissing Seth for the first time. *I knew it. There's a thin line between love and hate.* Listening to me agonize over Jeremy and Gen. *Your real friends don't leave you. The people who really love you don't do that.*

But she did.

Before she died, she'd pulled away from me.

What didn't she want to tell me?

I clutch her necklace. I was always holding out hope. That her obsession with dance would end at some point. I just had to wait. And someday I'd have my sister back.

Now I never will.

So this is all I have left. Finding out the truth. I owe her that.

I turn from the bench and run toward the park.

Gen. Thatcher. Seth's dad. Gen's mom. Jeremy. Seth. It's kind of unbelievable that just a few weeks ago, I thought Thatcher had to have been the one to kill Fiona, because I couldn't find a single other suspect. And now there are so many, I don't know where to look. It's like for every answer we uncover, ten more questions come with it.

If Fiona was having an affair with someone and she got the money for school from them—wouldn't there be some evidence of it? Some big bank transfer? But the police should be able to uncover that. They should have seen it when they took her computer and phone. Which makes me remember that they still have *my* computer and phone.

And then, at the edge of the park, I stop.

The phone.

Whoever gave Fiona the money for school—she must have had a way of communicating with them.

Like a secret phone.

Of course, I don't know if there was one for sure. But if she had a second phone, it must not have turned up in the cops' search—or it would have led them to somebody. Which means she didn't have it on her the night she was killed. And they didn't find it in her room.

Unless Fiona did have it on her, and it fell out by the ravine.

Was that why we were shot at? Was the killer there, too, looking for her secret phone so they could destroy it? Tying up more loose ends? Was that all Thatcher was to them? A loose end?

Or the killer could be looking for the phone at the ravine, but that doesn't mean it's there. Fiona could have hidden it somewhere else.

If I were Fiona—where would I hide something like that?

They didn't just search Fiona's room last summer. They searched our whole house. And while our house is old, it's not the kind of place full of charming little hidey-holes, the way the Montgomerys' house probably is. Also, it's not that big. And we don't have a pool house, or even a shed—

Then it hits me.

The tree house.

I turn on my heel and run straight into the woods, faster this time. Back toward Bier's End.

The woods are quieter than usual, as if all the birds and insects and woodland creatures are holding their collective breaths, watching me make my way deeper into the brush. My breath is loud in my ears. After what seems like both a long time and no time at all, I turn a bend in the path, and there it is: the abandoned tree house of our childhood.

It's about twenty minutes from here to the ravine on foot, so anyone looking for clues around the ravine itself wouldn't necessarily have come here. But it would be a good place to hide something if you were on the way there from our house.

I put my foot on the lowest plank nailed into the trunk of the tree. It doesn't feel as sturdy as I remember, but it doesn't wobble. Then the next, and the next. Five steps up, and I'm at the wooden platform below the tree house.

It's covered in dead leaves, sticks, years of whatever the woods have dropped onto it when none of us were here to sweep it clean. I put my palms on the nearest plank of wood, test it. It feels like it will still hold my weight.

I pull myself up gingerly. Look at the pile of wood debris. Start a slow, careful sweep underneath with my hands.

It takes less than a minute before my hand strikes something hard.

I grab it.

It's a small dark phone.

33

I WAS RIGHT.

I can't believe it.

It's inside a plastic bag. I take it out and stare at it. It's last generation, the same model as the secret phone Seth gave me. No case. But there isn't a scratch on it. With any luck there'll be no water damage.

I press the power button, stupidly. Nothing. But that's okay. It uses the same charger my phone does.

I'm just about to climb down the steps and run back to my room to plug it in when I pause.

Fiona's journal that the cops couldn't find. Could that be here, too?

After sticking the phone into the waistband of my shorts, I move cautiously forward on my hands, pushing leaves over the edge and onto the ground, until the entire platform is clear.

Nothing here.

I look up at the tree house. It's not safe to put my weight on the wood. But if I could just climb up the trunk, look around while keeping most of my weight on the tree—

I put my foot on the next wooden plank nailed into the trunk, then the next. Soon my torso is through the hole in the tree house floor.

The wood nearest me is all rotted. But over in the far corner, the part that hangs past the platform below, there's a huge pile of leaves, which means the wood underneath is intact. If I could just reach over there, sweep them aside—

I stretch as far as I can while still holding on to the tree trunk. But it's not far enough.

I test a piece of rotted wood near me. It holds under my hand. I put my other hand out. No falling wood. If I lie across the bottom of the tree house, maybe it will be able to hold my weight.

I lean forward, my feet on the plank, bracing myself against the least-rotted part of the wood. Sweep leaves aside. Nothing. Then, slowly, hesitantly, I lift one knee onto the tree house floor.

I test it. Still sturdy. I pull my other knee up, until I'm on all fours. Sweep the leaves in front of me aside. Nothing. I move forward, creeping cautiously. Again, nothing. Reach for the farthest corner of the tree house, where the biggest pile of leaves sits. Move my leg forward—

And crash down through empty air.

34

I CAN'T BREATHE.

I can't breathe.

The sky above me is black. Or maybe it's me. I can't breathe, I can't see—

Then a shadow above me, blocking out the sky—

Hands on mine, pulling me up.

"Deep breaths."

I inhale. Exhale.

A hand on my back, dark eyes peering into mine. Seth.

"Addie. You okay?"

I take another breath. "I . . . think . . . so."

"You sure? I saw you fall."

I look up. There's a hole in the rotted wood of the tree house bottom. I just missed the platform below it by a foot or so.

Then my hand flies to my waistband. The phone is still there, at the front of my body. I sigh in relief.

I look back at Seth. "Where did you even come from?"

He's dressed in a plain T-shirt and shorts, actual sneakers on his feet, baseball cap jammed over his curls. He scratches his eyebrow. "I was on my way to your place, actually."

I eye him suspiciously. "This way?"

"I was trying not to be seen."

"Why didn't you just text me?"

"I did. You didn't answer." He looks at the phone in my waistband—obviously mistaking it for the one he gave me.

I can't tell him about this phone. Not until I find out what's on it. If it really was Fiona's, if she was actually using it to contact some wealthy benefactor who may have killed her, I have to figure it out on my own. Make sure Seth's dad isn't said wealthy benefactor before letting him in on it.

I try to sound casual. "It died while I was running." In truth, I left it at home.

"Oh." He scratches his scar. "I figured you were mad at me."

My breath is slowly returning to normal. My heart rate, too. Seth isn't suspicious of anything. Just here to have the awkward morning-after conversation.

I need to run back to my house so I can charge the phone, but I can't do that with Seth standing in front of me, looking all concerned. And I know there's only one way to get rid of him.

"I'm not mad," I say. "I just went for a run to . . . clear my head."

He looks up at the tree house, the leaves still spiraling down. "And decided to hang out up there?"

"I had the idea to look for Fiona's journal, actually." It's not exactly a lie.

Seth's eyebrows go up. "Well?"

I shake my head. "Nada."

He looks disappointed. "Next time, maybe let me know before you nearly kill yourself climbing trees?"

"Will do." A beat. "I need to get home—"

"Wait," he says, as I knew he would. "We need to talk about last night."

"I told you. I'm not mad."

His brows come together. "Well, I am, a little."

Of course he is.

I take a deep breath. "I didn't mean to make you mad. I just meant that things are already complicated enough. I'm sorry if I acted like . . . I regretted it or something."

His voice is low. "Didn't you?"

"No." I don't know whether I'm lying. "I'm just . . . confused, I guess. With everything going on."

A pause. "Yeah, I get that," he says finally.

I pull my hair out of its ponytail, secure it back up again. "All I meant was, the time we spend doing—that—is time we're not spending figuring this out. Davy's never around anymore, I can't keep an eye on him, who knows what kind of case the cops are building against me, and even if they don't actually arrest me, Rutgers could rescind my acceptance, and I'm supposed to leave for college in a month, and if we don't figure this out by then, we—"

My spiral has its intended effect. Seth takes another step toward me, touches my arm. "I know. I get it." His voice is softer now. "That's why I came to talk to you."

I let out a breath. "So we're agreed? Just focusing on the case?"

His hand on my arm is warm. "If that's what you want. Sure."

That look is back in his eyes. My head is throbbing. I don't know if it's because of the fall or all the thoughts swirling around inside of it.

I would have noticed if he'd left.

That's what I told the cops. I swore up and down there was no way Seth Montgomery had left my side that night. But what Gen said is true; I *am* a heavy sleeper, especially when I've had something to drink.

Could Seth really have slipped away from me that night, come back before I'd even woken up?

In those seconds he ran ahead of me the night Thatcher died—was that enough time to push him?

No. Seth loved Thatcher like a brother. There's no way he had anything to do with his death.

And Seth couldn't be the person Fiona had gone to for money—he helped me figure out that that person even exists.

He told me he cared about me.

Unless all of that was an act, too?

I try to push the thought out of my mind. But it stays there, stubborn. Because when I actually think about it, it doesn't make any sense.

Why *would* he care about me?

"Addie?" Seth asks.

I step back. His hand drops. "I think that's for the best."

"Okay."

"Okay." I turn to go. "I'm going to go take some Advil. My head hurts."

"Do you want me to walk with you? You could have bumped your head—"

"It's fine. I'm fine. I'll charge my phone and text you when I get there."

Seth still looks worried, but he lets me go.

I run home as fast as I can.

35

I MAKE IT home in record time.

I go straight to my room and plug in the phone, then shoot off a text to Seth that I'm back. And then, heart hammering in my chest, I wait.

Even if I didn't damage the phone in my fall, it could've gotten damaged any number of ways, sitting out there for almost a year. It might not even be Fiona's at all.

After a minute, it turns on.

I seize it with both hands.

And then falter.

The passcode.

I try Fiona's birthday, mine, Dad's, Davy's, even Mom's. Nothing.

Then words. BALLET. Nope. I'm locked out for a minute now. When I get the chance to try again, I put in SADIE. Nothing. Now I'm locked out for five minutes. I can't keep doing it like this.

I'm just about to run upstairs to Fiona's room to look at the names of the dancers on her wall when I stop in my tracks.

That piece of paper with the random numbers I found in her jewelry box.

I haven't given it much thought since finding it, but now I dive for my nightstand drawer. I'm terrified it will be gone, the cops somehow recognizing it for what it was, taking it—but no, here it is, untouched.

I unfold it and enter the numbers, my heart in my throat.

It works.

Holy shit.

I'm in Fiona's secret phone.

As I suspected, it's a lot like mine: no apps on the home screen besides the ones phones come with. When I open up the messages app, there's only one message stream.

The number isn't saved to a contact in the phone. But it's a 212 area code.

Manhattan.

My heart beats faster as I click into the messages.

The very last message is outgoing, dated three days before she died. It simply says, **See you there.**

I scroll up to read more.

Can't wait to see you, my tiny dancer, from the 212 number right before. I feel a little sick.

I go farther up.

From 212:

You're all I think about, tiny dancer
Can't stop thinking about last night
Was it as good for you as it was for me?

Then Fiona:

Yes it was nice ☺

From 212: **When can I see you again?**

Fiona: **I don't know, I have a lot of practicing to do this week and then I have work**

I frown. She was also keeping up the work charade with this person. I wonder why.

Why work? I told you, I've got you covered. Anything you need, it's yours

I suck in a breath.

I was right.

It was about the money.

I keep reading.

Fiona: I appreciate that but I still need to save

212: You don't need anything anymore, babe. You've got me.

Vomit.

I scroll up more, and more. All the way to the beginning of their conversation, from April of last year.

Right around the time Thatcher told Fiona he wouldn't give her the money, according to Caleb.

She went into the city around then, I remember. Something about a tour at the American Ballet Academy. Maybe that was when she went to Thatcher's, asked him for the money. And maybe Harold Montgomery had been over that day, saw her leaving, overheard them, even. Thought she was pretty and saw his chance. Gave her what she wanted. And in exchange, she had to give him what he wanted.

I can't tell Seth about this.

"Addie?"

I jump a mile into the air.

Then turn to see Davy, standing in my doorway, a paper bag in one hand.

"H-hi," I manage, trying to calm my racing heart. "You scared me."

"A cop just dropped this off." He holds out the bag.

My laptop and real phone. "Oh. Thanks." I get up to grab them.

But he's frowning at something behind me. "Where'd you get that other phone?"

Shit. But I decide to tell a semitruth. "Seth gave it to me. We're not supposed to be talking to each other . . . but we want to. So, extra phone." I shrug.

Davy looks at me. "Are you guys, like, dating?"

"No," I say firmly. "We're just friends."

My brother's face is troubled. "Are you sure the police aren't about to arrest you?"

"Yes." I try to sound more confident than I feel. "They don't have any evidence. They can't." The last thing I need is Davy worrying about this.

"Okay." He doesn't look appeased, though.

I put a hand on his arm. "They can't arrest me for something I didn't do. I'll be fine."

"You'd tell me if you really thought you were in trouble, right?"

"Yes. It'll be fine, Davy."

It has to be.

"Okay."

Davy finally heads off to his own room.

I let out a breath and run back to Fiona's secret phone.

I have to read every single text. I have to find concrete proof that this is Harold Montgomery.

And after that, I have to decide what to do with it.

———

I spend the rest of the day and night, with a brief break for dinner, reading through Fiona's text stream.

I scroll faster. But the more I go on, the more my heart sinks.

I don't know if this guy was purposely not giving any info out about himself because he knew the phone might be discovered, or if he was just lucky. But there are no specifics, just **Meet me at the house at 4PM** or **7PM? Downtown office?** Which at least tells me it was someone with an office downtown. But that could be millions of people.

The guy was always calling Fiona things like *babe* and *sweetheart* and my personal least favorite, *my tiny dancer*. But she never called him anything. It's clear, at least to me, that Fiona had no affection for this guy. It was transactional for her. She needed his money and she did what she needed to do to get it. It's kind of amazing to me he never figured it out. But I guess people can talk themselves into anything if they want it badly enough, see what they want to see.

Then I'm still. Maybe he did figure it out. And that's why he killed her. Maybe it didn't have to do with the money. It had to do with the fact she didn't love him.

There *are* references to the money part.

212: **Check the mail, a little love from me** ♥

Fiona: **Thank you, I appreciate it**

But nothing that points to Harold directly.

Until I get to:

I'm in a meeting until then, but when you get here, call Patrice to let her know you're at the service elevator. Someone will let you in. Get off at the 12th floor. Then wait for me in my office.

I wonder if Harold Montgomery has an assistant named Patrice.

I turn to my laptop and google *Harold Montgomery*. Predictably, a bunch of old white men show up, so I add *New York, NY* to the end of the query.

Still more old white men.

Then I add *Wall St.*

Bingo.

There's a professional headshot of Harold Montgomery. Apparently, he's in the same office building as Thatcher Montgomery Sr.

And there's a phone number right here.

I start to dial—then remember it's Saturday. I'll have to wait until Monday.

But if Harold Montgomery does have an assistant named Patrice—I could take that to the police. That would be pretty strong proof. Wouldn't it? Or maybe they have a way to trace the number and prove who it belongs to. But if he's smart, Harold Montgomery would have gotten rid of his own phone a year ago.

Plus, there's nothing here that one hundred percent proves this phone is Fiona's. There could be more than one Patrice. There's the *tiny dancer* thing—but I didn't even find the phone in our house. I found the paper with the passcode here—but I have no way of proving that to anyone, either.

I need more evidence.

Then it comes to me.

I could head to New York City and straight up ask Harold Montgomery's assistant if she's seen my sister around the office. Maybe secretly record her answer.

Then, once I have actual proof, I'll head to the police.

36

I SPEND SUNDAY something of a wreck. Seth's not around; he went to the city because his dad wants him to meet someone on Monday for an internship next summer that he doesn't want. So at least I don't have to spend the day with him, pretending like I'm not planning on calling up his dad's assistant tomorrow and potentially sneaking into his dad's office.

Monday morning, I make the call. When the robotic voice asks me to whom I'd like to be transferred, I say, "Harold Montgomery, please."

After three rings, someone picks up.

"Harold Montgomery's office, this is Patrice speaking."

I rip the phone away from my ear and press end.

Now I just need proof my sister was there.

Which means I need to find a way to get to the city. I can't exactly borrow Dad's car without him asking me why. There's a bus, but the bus stop is a half hour away. Then it's two hours to Port Authority, and from there I'd have to navigate the subway or take a cab down to Wall Street. All in all, about three hours door to door, assuming I don't get lost in the city, which I almost certainly will. Whereas a car ride would take half the time.

An idea comes to me, and before I can talk myself out of it, I'm punching Gen's number into my phone—I deleted it last year, but I know it by heart—and pressing it to my ear.

"Hello?" She sounds wary. So either she didn't delete my number, or she has it memorized, too.

"Hey. It's me."

"I know."

"Listen, I've been thinking about what you said," I blurt out. "And I think—I need to go to Manhattan and look around Seth's dad's office."

"You think Seth's *dad* had something to do with this?" Gen's voice is skeptical.

"I don't know, just . . . Seth hangs out there, and I thought I might find something," I fib. I'm not about to tell her about the phone. I still don't know if I can trust her. I take a deep breath. "Can you give me a ride to the city?" Gen and her mom share a little old red car. "I know we're not exactly close right now, but . . ." I trail off.

"But you have no one else," she finishes.

No use denying it. "Yeah."

"Our car's in the shop," she says, and my heart sinks. "Something about the engine, I don't know."

"For how long?"

"Until Friday at least, they said."

I swear. "Okay, well—"

"We could ask Jeremy, though."

That idea hadn't occurred to me. His mom gave him a car last fall, I'd heard. "You think he'd do it?"

She sighs. "Probably. I'll check with him and let you know what he says."

With that, she hangs up.

Sadie scratches at my door then, so I go take her for a walk. I'm just coming back in when my phone buzzes.

It's Jeremy.

Pick you up tomorrow at 10.

37

AT TEN A.M. sharp the next morning, Jeremy pulls up in a silver two-door Honda Civic.

The boy in the driver's seat looks like the Jeremy I knew: football T-shirt, dark sunglasses, backward hat over his brown hair, which is damp because he'd have just showered after his morning run and workout.

But I can't get the image of the other Jeremy—the angry one in the woods, who insulted me, who was about to hit Seth again—out of my head.

Maybe you don't know him as well as you thought you did.

I push that thought aside. Either Seth is just pissed that Jeremy assaulted him—justifiably so. Or he's trying to throw Jeremy under the bus—to take suspicion off himself and his family.

Plus, Gen said she and Jeremy were together the night Thatcher died. So that murder, at least, cannot have been committed by Jeremy.

Gen gets out the passenger side of the car and looks me up and down. "Nice outfit."

I tug at my collar. I've dressed for the occasion, in a white blouse and the nicest pants I own. And I've curled my hair. I hate wearing clothes like this, doing my hair; I feel like a kid playing dress-up.

"Thanks," I say.

She pushes up the seat. "I get shotgun." I don't argue, just climb in the back.

Jeremy clears his throat. "Hey."

"Hey."

He pushes his sunglasses up onto his head. Now all I can see in the rearview mirror are his dark green eyes on mine. I break eye contact, try and tamp down the feeling that this is all a huge mistake.

Gen gets in and we pull away from my house. I shift in the faux-leather seat, look out my tiny window. Decide that I don't like two-door cars. No escape route.

No one says anything for a solid five minutes, until Jeremy reaches the highway.

Gen breaks the silence. "Oh good, I thought it'd be awkward."

An exhale from Jeremy, and a wan smile from me.

A buzzing comes from the front seat. Gen picks up her phone. "Yeah?" A pause. "Not yet, Mom."

I tense up. I'm fairly certain Gen didn't tell her she was spending the day with me. Though it's not like Mrs. Rodriguez can see me through the phone.

"I'm with Jeremy." No mention of me. I was right. "I don't know." Another pause. "Yeah, I told you, I'll do it later." She sounds annoyed. "I know, Mom. I gotta go." She hangs up.

Jeremy looks at her sideways. "She bugging you about college applications again?"

"Yup."

"You should go. Especially if you don't have to pay for it."

"I don't want my uncle's money."

That makes me still.

Gen only has one uncle. Ramsay.

"Ever since last fall, he's been acting like he's so much better than all of us. I'm surprised he hasn't spent it all already on his fancy new car, and that trip he took over the winter with his twenty-five-year-old girlfriend."

"It's stupid not to take it if someone's offering to pay," Jeremy says. "No matter who it is."

"I hate school and I suck at it."

"You want to work minimum-wage jobs the rest of your life?"

"You can end up doing that anyway even if you go to school. Might as well get a head start."

I try and concentrate on this newfound information, but I can't help but notice the easy rhythm to their conversation, as well as the fact that they've apparently forgotten I'm here. I feel an ache deep in my chest. It wasn't supposed to be this way.

Then I focus back on Gen's words. "Where did he get the money?"

Gen's head turns briefly. "An old friend left it to him. Some guy on the force."

"Left him enough to offer her a decent amount toward any in-state school," Jeremy adds. "And she's being too stubborn to take it. Hey, Addie, maybe you can talk some sense into her?"

And the conversation unspools from there. Almost like we're three normal friends again.

The highway flies by outside, and when I look at my phone, I'm surprised to see an hour has passed. We've hit a lull in our conversation, but it's way less awkward now.

I want to ask Gen what proof she has that this money Ramsay got is from "some guy on the force." But I don't want to ruin this sort-of truce we've entered into. Plus, I'm not sure how she'd know.

"I'm sorry about Seth," Jeremy says abruptly, into the silence. "I didn't mean for it to be that bad."

"What did you mean for it to be, then?" I ask. Gen's sitting at attention now. But she must know what happened if Jeremy isn't explaining it to her.

"I was just—pissed." He takes a hand off the steering wheel, tugs on his hat. "I wasn't thinking. My mom had just given me this car and I couldn't even really enjoy it because I was still so pissed, so I just got in and drove and . . . ended up in the city." A pause. "I didn't have anyone to talk me out of it yet." He looks at Gen, and something in that glance breaks my heart a little. "I didn't mean to hit him that hard. Or I thought he'd fight back more, I don't know. But I am sorry."

I guess that's the best he can do.

"I'm sorry, too," I say. "For . . . Seth."

A tight, quick nod. He doesn't want to discuss it further. So I shut up about it.

Another lapse of silence.

And then I can't help but ask: "So you guys are . . . hooking up, but not together?"

The back of Jeremy's neck goes red.

"Whatever we are, you don't have the right to be mad about it," Gen snaps.

"I didn't say I was mad. I'm just . . . asking."

I'm sort of telling the truth. *Mad* isn't the right word. I don't know how I feel. I don't really have feelings for Jeremy anymore, but we used to be a unit, the three of us. The One-Parent Club. The two of them together leaves me on the outside.

This is how Gen must have felt when Jeremy and I got together.

We lapse into silence again, and soon the skyline of downtown Manhattan can be seen over the stretch of highway.

I don't go to the city often. Besides there being no easy way to get there on public transportation, Manhattan doesn't appeal to me. Concrete and skyscrapers and crowds of people. Give me the woods of Bier's End any day. I used to try and find the silver lining in Fiona coming here for ballet school, tried to tell myself I could meet up with her and we could see a show together, go to a museum. But I could never muster up all that much excitement for it.

Once we're through the Holland Tunnel, we emerge into the chaos of downtown. It takes both me and Gen to help Jeremy navigate to the address I have written on my phone. There's a knot of nerves in my stomach the entire time.

That knot expands to a giant ball as we pull up to an imposing glass-and-steel building.

"So the plan is you're searching Seth's dad's office for something to prove he killed your sister?" Jeremy asks.

"I don't actually think Seth killed my sister—" I stop. That's still true, isn't it? "But I think his dad might have been involved," I finish.

"Why?" Gen asks.

I exhale. "I can't really get into it right now—I'll explain when I get back." I'll have to decide if I'm going to tell them the whole truth or make something up.

"I don't love the idea of you going in there alone," Gen says, looking up at the building.

I feel a little jolt of warmth at that, cutting through the nerves. "I'll be fine," I say with false confidence.

"So what's your plan?"

"My story is I'm looking for Kendall." I came up with this idea last night. "She interns here." Technically she interns in a different department, but I can pretend to have gotten confused and gone looking for her at her dad's office. "I'll say that I want to learn more about finance, which isn't a stretch."

"So what happens when you run into her?" Jeremy asks.

"I won't. She's not in this department. So I go up, pretend I mixed up where she works if anyone asks, and if no one's there, I look around."

"Doesn't sound like the most well thought out of plans," Gen says.

"Do you have any better ideas?" I demand.

Neither of them respond.

"I'll circle," Jeremy says finally. "Just message us when you're coming out and we'll be here ASAP."

"Thank you."

His mouth lifts at one corner. "No problem."

I take a deep breath. "Okay. Here I go."

Gen gets up to let me out of the back seat, and for a moment we stand there facing each other on the sidewalk. I have the urge to hug her, and for a moment I think she's about to do the same, but then she just nods at me, says, "Good luck."

I turn to face the building. Well-dressed people are streaming through the doors, and inside the tinted glass I can see a long reception desk.

But that's not where I'm headed.

Instead, I walk around the side of the building, onto a smaller street, more like an alley, and find a door labeled SERVICE ELEVATOR. And then I wait.

Not less than five minutes later, a truck pulls up. I exhale. Showtime.

A scruffy-looking white man jumps out and heads to the back of the truck. I wait as he unloads several brown packages, piles them on a dolly, and heads toward the service elevator without even glancing my way.

Once he opens the door, I jump forward. "Excuse me. I need to hitch a ride."

The man shakes his head. "This is the service entrance."

"I know, but I forgot my license and security won't let me in. I'm supposed to interview for my first job." I swallow, try and summon up fake tears. "And if I miss it, I'm totally screwed and this is, like, my one opportunity to get somewhere in life, and—"

"Okay, kid, okay." He nods toward the elevator. "Hop in."

It worked. I can't believe it.

I exhale and wipe away a fake tear. "Thank you."

We get in and I punch the number twelve.

We ride up in silence. When we get to the twelfth floor, I thank him and get off.

I'm let out onto a corporate-looking hallway. Beige carpet, white walls, framed black-and-white photographs. Finance people hate color, I guess. There's a man at one end walking with his head in his phone, a woman coming the other way doing the same. I straighten up and start off in a random direction, hoping I look like I know where I'm going. Neither of them even glance at me.

I couldn't find Harold Montgomery's office number by googling, but I figure the twelfth floor can't be that big. I walk along, passing office after office with nameplates out front. A handful of people glance up, then look back down when they see me. Apparently, I've done a good job fitting in.

Finally, I turn a corner and see the nameplate THATCHER MONTGOMERY.

I'm close.

I pass by the open office door, heart pounding. There's a middle-aged white woman with a neat brown bob sitting at a desk just outside who glances at me, then back down at her computer.

I walk three more feet and stop.

The plate outside the office next to it reads HAROLD MONTGOMERY.

The desk in front of his office is empty. But I'd be willing to bet that's where Patrice sits. Maybe she's in the bathroom. Or—just my luck—she called in sick today.

With no other choice, I backtrack to Thatcher Montgomery's office. I face his assistant, give her my best aspiring-intern smile, and say, "Excuse me?"

She looks up. "May I help you?"

"I hope so." My heart is pounding so loud, I'm afraid she can hear it in my chest. "I'm supposed to meet Kendall Montgomery. Have you seen her?"

The woman purses her lips. "Kendall doesn't intern in this department."

"Oh." I make a big show of looking embarrassed. "I must have—Downstairs, they must have sent me the wrong way, I'm so sorry, I'll just message her and let her know where I am—"

I look down at my phone and pretend to send a text. "She's going to meet me here," I report. "So I'll just . . ."

The woman gestures to a row of chairs along the hallway, directly across from Harold Montgomery's office. "You can wait there, if you like."

"Thank you."

I take a seat and wait, tapping my foot as I do. If Patrice is in the bathroom, she's taking a long time. Or she could be out today, since Harold Montgomery's office appears unoccupied. I wonder if the other assistant would notice if I just darted in there.

Or maybe she saw my sister last year, since she sits right outside his office, too.

I swallow, then clear my throat. "Um. Excuse me, Miss, um—"

"Patrice," the woman says.

My heart lurches.

Patrice is *Thatcher's* assistant. Not Harold's.

Maybe she got promoted. Or maybe Harold just used his brother's assistant to help him sneak my sister in because . . . because she's more trustworthy or something, I don't know. But the point is, the woman who can tell me what I need to know is right in front of me, right now.

I look down at my phone, open the voice memos app, and discreetly press record.

Then I step closer to her desk and paste a smile on my face. "I'm meeting Kendall because I wanted to apply for an internship here next summer."

Patrice nods, not especially interested.

"My, um, friend interned here last summer. Maybe you met her?" I pull up the photo of my sister I saved for this purpose. "Her name was Fiona?"

I hold my phone in front of Patrice's face. She looks at it for a long moment.

And then she shakes her head. "We get a lot of interns around here in the summer," she says, typing something on her computer. "I don't remember most of them."

My heart sinks.

She has to be the same Patrice. How many assistants named Patrice can there be around here?

Does she really not remember letting Fiona in through the service elevator a year ago?

Or—and as I think this, I take a step away—is she so loyal to Harold that she's lying to me?

I watch her typing and realize she could be alerting him, or Thatcher Sr., who might have even been aware of what his brother was doing, right now.

I need to leave.

"Oh, Kendall just told me to meet her downstairs," I blabber. "Thanks for your help."

I turn to head down the hallway—and then stop.

Because walking toward me are Kendall—and Seth.

And neither of them looks exactly pleased to see me.

38

"H-HEY."

Kendall tilts her head. She, at least, looks more curious than pissed.

Where Seth just looks angry.

"Um . . ." My heart is racing. "I was just looking for you. I—"

I glance at the assistant sitting at the desk outside another executive's office.

"Come on," Kendall says smoothly. She nods back the way she and Seth came, and with no other choice, I follow them, my mind racing.

What can I tell them about why I'm here?

Whatever I do, I absolutely cannot tell them about the phone.

Shit, shit, shit.

Kendall leads us around the corner, then opens the door into some kind of small conference room. It's empty, nothing but a round table and rolling chairs, windows looking out over lower Manhattan. I can even see the Statue of Liberty from here.

Kendall's closed the door, and it's silent. We might as well be the only three people on earth. The two of them are waiting for me to say something.

"It was just a theory I had," I blurt out.

"What theory?" Kendall still doesn't sound angry.

"Look, we thought Fiona was getting money from someone. No one has more money than all of you. So I thought I'd just come here and see if, I don't know, your dads' assistant recognized her, in case she got the money from them."

"What did she say?" Seth asks tightly.

His eyes haven't left me. This feels precarious. Like if I put one foot the wrong way, I'm screwed.

"She said she'd never seen her before," I say truthfully. "So this was all a waste of my time. But I just had to check."

Kendall and Seth exchange a glance. I hate this. I hate being on the outs.

"Why didn't you tell me what you were doing?" Seth's voice is quiet.

"Because I thought you'd react like this, maybe?"

His brows come together, and he's about to retort something when Kendall steps in.

"I get it." She looks at Seth. "Tell me the same thought didn't cross your mind."

"No, actually, I didn't think my dad was giving an eighteen-year-old girl money—and what are you implying?" he demands of me. "What do you think Fiona was doing for that money?"

"It was just a theory," I repeat lamely.

"Seth," Kendall cuts in. "You can't blame her for—"

"Let me talk to Addie alone, please."

Just then the door to the conference room opens. Adults in suits walk in, stop when they see us.

"We were just finishing up," Kendall says brightly. I keep my head down as we head out the door and down the hallway to an elevator bank—a normal one this time.

"How did you even get in here?" she wants to know as we step into the elevator.

"Service elevator," I mumble.

She looks impressed. Seth . . . doesn't.

We reach the lobby and head out through the double doors. I manage to shoot off a text to Gen not to come get me yet. If Seth sees Jeremy, it's only going to make things worse.

"Let's take a walk," Seth says tightly. Kendall bids us goodbye, a slightly worried look on her face as Seth propels me down the city block. I find I'm actually sorry to see her go.

When we reach the corner, Seth turns and faces me. There are people streaming by, but we might as well be alone; no one is paying us any attention.

"Addie. Are we still in this together?"

"Of course," I say, but even I don't believe me.

"So why didn't you tell me you were coming here?"

"I told you," I say, throwing up my arms. "I thought you'd be pissed. And I didn't want to deal with that."

"You came to search my dad's office—but did you ever consider searching Jeremy's place to find the gun he was shooting at us?"

"Seth, your theory that Jeremy was shooting at us is based on *nothing*. I told you, he doesn't even own a gun!"

Was this Seth's plan all along?

To pin it on Jeremy, while his dad gets away with it?

I look at Seth, his eyes serious and intent on mine. I want to believe he's on my side.

But why would he be?

What makes more sense—that the hot rich boy from the city has somehow fallen for me, when he could have basically any girl he wants—

Or that he's just using me to save his own family?

He's my only alibi for that night. For *both* nights. One word from him and that alibi goes up in smoke.

I go on, "Besides which, Jeremy doesn't have any money—"

"What if this money stuff is just a red herring? And it's him all along?"

"A *red herring*? Are you listening to yourself?"

He glares at me. "This is because we slept together, isn't it?"

"*No.* Just because I don't want things getting complicated in that way—"

He steps toward me. Now our faces are so close, we could be kissing. "If you haven't noticed, Addie, things are already really fucking complicated. In every way. Lying to me isn't going to solve any problems. A week ago, you'd have told me about this. But we get close again, and suddenly you're shutting me out. When are you going to grow up and start facing things instead of running away from them?"

I stare. "I'm not *running away*, I'm trying to find out who killed my sister—"

"And I'm trying to find out who killed my cousin! I thought we were in this together!"

His voice is rising. I don't think I've ever seen him this upset.

Part of me wants to relent. Tell him I'm sorry. Forget everything Gen told me.

But the part of me that thinks she was telling the truth, that's questioning every interaction Seth and I have ever had, that's picturing the trailer park she comes from alongside the mansion he comes from—that part of me won't be silent.

I close my eyes. "We were never really in it together, Seth. That's the problem."

"What do you mean?"

"I mean—you'll be fine!" I burst out. "People like you are always fine! Even if *you* were the one who did it, your dad or uncle would find a way to get you off. Probably by pinning it on someone like Jeremy—or me."

He's looking at me like he doesn't even know me. "So now you think *I* killed Fiona and Thatcher?"

"I didn't say that. I just mean—"

Then Seth's eyes go to something over my shoulder.

I spin. And see Jeremy's car directly behind me.

39

"SO THAT'S IT."

Seth's voice is flat.

When I turn back around, he's not even looking at me.

I swallow. "I needed a ride—"

"You spend two fucking hours with them and suddenly *I'm* the bad one. Not the guy who landed me in the hospital, or the girl who insulted your family—"

"They apologized for that—"

He holds up a hand. "Just . . ." And then he turns and walks away.

I stare after him. Even the set of his shoulders radiates anger.

I don't know what to think, what to feel. I've never made Seth any promises, but I know that doesn't matter to him. If he's sincere, if he's not in league with his father trying to set me up, set Jeremy or Gen up—I'm pretty sure I just hurt him in a way I didn't even know I was capable of.

That, or he's a very good actor.

"Addie?"

Behind me, Gen's leaning out of the car. "You okay?"

I swallow down my anger, my sadness. "Yeah. Let's just go."

She gets out of the car, and I'm about to crawl into the back seat when Gen surprises me by doing it first.

"What—"

"You look like you need shotgun more than me."

I'm not about to argue with her, so I slide in and we pull away from the curb, a car honking behind us.

"So what happened?" Jeremy asks.

I tell them I didn't find anything to incriminate anybody. And how Kendall and Seth found me instead. "So it was all for nothing. And now Seth is pissed at me."

I expect them to laugh, or at least say *I told you so*. But neither of them do.

"I'm sorry," Gen says, and Jeremy lifts his hand like he's going to give my arm a squeeze but then thinks better of it and puts it back on the wheel.

We're all quiet as we inch slowly back up through Manhattan, toward the Holland Tunnel.

"So why did you think his dad may be involved?" Gen asks then.

I hesitate.

This past year, ever since Jeremy and I broke up, I thought there was no one left on my side. And then Seth came along. And despite everything, he became the one person I could count on.

And now?

I look over at Jeremy's profile. Look into the rearview mirror and catch Gen's eyes.

What if my old friends are the people I should have trusted all along?

I remember thinking there was a tenderness in Seth's eyes that night in the clearing. That that's when it started between us, this weird, unnamable thing that bound us to each other.

But what if I'm remembering that wrong, too? What if there was no look in his eyes? What if it was just the cider?

How much can we really trust our memories?

So I tell them. About the phone I found. The messages on it. Patrice, who was no help at all. The gunshots in the woods. Seth's car.

(Would Seth have sabotaged his own car? So we'd have to spend the night together? And get close again? Did he book that place with only one bed on purpose?)

Jeremy and Gen listen to everything in silence. We're well out of the city by the time I'm done.

"Holy shit," Gen says.

Jeremy shakes his head. "Why don't you just take that phone to the cops?"

I knew Jeremy would be Mr. Do the Right Thing. "Because there's no names on it, nothing to prove that it was even Fiona's, much less that the guy she's texting is Harold Montgomery."

"Where is it?" Gen asks. "Can we see it?"

"I left it at home."

A pause. "You really shouldn't leave it where anyone can just find it."

"No one even knows it exists."

"Not even Seth?" Jeremy asks.

I shake my head. Then hesitate.

He did see it in my waistband that day. I thought he'd assumed it was the phone he'd given me. But I don't actually know for sure.

A little while later, Jeremy decides to pull over at a rest stop on the side of the highway so he can grab something to eat. I'm actually surprised he's lasted this long without food; he eats more than anyone I know.

"You guys coming in?" He looks from me to Gen.

"I'm not hungry," I say.

"Me neither," says Gen.

He gets out, leaving the two of us alone.

"Jeremy and I hooked up once before you ever got together," she says.

I'm startled. I twist around in my seat to look at her. *"What?"*

She nods. "Summer before junior year. You were at Fiona's recital. My

234

mom came home drunk, and I was upset, so I went to Jeremy's, and we started drinking and it just . . . happened."

I don't know what to say except, "Why are you telling me this now?"

"Because he wanted to keep hooking up. And honestly? So did I. But I said no." She looks me in the eye. "I didn't want it to mess up what we had."

By *we*, I understand she means the three of us.

"I . . . never asked you to do that," I say.

"Yeah, you didn't have to. I knew it would upset you. So I said no." She crosses her arms and looks out the window. "But you couldn't do the same for me."

"I did think of you, I just—" I squeeze my eyes shut, then open them again, make myself look at her. How to make her understand? "After my mom left, Fiona was gone all the time, and I had that on-again, off-again make-out thing with Seth that he wouldn't even, like, acknowledge existed—I just felt like there was something wrong with me. And then there Jeremy was, one of my oldest friends, and he was Jeremy *Reagan*, and—he wanted me. Like, in public. I did it because—I guess I just wanted to know that someone could love me."

"I loved you," she says quietly.

"I know, but—"

"No, Addie, I don't think you do know. Because if you knew, you wouldn't have done what you did. You and Jere—you were all I had. I didn't want to risk losing you, even if it meant I didn't get to go out with the star quarterback."

"It wasn't just because—"

"Let me finish," she interrupts. "The thing is—I chose *us* over what I wanted. Because I thought either of you would do the same for me. And then you and him both went ahead and did the exact opposite, leaving me all alone. I didn't mean what I said about you, or your mom, I really didn't, I just—I was losing both of my best friends at once and I just snapped."

"I'm sorry" is all I can think to say.

She looks at me. "Thank you."

Neither of us speaks for a moment.

"I have to pee," Gen says. I start to get out of my seat, but she waves me off and climbs out Jeremy's side instead.

Leaving me alone to think about everything she just said.

When she puts it that way—

Yeah, I can see where I'm the asshole.

If I hadn't been so desperate for someone to prove to me that I could be loved—maybe I wouldn't have put that desire ahead of Gen.

Then maybe she would have been here all along.

Maybe they both would have. And it wouldn't have mattered what I did with Seth last summer; they'd have stuck by me anyway.

Why am I so incapable of seeing what's right in front of my face?

It always comes back to me. It's all my fault my fault *my fault*—

I bang the console of Jeremy's car. The glove compartment falls open.

I go to close it—then stop.

Something silver is glinting inside. I reach in—

And pull out a gun.

40

I BLINK.

It's still there.

It's a handgun, small and silver, and that's all I can tell about it. Despite living in an area where a lot of people hunt, I know nothing about guns. My parents never owned one.

And neither, I thought, did Jeremy.

What's it doing here?

I let go hastily, letting it fall back into the glove compartment, then close it afterward.

Why does Jeremy have a gun in his car?

Why does Jeremy have a gun at all?

"Addie."

I jump a mile in the air.

Jeremy's peering at me from the driver's side. "You okay?"

"Um, yeah, you just scared me."

"I got you curly fries." He holds out a greasy paper bag. He knows I love curly fries.

"Oh—thanks." I take it from him and clutch it tight.

"Where's Gen?"

"Bathroom."

He nods, takes his hat off, runs a hand through his hair. "You sure you're okay?"

"Why's there a gun in your glove compartment?" I blurt out before I can think about it. "I wasn't snooping, I just—bumped into it and it fell open and I saw it."

Jeremy's eyebrows go up. "It was my dad's."

"Oh." My mind is racing. "It's just—I've never seen it before."

"My mom had it locked up. She said I could have it when I turn eighteen. Gave it to me on my birthday. But I haven't done anything with it except target practice, at that range over in Merriman."

"Oh." But—"Why's it in the *car*?"

His cheeks go a little pink. "I guess I got spooked, coming to the city, to their office, and Gen's convinced they're all behind this, so I thought I should, I don't know, have protection or something."

I nod.

It makes sense.

Just the fact that there is a gun here does *not* mean Jeremy was the one shooting at us in the woods.

Why am I letting Seth and his out-there theories get to me?

"Sorry it freaked you out." Jeremy glances at the glove compartment, then looks back at me. "Is anything else wrong?"

"No," I say, too quickly. "I just need to get home."

Gen returns then, and we head out. Conversation on the way back is surprisingly normal. We hit a little traffic but are driving into Bier's End by four.

Jeremy drops me off first. I look at him, at Gen, as they pull up to my house. "Thank you. For driving and for . . . everything."

He nods. "You're welcome," Gen says, looking at me. She raises an eyebrow and—for the first time in almost two years—smiles at me.

I smile back, all the while trying to push the image of that gun, glinting silver, the weight of it in my hand, out of my mind.

"Keep us in the loop," Gen says before I get out of the car. I promise them that I will.

When I step into my house, no one's home.

Dad's still at work, and I don't know where Davy is, as usual. Sadie's whining to be let out, so I grab her leash and head right back out the door.

I take a path through the woods, a longer one than I usually go on. Try and put everything out of my mind, if only for an hour.

When I get back to my house, from far off I can see a note stuck to my door. Not the main door of the house, but the outside door to the extension of our house, the one that goes straight into my bedroom.

When we were little, Jeremy, Gen, and I used to leave notes for the others to find, on our doors, in the woods, but that all stopped when we got phones. I feel a ping of warmth, thinking maybe it was them, maybe this is the sign that our friendship really is back on track.

And then I get close enough to see what it says, and my blood goes cold.

It's a white piece of paper with two words scrawled in big black letters.

STOP DIGGING

I walk up to it, hardly believing my eyes.

Seth's car, the gunshots—they weren't accidents. And they weren't meant to kill us.

They were a warning, telling us to stop.

With a shaking hand, I grab the note, and something falls out behind it.

I stoop to pick it up—and lose my breath.

It's a photo of Davy, asleep somewhere. His gold hair is mussed on the pillow, and it's dark in the room, but not so dark I can't tell it's him.

What the *fuck* is this?

I pull out my phone, fumble with it, drop it on the ground. Finally, I manage with shaking hands to press my brother's name.

"Hello?"

"Davy!" I nearly collapse with relief. "Where are you?"

"Um. Home?"

"What? Where—"

I run around to the front of the house and bound in the front door, Sadie fast on my heels—

To find Davy, sitting at the kitchen counter, eating a peanut butter and jelly sandwich and looking mildly bewildered.

"Davy." I run over and grab him from behind in a hug.

He actually laughs. "What are you doing?"

"Just—glad to see you." I force a smile. "What are you doing tonight?"

"Um. Nothing?"

"Good. Good, I'll . . . make us dinner. Let me just . . ."

I hurry back outside and grab the note and photo—only belatedly realizing I probably shouldn't have touched them, in case they have fingerprints or something on them. But the person who left them probably made sure to wear gloves.

I need to take all this to the cops. To Carter. Between this and the phone—they *have* to take me seriously now, don't they?

I head to my room, then make a beeline for my nightstand drawer.

But the phone's not in there.

A surge of panic goes through me.

Fiona's phone. It has to be here.

I push aside the junk in the drawer, bookmarks and ChapStick and old pieces of paper and pens. Then pull the drawer out and empty it onto my bed.

But there's still nothing there.

Fiona's phone is gone.

41

I TEAR MY room apart.

Sheets everywhere, bed shoved aside, every box of random stuff under it upended. Closet torn through. But even as I'm doing it, I know there's no point.

The phone is gone.

I stand in the middle of my mess of a room, panic threatening to close my throat.

That was the only thing I had. It wasn't the most concrete proof, but those messages to "tiny dancer," the mention of Patrice—it was *something*, at least.

And now I have nothing.

I run to the outside door to my bedroom. It's bolted from the inside, the way I keep it. The front door to the house was locked when I got in. I run to the back door. Locked. Check every window on the ground floor. All locked.

Which means no one broke in here.

The person who took the phone had a key.

"Addie?"

I jump, then turn to see my brother.

"Was anyone here?" I blurt out.

He looks at me warily. "What's wrong?"

"The phone. I mean—my phone. The one I used to text Seth. Have you seen it?"

Davy shakes his head, looking mystified.

"Was anyone here?" I repeat.

"Just Marion, but then she had to leave for dinner."

Marion. Again.

Would *she* have stolen the phone? On the instructions of her uncle? Her father?

Or Seth himself?

"Did she come inside?" I ask.

His eyebrows go up. "Yeah, for a little, but—why would *Marion* steal your phone?"

I'm not about to go into it with Davy. "I— You're right. I probably just . . . misplaced it . . ."

I've turned away from my brother, and my heart is sinking like a stone.

Maybe Marion took it. Or maybe someone else did, before my brother got home. But if the house was locked—

Jeremy and Gen both know where we keep the spare key. And they're the only people I told about the phone.

I squeeze my eyes shut. *No.* They were *helping* me.

But then I see the glint of that silver gun in my hand.

What if they pretended to be on my side again—just to find out what I know?

To help sow seeds of doubt between me and Seth?

Or—what if it *was* Seth, somehow? He came back from the city after me, followed me here, saw me leave with Sadie, and decided to search my room while I was gone?

But *Seth* doesn't know where our key is, at least.

And then I remember.

Under the rock by the maple tree in the backyard.

I told Seth that myself.

So it could have been him.

And now I have nothing to bring to the police except that note and photo.

I'll have to just *tell* Carter about the phone. I can testify that I had it. Take a lie detector test or something. Would that work?

I have no idea.

I almost pick up my phone to text Seth and ask him. And then I remember.

I'm on my own.

———

I go outside and remove the spare key from under its rock. Then, once Dad is home, on the guise of walking Sadie, I head to the police station.

I ask for Carter inside, but the woman behind the desk tells me he's off duty until tomorrow. "If this is about the Montgomery case, Detective Ramsay is—"

"No," I say quickly. "I'll come back."

"And you can't bring dogs in here."

I leave, feeling lower than ever.

No way am I taking this to Ramsay. Not now that I know about his sudden windfall last fall.

I'll come back tomorrow. I'll tell Carter everything.

And I'll hope that'll be enough.

That night, I push my dresser up against my door to the outside. Just in case.

I try and reconcile the note, the photo, and the gunshots in the forest with Jeremy and Gen. Maybe it was like Seth said. Jeremy got drunk, thought he was going after me, accidentally pushed Fiona, and has since been desperately trying to cover up his tracks, with Gen's help.

Or maybe—and this gives me a little hope—Gen has nothing to do with this. Maybe it's just Jeremy acting alone. And Seth was right, and the money Fiona needed had nothing to do with why she was killed.

Or maybe it's been Seth all along.

He couldn't have shot the gun, of course—but if he's doing this for his father, he's not working alone. He might not even have left the note himself. Taken the phone himself. Maybe he got Marion to do it. Maybe she's just been pretending to be into my brother this entire summer to get close to us, get access to our house.

Or maybe it was Seth's role to get close to *me*.

And I was stupid enough to let him.

42

THE NEXT MORNING dawns cloudy and gray.

I rise early, but I barely slept anyway. I kept thinking I heard someone coming into the house and went upstairs half a dozen times to make sure Davy was okay.

I need to go tell Carter. Now, before Dad and Davy are even awake. I throw on shorts and a T-shirt, take Sadie for the shortest walk ever, then run upstairs to check on Davy one last time before I go.

I creak open the door to his bedroom—

To find it empty.

I panic for a moment, then run to the bathroom, surely he's just—

The bathroom is empty.

I tear through the house, checking Fiona's room, the kitchen, the sunporch, the downstairs bath.

But it's no use.

Davy's gone.

My breaths are shallow in my chest, and there are spots at the edge of my vision. This can't be happening, maybe I'm still dreaming, a nightmare made of everything I've gone through the past few weeks, maybe I can just shut my eyes and it won't be real—

My phone buzzes in my pocket.

Of course, maybe Davy just ran out to get bagels, or— I tear out my phone.

But it's a number I don't know.

"Hello?" I sound frantic.

"Addie? It's Kendall."

I deflate. "Hi, I can't talk, I have to—"

"Davy's missing, isn't he?"

My body floods with relief. Of course. He's at Marion's, he must have snuck out early this morning. "Oh thank God, is he at your house?"

"No, I'm calling because Marion's missing, too."

My heart stops. "What—what do you mean, when did she—"

"I think you'd better get over here. Now."

————

Nothing stirs outside the Montgomery mansion as I approach through the trees.

I went through the woods, running as fast as I could. The house is silent in the hazy morning. The sun filters in weakly through the clouds overhead.

I knock on the kitchen door. "Kendall?"

No answer, so I let myself in. No one in the kitchen or anywhere I can see.

"Kendall?" I call again. And then: "Seth?"

I hear footsteps on the stairs. A moment later, Kendall bursts into the kitchen, wearing leggings and a crop top, a leather bag slung over her shoulder and a worried look on her face.

"They're in the woods," she reports.

"What?"

"Follow me—I'll explain on the way."

With no other choice, I follow her back out the kitchen door.

She's talking as she jogs into the backyard. "Marion left a note saying she couldn't be here anymore and she and Davy were running away together, she was sorry, and not to worry about her."

I exhale.

Relief—Davy hasn't been hurt, or kidnapped, or anything like that.

Fear—now he's out there on his own, with no one but Marion for protection against whoever is threatening him.

If she'd even protect him. If she, too, hasn't been a part of this all along.

I pull out my phone again. I tried calling Davy half a dozen times on the way over here—then curse. It's dead. I didn't bring my Seth phone with me at all.

"Did you try calling Marion—"

"Yeah!" Kendall shouts back at me. We're passing the pool house now. "No answer. But then I saw them from my window—they're heading into the woods. Backpacks on. They must think they're going to get on the Appalachian Trail or something, live off the land." She shakes her head. "Marion's never even been camping."

I take a deep breath. Davy's safe. He's just ahead of us in the woods. All I have to do is catch up to him and then not let him leave my side until we go talk to Carter.

Kendall and I make it to the clearing. I scramble up the wall, Kendall right after. We pause at the bottom, listening, but there's nothing save the sounds of Bier's End: insects buzzing, birdcalls, the rustling of the wind. The sky overhead is gray, getting darker by the second. "Which way did they go?"

She points. "Toward the ravine."

That doesn't really make sense—the easiest way to get to the Appalachian Trail is through the woods, then on through the state park.

But it's not like Davy has the best sense of direction. We turn toward the ravine.

"Where's Seth?" I ask as we run along. "And the rest of your family?"

"Still in the city. I came back last night with Marion because she threw a fit, saying she couldn't be away from Davy for another day." I'd expect Kendall to roll her eyes at this, but she just looks worried. "Now I know— they must have been planning this."

We continue to move at a jog through the woods. I'm afraid, even though there's no need to be. We'll reach them before they get far. We'll stop them.

Still—I don't want Davy anywhere near that ravine.

I don't want to picture it, but the image rises in my mind: Thatcher, thin legs sticking out at an odd angle, blue eyes wide and staring. Then the image shifts, the boy's hair turning blond, and it's my brother I see lying there, motionless, blank, dead.

I clutch Fiona's necklace to me, then run faster.

"Addie!" Kendall gasps behind me.

"We need to catch up—"

"No—I thought I heard something."

I freeze, Kendall pulling up beside me. We're both still, listening. But all I hear is the blood pounding in my ears.

"What'd you hear?"

"I'm not sure."

We listen for another moment, but there's nothing.

We continue on our way. As we get farther into the trees, I keep my ears pricked, my eyes darting around for any sign of human life, but there's only a squirrel scurrying in the undergrowth, the call of a bird. I wait for that feeling of eyes watching me, that prickling on the back of my neck, but there's nothing. It feels like Kendall and I are totally alone.

Suddenly I hear a rustling not far off. Kendall and I both freeze.

I strain to hear, thinking it's just my imagination—but no, there it is.

Footsteps through the woods, coming from behind us. It sounds like the person is running.

Chasing us.

Kendall grabs my arm and pulls me behind a thick bush.

I don't know what to do. I don't know who's coming, if it's friend or foe, if we should call out that we're here, if we should hide. And so I wait, breath held, poised to run if I have to.

A figure bursts into the clearing in front of us.

Holding a small silver handgun.

Jeremy.

I'm frozen.

Jeremy—it was *Jeremy*, this whole time—

And somehow he knew we were here—he's hunting us—

He stops, the gun pointed out in front of him. Listening for something.

I steal a glance at Kendall. She's watching him, her eyes narrowed. She looks at me, puts a finger to her lips.

Then, before I can say anything, before I can do anything, Kendall steps out from behind the bush, pulls something out of her bag—

A small black gun.

I've barely registered the fact that Kendall has a gun when she holds it out in front of her.

And shoots Jeremy.

43

SOMEONE, SOMEWHERE, IS screaming.

It takes me a moment to realize it's me.

Jeremy's dropped to the ground. Without even deciding to, I'm leaping out from behind the bushes and running toward him.

"You shot him!"

I don't hear whatever Kendall says. I don't even think about how a moment ago I thought Jeremy was here to kill us. All I know now is—I don't want him to die.

He's clutching at his shoulder. The bullet hit him near his collarbone. I have a moment to be grateful it missed his heart, missed his head, but his face is sickly pale, and the blood, there's so much blood—

I look wildly from Kendall, standing not far away, the gun in her hands, back down to Jeremy. I have to—stanch the bleeding—

"Call 911," I order Kendall.

I pull my T-shirt off so I'm in just my sports bra, ball it up, press it into Jeremy's wound. Within moments it's soaked through. Jeremy is whiter than a sheet, gasping. It's like he can't even see me.

"Ah—"

I grip his hand. With my other hand I'm still pressing my T-shirt into his wound. "It'll be okay. You'll be okay. You hear me? You're going to be *fine*."

I look back at Kendall, expecting to see her on her phone.

But she hasn't moved.

"What are you doing?" I practically scream. "He needs help!"

"Keh—"

Jeremy's trying to talk again.

"Kendall will call for help." I squeeze his hand. My other hand is stained with his blood. "You're going to be okay—"

But his head is thrashing back and forth.

"Jeremy, just *hold on*—"

"Addie."

Kendall's voice, coming from behind me.

"What are you doing?" I half scream. "Why aren't you calling anyone?"

Her voice sounds funny, higher than usual. "There's nothing you can do."

A gasp comes from Jeremy.

His eyes roll back into his head.

And then they close.

"No," I say firmly. *"No."*

I say it like a prayer. I fumble for his wrist, press my ear to his heart, listening for a heartbeat, a sign of life, anything—

It's there. Faint. But it's there. He just passed out.

I rise, tears blurring my vision, stumble toward Kendall. I have no idea what's wrong with her. In that moment, I don't even care. I just want him to live.

"Give me your phone," I order.

Her face is blank. "No."

Kendall raises her hands slowly.

And brings her gun up to point at me.

I can't comprehend what I'm seeing.

My hands are shaking at my sides. "Kendall, what— It wasn't me! Even if it *was* Jeremy—we need to call 911, we need to get him *help*—"

"I'm the one in charge right now." Her voice is calm. Her hands steady. "So I'm the one who says what we need to do. And right now, I need you to walk toward the ravine."

It hits me all at once.

The person who did this knew Fiona. Knew Thatcher. Knows these woods. They have money. They have insider info on Seth's and my investigation.

I stare at Kendall.

"It was you."

44

MY MIND FEELS slow, like I'm in a dream.

Jeremy, dying on the ground in front of me.

Kendall, with the gun pointed at my face.

"Move," she says softly.

I look from Jeremy to her. "Can you just— He had *nothing* to do with this—"

"I panicked." She frowns at his still body. "But it's too late now. I can't have him telling people I shot him. Now *move*."

I look back down—and register the handgun lying at his side. I freeze. If I could just—

"Don't even think about it." Kendall steps toward me, making me flinch. "Move. *Now*."

I take a step, trying not to look at my ex-boyfriend, ex–best friend, dying or dead on the ground. He was trying to say something just before he passed out.

He was trying to warn me.

"Addie, I swear to God, I will shoot you if you do not walk the way I tell you to," Kendall says tightly. *"Move."*

With one last look at Jeremy's inert form, I take a step forward, and then another. I don't know how I'm doing it. Walking away from him. Moving, with a gun pointed at my back, by someone I thought was—if not my friend—someone I at least thought I could trust.

"Are you going to shoot me?" My voice sounds funny in my ears, too breathy. The sky is no longer gray, but a bright white, unearthly. I can't hear anything in the woods, no insects, no birds, no animals. There's nothing out here except Kendall and me.

"That depends on whether or not you jump."

I look back. Her face is still in that tight, concentrated look I've never seen before.

"Why?" I'm surprised at how calm I sound. I touch Fiona's necklace, realize I'm getting Jeremy's blood on it.

"I was supposed to be getting away with this." The padding of our feet on dirt. "But things don't always go as planned. I wasn't as careful as I thought. So I need a scapegoat."

I.

Kendall did this. She did it alone.

"Seth had nothing to do with this," I say softly.

She laughs. "No."

A wave of shame goes over me. Seth. He was on my side this whole time. Maybe if I'd never doubted him, I wouldn't be here right now.

About to be killed. By the same person who killed my sister.

"Honestly? I'd have loved to throw Seth under the bus. But my family would never stand for that. It could never be one of us."

It clicks into place. "Me. You're going to say it was me. And I—"

"Couldn't live with your guilt any longer. Correct."

My mind is spinning wildly. I need to figure a way out of this. But also—I need to know *why.*

"Why Fiona?" I ask. "She was your friend. Why would you kill her?"

Kendall frowns. "She wasn't innocent in all of this."

"So tell me." I need to know, and I need to keep her talking. Maybe if she's distracted enough—if I can buy myself enough time . . . "What did she do? Why did you kill her? Why did you kill your own brother—" It comes to me. "You were the one who had us shot at in the woods? Seth's car—the picture of Davy—that was all you?"

"The car was because I didn't want you talking to Caleb," she says. "It was stupid of me to mention him to you. But I thought Seth already knew. I had no idea what Thatcher might have told him last year. So I messed with Seth's car the night before you left. He didn't know I was home; he thought I'd already left for the city. But since I was one of the only ones who knew where you were headed, I was afraid that made Seth suspicious of me. So I guided us to the ravine that night we were all together. I'd hired someone to shoot at us while we did. It worked. Seth started trusting me. Telling me things."

"What things?"

"How worried he got when you began distancing yourself. And how he was pretty sure you'd found something in the old tree house and weren't telling him about it."

I exhale. I thought I'd fooled him—but he knew me better than that.

"So you were afraid, what—I'd found Fiona's journal?"

"No. *I* have Fiona's journal. I took it from your house the night she died."

I turn to stare at her, but she prods me forward again.

"The night you killed her." She still hasn't told me why.

"I was afraid of what would be in it. Fiona's phone I stole just yesterday, right after I dropped Marion off at your house. She and Davy were busy making out and didn't even notice when I slipped into your room. I was looking for the phone you and Seth were using, to see if there was anything he wasn't telling me. It was very lucky I found *that* phone instead—next to the piece of paper with the password on it."

I curse myself for being so stupid. Not just leaving it in there, unprotected, but leaving that paper, too.

But I'm still confused. "So it wasn't Seth's father sending those texts to Fiona?"

I twist my head around and see her mouth go up at one corner. "You weren't far off, you know. You and Seth were actually pretty good little detectives. Fiona didn't get a scholarship. She *did* find herself a wealthy patron. But it wasn't Seth's father. It was mine."

"*Your* father." Thatcher Montgomery Sr.

"Correct." She gestures with the gun. "Keep moving."

I do, swallowing. I don't hear anyone, but we have to be getting close—

"Davy and Marion," I say suddenly. "What if they see you? What if—"

"They're not here. I said that to get *you* here."

"Where are they?" I see red. If she did anything to Davy . . . "What did you do to them?"

"I was telling the truth about them running away. I imagine they're just off on some stupid little lovers' trip. They probably headed down to the bus station or something equally cliché. My parents will find them and bring them back."

I let out a breath. Davy—safe, thank God.

But that means we're truly alone.

No one is coming to save me.

Kendall goes on: "This all happened because no one cared about what *I* wanted. We all could have saved ourselves a lot of trouble if anyone had just listened to me."

"I'm listening." I have no idea if I can talk her out of this. If she killed her own brother—I don't think I have a chance. But keeping her talking is buying me time. "Tell me."

She's quiet for a long moment. And then she starts to speak.

"I didn't want to work for my father," she begins. "I didn't even want to go to college. I wanted to start my own business. But when I turned eighteen, Daddy refused to give me access to my trust fund. Said I was 'too irresponsible.'" There's a quiet undercurrent in her voice: rage. Kendall is absolutely furious. "So I got my act together, got into school—with his help—stopped basically, like, *all* my spending, started working for my dad's company, and what happened? Still no trust fund."

Kendall's sudden revamp on her social media. Her partying pictures changed to serious student pictures. That was all for her father's benefit.

"He didn't want to give me what I deserved," she goes on. "Nothing I said or did would move him. My mom wouldn't help. Thatcher wouldn't help. So I was stuck living a life I didn't want. And there was nothing I could do about it."

The rage in her voice is growing. I keep walking.

"And then—I stop by the office last summer and find one of my best friends, Fiona, making out with my *father*."

I flinch.

Kendall catches that. "Yeah. Gross. Also, what a fucking hypocrite my father is. Telling me how to live my life, denying me my trust fund, and all this time he can't even keep it in his pants?" She snorts. "But that gave me an idea."

I step on a twig, which makes me jump.

"I went to your sister the next day," Kendall goes on. "Told her what I saw. Asked how much he was paying her. Because he was definitely paying her. I could see it in her eyes. She wanted his money. Nothing more."

I swallow. I knew it was all true. The phone proved it. But still, the confirmation of what Fiona did to get what she wanted makes me want to throw up.

"She begged me not to tell. And I said I wouldn't. For a small fee."

I glance back at her, nearly tripping on the undergrowth.

Kendall shakes her head. "It was such a simple idea. I can't believe I didn't think of it sooner. He paid Fiona—and Fiona paid me." Her face darkens. "Until she stopped."

"Why did she stop?"

She prods me forward with the gun. I have no idea how close we are to the ravine. But my only hope is to keep her talking. Maybe she'll get distracted, maybe she won't notice how slowly I'm walking, which will give time for someone to come—

But who would come? No one knows I'm here.

"Fiona told me she didn't want to pay me anymore," Kendall goes on. "She said she was the one who was putting it all on the line, sleeping with a guy she didn't even like. She didn't think it was fair that she was doing all the work and I was just collecting the money." She snorts. "Like anything is ever *fair*. She said she didn't care who I told—she was done paying me off to be quiet. She was going to keep all the money for herself. For her stupid ballet school."

Her voice has dropped to a whisper in her outrage.

"So that's when you decided to kill her?"

Kendall scowls. "She was sleeping with a married man. Not only that—the *same* married man her own mother used to sleep with."

That stops me in my tracks. "What?"

"Oh, you didn't know that?" She smirks. "Yeah. Your mom and my dad were sleeping together, back in the day. My mother paid her off to disappear. Maybe it will give you some small amount of comfort? Knowing your mother didn't just abandon you for nothing—she abandoned you for a bunch of money?"

Before I can even process this, Kendall goes on. "Your mom wasn't the first, either—but she was the only one my dad fell in love with. Maybe that's why he went for her daughter. Trying to relive his glory days or something." She snorts. "Fuck him. And fuck the sluts in your family who fell for him."

A bolt of anger goes through me. "Don't—"

"I'll do what I want. I'm the one with the gun." She gestures again. "Walk."

But I don't move. "How are you going to get away with killing me, too?"

"I have a plan," she says calmly. Her voice is deadly soft. "Now *move*."

I want to call her bluff. But I'm afraid I'll come out on the losing end. If she shoots me right now, I'll be gone, and no one will know the truth.

I keep walking. "So Fiona stopped being useful, so you decided to kill her?"

"Not exactly. First I had to come up with a plan." Kendall pauses. "And then it came to me. How easy it would be to keep this going. Find some dumb, pretty young girl who needs money. Put her in front of my weak can't-keep-it-in-his-pants father. Tell her I won't say anything—for a cut."

I look back. She's actually smiling now.

Her expression darkens. "But I couldn't do that while he was still obsessed with your sister. And she wouldn't agree to end their deal. I *gave* her a chance to walk away. It's not my fault she refused. Basically sealed her own fate."

My heart is pounding in my chest. Every bad thought I've ever had about Kendall is going through my mind. This past month I'd started to reframe how I thought of her, decided maybe she wasn't just some vapid rich girl, the way I'd seen her while we were growing up.

And now I know.

She's so much worse.

"It really isn't even my fault," she says. "I was just trying to get what I want. What I deserve. That's how the world works for powerful men. It's what I had to do to make it work for me. I'm no worse than anyone who has any power. That's how they get there. They step on people. It's what I had to do."

I swallow down my venom-filled reply.

"I came up with the idea of the ravine," Kendall goes on. "I told Fiona I wanted to talk to her about it one last time. Made it sound like my dad was getting tired of her, like he'd be cutting her off soon. She was scared, so she came. I wore gloves. I made sure she was dead. Then I ran.

"I thought an accident or suicide would be an easy conclusion for them to draw. And it would have been—but then my stupid fucking brother had to go and get in the way."

"He saw you?"

"I don't know how he found out. All I know is he did. And my father knew, too. Thatcher must have told him. But Daddy never would have turned me in. My brother, however—he wanted me to confess." She makes an annoyed noise. " 'I'm sure they'll go easy on you, K. Dad will get you a good lawyer, it'll be fine'—what an idiot." She shakes her head. "I didn't *want* to kill him, too. But he wouldn't shut up. There was no other way."

"So you pushed him. The same way you pushed her."

She lifts her shoulders. "What choice did I have? Things were going well after Fiona died—I gave my dad a couple of months to mourn, and then I invited 'a friend' over—and I repeated the scheme. That worked, until he got sick of her. Then a few months later, there was another. And then another." I can hear the smile in her voice, turn to marvel at it. "I'm a fucking *genius* is what I am." The smile fades. "I just had to kill my big brother to make sure everything kept going smoothly."

I swallow. "How'd you manage that?"

"That night, *he* brought *me* to the ravine. To, I don't know, spook me? He didn't think he was in danger. He wasn't afraid of me. Even knowing what I did, he wasn't afraid. He underestimated me. The way everyone does." She pauses. "He saw the push coming. He screamed. That was unfortunate. I wouldn't have done it like that if I'd known you and Seth were fucking right on the other side of the wall—"

"We weren't—"

"When you came running, I had to hide. Making my way back to the house with the police and the paramedics crashing through the woods—it's a good thing I know this place like I do. I didn't get caught. Obviously." She scowls. "But my dad figured it out. He thinks the cops are in the process of figuring it out, too. And we need to give them a scapegoat.

I'm sorry it has to be you. Really, I am. But we agreed you were the best option. That's why I planted all those theories about you online."

I turn. "*You* were—"

"RdHerrng41. And a few other usernames. But that wasn't enough to get you arrested. I didn't want to have to kill you. My plan was to try and get Seth to turn on you. Retract his statement that you were together that night. But even with all the seeds of doubt I sowed between you, even when I tried to convince him *you* were about to turn on *him*, he never wavered." She snorts. "Pathetic. And then, when I saw you at my dad's office—I knew it was only a matter of time before you figured it out. So this is the solution. You turn up dead. Suicide, from your guilt. It'll give them a scapegoat. All of this will finally be over."

"Why would they think it's suicide?"

"We have a friend on the case." Her voice is placid. "He'll make sure that's what it looks like."

"Ramsay." I knew it.

"My father paid him off. It's easy to get what you want when you have money. It's so, so easy."

I know where we are now. Know I only have a few minutes before we're at the ravine.

"What if someone finds out?" I try. "Seth, or someone else in your family?"

"Seth's not as stupid as my brother. He knows how powerful my father is. Once you're gone, he won't say anything."

I open my mouth to argue—then snap it shut.

Because I don't think Kendall is right about that. If Seth found out Kendall killed me, too, I don't think he'd be quiet about it.

Of course, that's little comfort if I'm already dead.

"Poor motherless Addie," Kendall says. "Always jealous of her big sister, Fiona, who was prettier, thinner, more talented than she was. One day, she just snapped. And then there's Thatcher, the boy who always loved Fiona, who spent a year trying to figure out who killed her. And he did figure it out, in the end—but not in time to tell anyone. She killed him, too.

"But since then, Addie's having nightmares. She can't live with the guilt. Plus, the police are on her tail. She's eighteen now. No juvie for her. So she decides to take the easy way out, in the same place she committed those terrible crimes. Her ex-boyfriend followed her. Tried to talk her out of it. But she shot him, too. Right before jumping. Or shooting herself. Tragic, really. But at least it's all over now."

She prods me forward.

We turn at a bend in the trail, and then there's the stone circle. The biggest rock is centered exactly along the north-south line, according to Seth. It might have been a place of great importance. A place where they made human sacrifices.

This is one of the last things I'll ever see.

If I don't fight back.

I touch Fiona's necklace. Kendall made a mistake. She panicked and showed her hand when she didn't need to. If Jeremy hadn't showed up, I'd still be walking along unsuspecting, searching for Davy. It would have been easy for her to push me.

She made a mistake.

And I can use that.

Too soon, I hear the running water of the ravine.

We aren't at the exact spot Thatcher died, but close to it. I don't know the exact spot Fiona died.

There's a rocky outcropping just ahead of me. And from there it's a straight, sharp drop to the shallow stream and rocky bottom below.

"Stop," Kendall calls.

I stop.

And for a moment, I think about it.

Because I'm not innocent in all this. If I'd been able to figure out what was going on with Fiona before that night instead of being wrapped up in myself, maybe I'd have been able to save her. If I hadn't been so dead set on accusing Thatcher this past year, maybe I'd have figured out who the real villain was sooner.

I could do exactly as Kendall planned. Davy would be safe. Everyone would hate me forever, but the people who knew me, at least, would know it wasn't true: Dad, Davy, Seth, Gen, Jeremy—

Jeremy.

I look out through the trees at the waving green. Imagine the ghosts of our small selves darting around this place, looking for something they would never find. Think of the ghosts of Fiona, of Thatcher, hovering near the places they died.

I don't know if there's a heaven, but if there is, I like to think Fiona is there.

Is she waiting for me?

Or would she want me to stay?

Fight, Addie.

Did I hear that voice out loud? Or only in my mind?

"What is it?" Kendall calls.

I turn to look at her. "Nothing," I say.

I don't know if I'm going to survive this. But I'm not going out like a coward.

"It'll be easier if you jump," she says softly. "Less messy. I'll climb down and get your fingerprints on the gun. Then I'll be gone before anyone even knows you're missing. It'll all be over. You'll see Fiona again." She nods toward the cliff. "It'll be quick. It was for them."

I take a step backward. There's a lump in my throat. Tears in my eyes.

Kendall starts to lower the gun.

I look down, as if closing my eyes in prayer. She's standing less than four feet away.

And then I attack.

45

SHE WASN'T EXPECTING it.

I launch myself at her, knocking her to the ground. The gun clatters to the rocks beneath us.

Kendall screams. Claws at my face. I turn to the side, but I still feel her nails rake my skin. The gun is just a few feet away—if I could just—

But as soon as I reach for it, she grabs me, pulling my hair, kicking, scratching.

Fighting like the animal she is.

I let out a yelp as her teeth sink into my arm. I get a fistful of hair, kick at her legs beneath mine, reach for the gun.

But Kendall is stronger than I thought.

With a grunt, she rolls herself on top of me, and now I'm on the bottom, trying to stop her from getting the gun. I tear, scratch, grab hair—but she's lunging for the gun—

Then her weight is off me. I dive toward her, but it's too late.

Kendall has the gun.

And it's pointing at me once more.

A hysterical giggle rises out of her. It sounds alien, subhuman. She has grass in her hair, dirt on her arm, a line of blood blooming on one cheek. "Not bad, Addie," she says, panting. "I didn't think you had it in you." Keeping the gun trained on me, she motions toward the ledge. "Now. You love your sister so much—you can join her."

"I'm not jumping." I try to sound braver than I feel. She has the gun pointed straight at my chest. "You're going to have to shoot me."

Kendall looks uncertain for a moment—then she takes a step toward me. I take a step back. The ledge is less than a foot away.

She's really going to do it.

Suddenly, there's a rustling in the bushes nearby.

And Seth bursts through the trees.

I've never been so happy to see anyone in my life.

But my relief is short-lived.

Kendall wings the gun from me to Seth. She looks furious—but not shaken.

Seth stops where he is, holds his hands up. "Kendall." His voice is eerily calm. "You need to give up."

"I don't think so, Sethy."

"You can't shoot both of us." He takes a step forward, closer to me. "How're you going to explain that?"

She keeps the gun trained on him. "You couldn't have just minded your own business, Seth?"

"You killed Thatcher." His voice is still calm, but there's a timbre underneath it I recognize: rage. "You killed Fiona, and you killed Thatcher, and you tried to kill Addie. That *makes* this my business."

"I did you a favor," she snaps. "How much money are you set to inherit now?"

"Thatcher was my best friend—"

Her laugh is hysterical. "Oh please, Seth. He could've minded his own business, too. Or better yet, my father could've given me what was mine in the first place and *none of this would have happened*!"

Seth's entire body is tense. Kendall is becoming increasingly unstable. Which could work to our advantage, if she lets her guard down—or it could lead to her shooting us dead, just like that, without thinking through the consequences.

My heart is thudding in my chest. Death is close now, closer than it's ever been. I can smell it in the air, taste it on my tongue. Our only hope is to reason with her.

"No one gives a shit about me," Kendall says. "So I have to look out for myself."

I look into Kendall's eyes, at her trembling chin. And an odd feeling moves through me.

"Kendall," I say. "I know what it's like to feel totally alone—"

"You have no idea what it's like to be me," she snaps. "You *can't*. You were born here. You were never going to be anything. But I'm supposed to *be* someone. All I'm doing is taking back what's mine, and no one's going to stop me. Not *him*"—she points the gun at Seth—"and definitely not *you*. You're nobody. *Nobody*."

She trains the gun back on me.

In one fluid motion, Seth is in front of me, covering my body with his own.

The gun wobbles in Kendall's hand for a second. But then she points it straight at Seth's heart.

"They'll know," he says hoarsely. It's the first time I hear fear in his voice. "Do you really think you can get away with this?"

"I don't have a choice."

"You do. You don't have to kill us."

"Run," I say. "We'll send you money. We won't tell anyone. We'll keep it between us."

Her laughter is maniacal. "You expect me to believe that?"

"Kendall, I just want this over." My voice breaks. "Fiona's dead, Thatcher's dead, Jeremy's—" I choke on his name. Then inspiration strikes. "We could say it was him," I go on, inventing wildly. "We could swear that he led us here at gunpoint and we shot him before he could shoot us. None of us have to go down for this. I'll swear to it."

I'm lying. Of course I'm lying. The moment she lowers her gun, I'm going to do everything in my power to make sure she's punished for this. I can only hope I'm a good enough liar, that Kendall is desperate enough to believe me.

"You're not going to be able to explain *three* more bodies," Seth says.

For a moment, I think we've gotten through to her. The gun slips an inch.

But then she catches herself, trains it back on Seth's chest. "Nice try. But it won't be that hard. I shoot you. I shoot her. I wipe the gun clean, put it in her hands. You and Jeremy went after her, tried to stop her. She shot both of you, then felt so terrible about it, she shot herself." She mock-frowns. "And me? I won't be anywhere near here when you're found. And if the cops start getting close, Daddy will cover it up. He always does."

"You think my dad's going to go along with it this time?" Seth asks tightly. "When it's *me*?"

"People in power do what they have to do to stay there. You of all people should know that by now."

Seth's hand reaches back, finds mine. "Remember when I said I still didn't know what I love?" he says, low so only I can hear.

I swallow. "Yeah?"

"I lied. It's you. It's always been you."

The click of the gun distracts me from whatever I might be about to say.

Kendall's finger is on the trigger. "Goodbye, Addie. Goodbye, Seth."

I close my eyes.

46

AND THEN A new sound meets my ears.

Footsteps, running through the woods.

Hope flickers in my chest.

"Here!" I call.

Kendall's eyes widen. "Shut—"

"We're here!" Seth hollers.

The footsteps grow closer.

And then a figure comes bursting through the trees.

It's Gen.

She's the last person I was expecting to see. She's out of breath and red in the face, and it's clear she's been crying.

And she has Jeremy's silver gun in her hands.

"Gen." Kendall's voice is a broken whisper. "Thank God you're here. It was them—they killed Fiona and Thatcher. They brought me here to kill me—"

I find my voice. "Gen, *no*," I say loudly. "She's lying—"

"Do you have service?" Kendall's eyes are fixed on Gen, even as she keeps the gun trained on Seth and me. "Can you call the cops? I don't know how to work a gun, Gen, I'm scared—"

Gen looks from Kendall with the gun to Seth and me frozen near the edge of the ravine. "I—I don't—"

"Call your uncle," Kendall orders. "Tell them we heard everything, they confessed, they told us how they planned both murders, and why. If both of us swear to it, they'll have to believe us."

Gen reaches into her pocket, looks at her phone, then back at us. "But they—"

"Gen, you *know* me." I swallow. She can't really believe Kendall right now, can she? "I didn't kill Fiona. I didn't kill *anyone*. It was Kendall. She shot Jeremy!"

"She's lying," Kendall breaks in. "*She* shot Jeremy. She's such a good liar, you know that—"

"Gen, call your uncle," Seth orders. "Do it, before she kills us all."

Gen stands with her mouth open, phone in hand. "I—don't have service," she finally whispers.

"Okay, so here's what we'll do," Kendall says. "I'll keep my gun on them while you go find service, then you call—"

"Gen, please don't leave me." My voice chokes up. "She's going to kill us."

"I'm trying to keep myself *safe* from you—"

"Gen, *please*—"

"She's a liar, she lied to you about Jeremy because she wanted him to herself, and now he's dead!"

"Because of you!" I scream at Kendall. I'm full-on crying now. "Jeremy's dead because of *you*."

"I could never do this!" Kendall's crying now, too. "My brother, my best friend—Gen, please, you have to believe me."

Gen looks between us, her phone still limp in her hand. Then a look comes into her eyes I don't like.

She turns to Kendall. "I believe you."

I feel like I'm going to throw up. "Gen, no—"

But she's walking toward Kendall, then standing right next to her. She aims Jeremy's gun at us.

My heart sinks.

Kendall's face shows a flash of triumph. "We need to get our story straight—"

It happens fast.

One moment the two of them are standing there—and the next, they're on the ground.

A gun is sailing through the air.

It clatters to the rocks.

And goes off.

47

"ADDIE!"

I force my eyes open. Clutch at Seth, in front of me.

Alive. Whole.

"Seth!"

His hands are on my face, his eyes going up and down my body. "You're okay?"

"I'm fine—"

And then he's gone, diving to the ground for Kendall's handgun as it skitters toward the edge of the ravine.

A scream comes from behind me.

I spin.

Gen, grappling with Kendall, the two of them rolling, kicking, Jeremy's gun between them—

Gen, who saved us—

I launch myself on top of them, trying to help Gen keep Kendall down. I have one arm, and Gen has the other, but Kendall is fighting with every ounce of strength she has—

"Stop."

Seth's voice comes like from a dream.

All three of us freeze.

I turn to see him standing above us, steady as a rock, Kendall's gun his hand.

Kendall goes limp underneath me. I take my hands off her, and so does Gen, Jeremy's gun safely in her hands. We rise from the ground, and I go to stand beside Seth while Gen slowly backs away. Kendall gets to her feet, brushing dirt off her legs. Her hair is a mess. Her face is a mask of rage.

"You don't know what you're doing—" she starts.

"Shut up, Kendall." Seth sounds weary. "It's over."

Her eyes go from Seth's face to the barrel of the gun. "Not until I say it is."

And then she turns and runs.

I'm frozen in place, not quite believing my eyes. Seth, too, seems in utter shock. His eyes go to the gun—and then he's shoving it into my hands and taking off after her.

I stare at the heavy object in my hand. I want to run after Seth, help him, but I don't know—

"You should put the safety on if you want to run with it," Gen says.

"I don't— Do you know—"

"Yeah." Gen holds out her hand.

I hand the gun to her, watch as she flicks on what I assume is the safety. Then I take it back and run off after them.

Kendall ran north, farther into the Bier property, toward the state park. Without the gun, she's no match for Seth—or so I believe. Still, I don't want to leave him alone with her.

Gen's breaths are behind me. I have to ask her how she knew Kendall was lying, thank her for saving our lives. Jeremy wouldn't—

Jeremy.

I trip on a tree root and go down, hard, onto my knees.

At once, Gen is at my side. "You okay?"

I swallow. "Yeah." I can't fall apart. Not yet. "But Jeremy—"

"He was still alive."

Hope washes over me. "Oh—"

"I called 911. They should be here soon. I was going to stay with him, but then he told me about Kendall—and how she was with you." Her voice is tight.

She helps me up as she pulls her phone out of her pocket. "I have service now," she reports.

"Call Detective Carter," I say. "Not your uncle. They paid him off."

Her eyes widen, but understanding comes into them. "That money."

I nod.

I strain my ears, but I don't hear anything. I want to keep running after Seth and Kendall—but I'm not about to catch up to them now, and if we want to get Kendall, we need more than just us.

"Detective? Yes, this is Genevieve Rodriguez. We're in the woods behind the Bier house and we need help . . ."

Gen keeps talking. I look up at the sky, the white turning to gray above the trees, clouds swelling with rain. I feel the weight of the gun in my hand. I can smell ozone on the air; a storm is coming.

In the distance, I hear the rumble of thunder. We'll likely still be back here when the rain hits.

But I don't mind.

The storm will pass.

I touch my necklace.

I'm not alone anymore.

48

SETH DIDN'T CATCH her.

But the police did, two hours later, in the denser part of the state park, along one of the hiking trails.

By that time, Gen, Seth, and I had been pulled into the police station, each in our own separate rooms, to give our statements. Detective Carter is with me. Only Detective Carter; no Ramsay in sight.

I tell him everything. When I'm finished, he sits back, dark hands folded, and looks at me.

"Addie." His voice is quiet. "You should have come to me sooner."

"I didn't trust you." I've already told him my theories about Ramsay. He didn't say anything while I talked, just watched me with that same calm expression.

"You should know that Detective Ramsay has been, ah, excused from this case." I open my mouth to ask questions, but he goes on. "I can't discuss any details pertaining to his absence. I just wanted to let you know. It's just me. Or if you're not comfortable with me, I can send in someone else. Officer Cortez—"

"No. It's fine." I let out a breath. "Do you know how Jeremy is?"

"I've heard nothing since he was taken to County Medical."

He's in critical condition, according to the last update. But he's not dead. Not yet.

"All I want now is to know where my brother is."

"As I told you, we'll let you know as soon as we find anything."

With Kendall in custody, there's no immediate danger to Davy. I have to keep telling myself that. Carter told me they believe Kendall was acting alone.

She hasn't confessed to anything, as far as I know. I had a glimpse, through the window in the door, of Thatcher Montgomery Sr., white-faced, marching down the hallway, with two men who are presumably lawyers trailing behind him. I'm sure Kendall will have the top defense money can buy. But with my testimony and Seth's, not to mention Gen's, I hope it will be enough to put her away for a long, long time.

A knock comes on the door, and Officer Cortez pokes her head in. "Detective Carter? Miss Blackwood's father is here."

Carter thanks her, then turns to me, an eyebrow raised. "Just so you know, Addie—I never believed you committed these crimes."

I stare. "Then why did you get a warrant? Take my stuff?"

"I was surprised when the judge approved the warrant only for you and not for the Montgomerys." He frowns. "I'm looking into whether something else was going on there."

Meaning—someone paid off that judge.

"But I did believe you might be hiding something. And as it turns out, I was correct about that."

I shrug uncomfortably.

"But we were not on the verge of arresting you. Or Seth Montgomery. Now. Is there anything else you want to tell me? Or ask me?"

I shake my head.

"Well, then I think we're done for now. I don't have to tell you to stay close to home, that we'll want to talk to you again . . ."

Detective Carter goes on, telling me things I already know. Afterward, he escorts me out to the lobby, where my father waits, his knee jiggling.

I tell him the whole story on the way home. He listens, not interrupting. And then I get to the part about Mom. Mrs. Montgomery paying her to go away.

He's still, not saying anything.

Then I can't help but ask, "You really didn't know . . . anything?"

"No. I didn't know anything." He swallows. "Just that she wasn't coming back."

I reach out a tentative hand, touch his sleeve. "Davy *will* come back."

But I don't know whether that's true.

———

We get home late in the afternoon. I walk in the house feeling as though I've aged a year in a day. I start toward my room.

"Addie."

Dad's voice stops me.

I turn to find his face a mask of misery. "Why didn't you tell me?" His voice sounds like it might break at any moment. "Why didn't you come to me for help?"

I don't want to put him through any more of this. But I have to know. "You thought I killed Thatcher, didn't you? As revenge for Fiona."

He opens his mouth, closes it. Then he sighs. "I didn't think you'd deliberately plotted murder, no. But the idea of you getting into an argument, it getting out of hand . . . and the police, coming here with a warrant—I thought maybe it was a possibility." He meets my eyes. "I'm sorry."

I have so many other emotions in me, I don't have the space to be angry at him, too.

"I should have come to you," I say. "I should have told you all of it. But I guess I felt like I had to handle it myself."

"We're broken," Dad says. "This family's been broken a long time. But once Davy gets back—we're going to fix this." There's a fierce look on his face I don't think I've ever seen there before. "I promise you, Addie. Things won't be this hard. Never again."

I'd like to believe him—but if I've learned anything, it's how life can surprise you. How things can get so much worse, so fast.

We still don't know where Davy is.

"I'm going to shower," I say instead.

I go to my room. Jeremy's blood is caked under my nails.

I look at myself in the mirror. I'm dirt-streaked, hollow-eyed. There's blood on my necklace. For the first time in a year, I take it off. Then I shower.

Afterward, I collapse on my bed, bury my face in Sadie's fur, and cry.

49

JEREMY IS STABLE.

Gen calls to tell me that the next day. She saw his mom on her way to the hospital, who relayed the news. She's going to visit him tomorrow, and do I want to come?

I say yes.

It's been a strange twenty-four hours. Kendall's arrest has been all over the news, local, national, and everything in between: *Millionaire's Daughter Being Held for Fratricide* and headlines like that, twisting the story every way it can be twisted: a Greek tragedy, a jealous best friend, even some hints at incest. I've been ignoring messages from journalists, gossip columnists, true crime podcasters. I don't know how to talk about all of this and what it's cost me, and I don't want to try.

Seth texted me last night on my burner phone. I saw it after I finished crying.

How are you was all it said.

I don't know, I wrote back. **You?**

Ok. Do you want to talk?

Not yet.

And he's respected that. It's the next day and he hasn't tried to contact me again.

I thought I'd feel better knowing Jeremy's stable, knowing I won't be going to jail for something I didn't do. But the cloud of Davy's continued absence mars everything. I'm still having bad dreams, waking bathed in sweat. But waking up doesn't help. It just reminds me that it's all real.

Dad said he's taking some time off work. He told me not to worry about dinner, is checking in on me, taking Sadie for her walks when I don't feel up to it. All that while he's calling the police for updates on Davy.

Two days after the woods, on the second day of August, Gen comes by to pick me up in her mom's car.

I get in without speaking. The circles under her eyes are dark.

She glances at me as we pull away from my house. "You okay?"

"No."

"Me neither."

"I didn't thank you," I say abruptly. "If you hadn't shown up—Kendall was about to shoot us." I still can't believe it's true. "But what I don't understand is—how did you find us?"

We pull out of my neighborhood, and Gen rubs one eye. "Jeremy," she says. "I saw him run to his car, and I asked him where he was going. He was already driving away, but he said something like, 'It was Kendall the whole time.' I had to think about it for a minute—but then I followed him. When I got to the Montgomerys' and no one was there, I took a chance and headed into the woods."

I frown. "But how did *Jeremy* know?"

"I don't know." She lets out a breath. "But I'm glad we get the chance to ask him." Her voice drops. "If Jeremy died—I don't think I'd ever get over it."

"He didn't. And this isn't stuff you get over. It's stuff you live with."

Gen looks at me. "I lied to you," she says then. "About seeing an email from my uncle that they were going to arrest Thatcher? That they were looking at Seth? That was all a lie."

I stare at her. "What? Why?"

"Kendall." Her face hardens. "She told me—we were hanging out one night, drinking—and she started telling me shit. That she suspected Seth killed Thatcher and Fiona. That she was scared of him. She was so . . . *convincing*. Then she told me he had you fooled and she was worried about you but couldn't think of a way to make you see you'd partnered up with the wrong guy . . . so I came up with the idea of saying I saw something in my uncle's things." She shakes her head. "I played right into her hands. I'm so stupid."

I lean my head back. "Is that also why you went with me to New York?"

"Yeah. I wanted to, I don't know, keep an eye on you."

I feel a tiny flame of warmth. "Well. Thanks. And you're not stupid. She was just . . . smart."

Planting the seeds that it was Seth with Gen, knowing Gen would tell me. Getting me to suspect Seth and leave him out of what I was doing had almost gotten me killed. Almost let her get away with it.

We hit a red light a block from the hospital. Gen's eyes close, then open. "I'm sorry, Addie," she says. "For everything. But most of all—I'm sorry I spent the past year and a half not talking to you. Even with the way I felt, with Jeremy and all . . ." She trails off, swallowing whatever she was going to say next.

The light changes, and we move forward. There are tears rolling down her cheeks.

I wonder what would have happened if she and I had stayed friends. Maybe with Gen on my side, I wouldn't have been so upset at Fiona for leaving. Maybe we wouldn't have gotten into a fight that night.

But there's no use in thinking about what might have been. There's only what is. Only what I can do now, with what's in front of me.

"I'm sorry, too," I say.

"Never again?" she asks, looking over at me.

"Never again."

50

JEREMY IS PROPPED up against a pillow, hooked up to some tubes, paler than I've ever seen him. Except for the moments I thought he was dead.

He smiles when Gen and I walk in. "My girls."

That's what he used to call us before everything went wrong. It makes tears spring to my eyes.

Next to me, Gen is crying; she hasn't stopped since we got out of the car, since she grabbed me in a hug so tight I felt I couldn't breathe. I get a tissue from Jeremy's bedside table and hand it to her, then grab one for myself.

"Are you okay?" Jeremy asks then.

Gen nods. But I shake my head.

Jeremy opens his arms—as best he can with one of his shoulders entirely bandaged—and Gen and I walk over and gingerly lean into them.

"I'm not about to break." His voice is huskier than usual, weaker.

"You look like you are," Gen says, sniffling.

He lets out a hoarse laugh. "Thanks so much."

"You scared the shit out of me." My voice is low. I'm angry, I realize.

It's not fair to be angry at him—but I am. "What were you even doing there?"

"I came to save you." His smile is wry. "Great hero I turned out to be."

"How did you even know where I was? Or that I needed saving?"

"Seth told me."

Gen and I stare. "He did?" I ask.

He nods, which makes him wince. "He didn't tell you?"

"I—" I don't want to tell them I haven't talked to Seth yet. Because I don't know how to tell him how grateful I am. And how sorry I am. "I've been busy," I say instead.

Jeremy says, "He was at his place in the city when he heard his dad and uncle arguing about Kendall. And he put two and two together. He called you, but your phone was dead. Then he called the cops but got Ramsay on the phone. Then he tried Davy, your house phone, Marion, but when no one picked up—he DMed me. Told me to find you and warn you."

"But *how* did you find me?"

"You weren't home, and so I figured you were on one of your runs. It was just luck that I happened to head toward the ravine. I heard you and Kendall, and ran after you—and then I fucked it all up."

"No." I try to smile. "You're a hero."

"I'm a victim." He nods at his shoulder with a wry smile. "A lucky one, that Kendall's such a bad shot." Then he sobers. "I can't believe all of this. We've known her almost our whole lives."

"You think you know someone, and then they turn out to be someone else entirely," Gen says.

"But not always," I say. "Sometimes people are who you thought they were all along."

Now they're both looking at me. Jeremy tilts his head.

"Are you in love with him?" he asks me.

"I don't know," I say honestly.

Gen shrugs. "Well. At least he's not a murderer."

I let out a choked laugh. "Pretty low bar."

Her smile fades. "How do you know he's not like them?" she asks. "That they're not all the same, deep down?"

The privileged. That family has hurt so many.

I search for the answer I know must be there.

"No one asks for the life they're born into," I say finally. "You can't blame him for who his family is."

They think about this, and then Jeremy nods, wincing again.

"Stop doing that."

"I keep forgetting."

A nurse comes in with medication for Jeremy. She doesn't tell us to leave, but I can tell from her expression that she wants us to let him rest.

I look at Gen. "Should we go?"

"I want to stay a little longer." The look that passes between her and Jeremy has something new in it. Something that doesn't involve me.

And for the first time, I don't begrudge them that.

Not all relationships are meant to stay the same forever. And that's okay. As long as there's still a place in their lives for me—and I know now that there is—I can handle whatever other changes come along with that. The three of us aren't back to what we used to be. We've been through too much. But we're *something* again, and that's more than I could have asked for.

"I can walk home," I say.

"I can call you a cab—" Jeremy starts, but I shake my head.

"It's a mile. I can walk." I look at Gen. "So . . . I'll see you soon?"

"I'll call you later."

I lean forward and kiss Jeremy lightly on the cheek. Then Gen and I hug, and I rise from his bed and head out of the room.

Once I'm out in the gray summer day, I check my phone, like I do constantly now, but there's still nothing from Davy.

"Where are you?" I ask the empty afternoon.

I turn the corner onto my street twenty minutes later. I'm four houses away when I see them.

In front of our house, three people.

One of them is Davy.

The second is Marion.

The third is Caleb Jones.

51

"I CAN EXPLAIN." Marion's voice is soft.

She pushes a strand of brown hair out of her eyes and looks from me to my dad to Seth, whom I called right away.

We're in our living room. Davy sits next to her on the couch, his hand clasped in hers. I'm pacing the living room, too agitated to sit, Seth leaning against the doorframe behind me, while my dad and Caleb are in the two armchairs by the window. Caleb is stiff, trying to look composed, and failing. My dad leans forward, as if he wants to walk over and reassure himself that Davy is really here.

I'd run immediately up to Davy and thrown my arms around him.

Then I had to resist the urge to scream at him.

"I know," he said before I could do so. "Just let us explain."

Parts of the story have come out already: how Davy and Marion decided they needed to get out of town but didn't know where to go, who they could trust. It was Marion's idea to message Caleb and ask if they could come talk to him. It wasn't until they'd already taken the bus to Philly that Caleb realized they'd run away. But once Marion told him what she knew, he agreed to let them crash on his couch until it was safe to come back.

"I knew," Marion says now. She looks down at her feet. "The night Fiona died—I was . . ." She looks at Davy, who nods at her to go on. "I was here. I heard something in the middle of the night and I got up and I saw—my sister coming out of Fiona's room. She had something in her hand. Later I realized it was Fiona's journal. That the police were looking for. I didn't know what was going on then, so when they were asking me questions, I didn't know what to say or what to do, so I—I didn't tell anyone."

She's trembling a little. Davy pulls her close, whispers in her ear. I'm taut, watching them. I want to shake her, tell her we could have used this information a year ago. But I know complicated relationships between sisters, maybe better than anyone. I touch my necklace as she goes on.

"I kept quiet for almost a year. I broke up with Davy and stopped talking to him. I just couldn't stay with him when I was keeping a secret this big. I thought about asking Kendall, like maybe she had a good explanation, but I was too scared." She takes a deep breath. "Then when we came back here this summer, I couldn't handle keeping it to myself anymore. So I told Thatcher." She says his name like a sigh.

"When was this?" Seth asks.

"The night before we came. I told him what I saw. He told me not to worry about it, that he would take care of everything." She inhales sharply, and a tear spills out of one eye. "And then . . ."

The room is silent.

"Then I knew." Marion looks up at Seth. "I knew it was her. I think I already knew, but then—I knew for sure."

"And Kendall didn't know you knew?" I ask.

Marion shakes her head. "She never pays much attention to me. I don't think she had any idea. But I was scared. So I—" She looks at Davy.

I stare at my brother. "You *knew*?"

"I lied to him," Marion says before Davy can speak. "I told him it was Thatcher who killed Fiona, and that Kendall killed Thatcher. I needed someone on my side, and I thought if I told him the whole truth, that it was my sister who killed his sister and I didn't turn her in—I didn't think he'd ever forgive me. So I lied." She hangs her head.

"It wasn't her fault," Davy breaks in. "She was—"

"It's okay," Marion says quietly. Davy falls silent. "I know I screwed up. I just— I was so scared. She's my *sister*. My brother was already dead, and she's my sister, and I didn't know what to do."

"You could have come to me," Seth says.

Marion looks at him. "I didn't know who I could trust. I thought my parents might have been protecting her. I didn't know whose side you'd be on. The police kept asking me questions, especially Detective Carter, after they found out I was here that night. I kept telling them I didn't see anything. But I don't think I'm a good liar. And I didn't know how long I *could* lie about it. Kendall killed Thatcher to keep it a secret—how did I know she wouldn't kill me, too? So—" She looks at Davy.

"So we decided to run." Davy looks at me now. "She told me the truth when we were on our way. But I didn't think— You told me you'd be okay. That they weren't going to arrest you."

"They weren't," I say.

"Kendall tried to kill her, though," Seth says. His voice is calm, not angry or threatening. But his words fall like stones into the middle of our living room. "She tried to kill me, too."

"I'm sorry, Seth," Marion whispers. "I just felt so alone."

"You're not anymore," he says, more gently this time.

"My parents are so mad at me—"

"You don't need them," he says. "You've got me."

Marion gives him a tremulous smile. "Thanks," she whispers. Then, to both of us: "And I'm sorry."

And I realize—I'm not angry at her. I don't know what it's like growing up in a family like that. The poison that comes on those silver spoons. And I don't have it in me to carry around resentment for Marion, too.

Just then the doorbell rings.

I'm nearest, so I open the door to find Detective Carter on our stoop.

"Addie." He hands me a brown paper bag. "Thought you might want this. The phone we need to keep for evidence, but we made copies of Fiona's journal, so if you want to keep the original—it's yours."

I stare down at the bag, then take it from him. "Her— You—you found it?"

He nods. "Hidden under the floorboards in Kendall's room."

I swallow. "Thank you."

52

DAVY ASKS IF Marion can stay with us for a little while, and Dad says okay, even though Seth said she could return to the house anytime she wanted. Thatcher Sr. and Seth's aunt have moved out, while Seth's own father is in the city. Seth's mom knew nothing about anything, apparently, so it's just the two of them there. Seth said they could get Marion her own lawyer, someone not controlled by her father.

Caleb rises and says he needs to get home. "Thank you for bringing them back," my father says, shaking his hand. I wonder if being able to help Thatcher's sister has given him any amount of peace or closure, but I don't know him well enough to ask. So I just give him a nod and let him go.

Then it's just us and Seth and Marion. I have the journal in my hands. "I'm going to order a pizza," Dad says. "You're welcome to stay, if you want."

Seth looks at me.

"Stay," I say. "I just need a minute."

He nods, and I flee to my room with Fiona's words between my hands.

I don't know if she'd want me reading it. But she isn't here anymore to tell me not to.

I sit down on my bed, touch my necklace, and open it.

The journal begins last winter, a year and a half ago. It's a lot of dance, a lot of hopes about ballet school. Almost nothing about us. At first. I read about her despair at the money, her deciding to ask Thatcher, her rage when he said no.

It's not fair that some people get everything they want and others don't, just because of who they were born to. If I were Kendall, this wouldn't even matter. I would be set. It's not fair.

Then her conflict. *Mr. Montgomery said he can help me out if I'd be willing to "spend more time with him." I'm not an idiot, I know what that means, and it makes me feel sick—but I'll do anything for ABA. Life isn't fair, so isn't it up to me to make it fairer for myself?*

There are almost no details about the affair itself. I guess she didn't want to relive any of it here. Just a lot more about dance. Trying her best to disassociate from what she was doing by retreating into the thing she knew best.

Then I get to this line:

It's the only thing I'm good at. I'm not a good sister anymore, and I'm not a good daughter, my mom left me, and Addie is better at taking care of people than I'll ever be. I'll go do the only thing I can, and they won't miss me.

I touch my necklace again. I want to tell her she was wrong. That no matter how bad we feel about ourselves over the things we've done or failed to do, there are people who still love us. Who still need us. I wish she'd talked to me about it. I wish I'd gotten over my resentment toward her in time to talk to her about it. I wish so many things had been different.

But wishing doesn't change the past. Nothing does. All I can do now is move forward, taking everything I've learned with me.

And I know where I have to start.

53

DAD, DAVY, MARION, and Seth are standing around the kitchen counter, eating pizza. They look up when I come in. Seth has questions in his eyes, but I know he'll wait until I'm ready. He won't push.

He's so good to me. He has been for years now. Why couldn't I see that before? Because everything that happened when we were little kids blinded me to it? Because I thought someone like him could never love someone like me? Or is it because I didn't think I deserved it?

I'm not all that hungry, but I haven't eaten all day, so I grab a slice of pizza and take a bite. Conversation resumes; something about Marion's school starting, Seth saying they could redo a bedroom in their apartment in the city so she could stay with them.

When we've finished eating, Dad clears his throat. "There's something I've been meaning to tell you kids."

We wait. Seth and Marion look uncertain, like they aren't sure they should be here.

"I've been seeing someone."

I blink. That's the last thing I was expecting him to say. "Really?"

"I didn't want to say anything before I . . . knew. And I know the timing is terrible." He's silent for a long moment. "But I met her through work, and she's quite, ah—I like her," he finishes. "I didn't think I'd ever feel anything for anyone again. But now I think maybe—maybe I can."

He's clearly flustered, his face turning pink. I've never seen him like this before.

Even though Dad isn't a hugger, I go over and hug him.

He stiffens, then hugs me back. "I'm happy for you, Dad."

"Are you?"

"Yes."

Across from us, Davy nods.

Soon afterward, Dad goes off to bed. Davy does the same a little while later. He gives me a hug and then he and Marion head upstairs. It's on the tip of my tongue to tell him Marion needs to sleep in Fiona's room, but I let it go.

Then it's just Seth and me in my kitchen, looking at each other over an empty pizza box.

"I can go—" he starts at the same time I say, "You can stay."

His ghost of a smile. He looks as tired as I feel.

Then he takes a deep breath. "I need to apologize."

I look at him. "For?"

"Kendall's my cousin. We lived in the same house. It did occur to me that someone in my family could have been involved, especially after we found out about that money. I even thought Kendall might have known something at some point, the way she was so eager to 'help' us, how she was one of the only ones who knew we were going to Philly . . . but then she was supposed to be in the city the night before we left, and she was with us when we were being shot at in the woods . . . but I should have seen past that. I should have *known*."

I shake my head. "I'm the one who should apologize."

His brow furrows.

I inhale. "You were right. I *was* shutting you out. I don't think I really believed you did it, but at some point I started to wonder if you might be covering up for someone in your family. If I'd just trusted you—maybe we'd have figured out it was Kendall sooner. Our whole life it's been you versus us. I guess that's a hard pattern to break."

His eyes are intent on mine. "Yeah. I guess it is." His face hardens. "My uncle knew. He knew it was Kendall and was covering for her. He would have let you take the fall. I'm never going to forgive him for that. And if they cut me off"—he lifts his shoulders—"I've got my grandma's money, but even if they find a way to keep that from me, too—I'll survive."

Something Kendall said comes to me: *Powerful men don't get that way by playing fair.*

Seth rubs a hand over his face. "My dad knew about the affair. Both affairs, I mean—he knew my uncle had been with your mom and then your sister. He thought maybe my uncle had paid someone to—to kill Fiona . . . but when Thatcher died, it threw him. He didn't think my uncle would kill his own son. But he swears he had no idea about Kendall until my uncle confided in him a couple days ago, the day I overheard them." He exhales. "I don't know what to believe. But at least Kendall can't hurt anyone anymore."

I know that. But it doesn't make things okay. Fiona is dead and Thatcher is dead and even if Kendall is punished to the fullest extent of the law, it won't bring them back.

Tears spill onto my cheeks. And then Seth's thumb is on my face, brushing them away. Through my tears I can't be sure, but his eyes look shiny, too.

I haven't let what he said right before we thought we were going to die enter my head. But now I let it in.

Remember when I said I still didn't know what I love?

I lied.

It's you. It's always been you.

"I meant what I said, you know," Seth says quietly.

I almost laugh. How does he do that? Read my mind that way?

But I have to let him off the hook. "It's okay. People say all kinds of things in life-and-death situations. I mean, I guess they do. It's not like I've ever been in one before—"

"What part of *I meant what I said* do you not understand?" He frowns at me.

For once, I'm speechless.

"I'm not expecting you to say it back," he adds. His hand is still on my arm, warm against my skin. "I just wanted you to know. Even if you don't feel that way, even if you never want to see or speak to me again, if you want to put all of this behind you, even me—I'd understand. And it wouldn't change the way I feel."

I stare at him, wiping the last of the tears from my cheeks. "Since when? I mean, when did you know?"

"I think maybe in some way, I always have." At my confused look, he goes on. "Addie—you're smart. You're stubborn. You recite prime numbers when you're nervous. You love your family more than anything in this world. You make me laugh. I like kissing you." His fingers move to my chin. "And when I thought you might be gone"—his voice is hoarse—"I didn't know how I was going to live in a world without you in it."

I find my voice. "Could've fooled me."

He shrugs. "Well. You were with Jeremy."

"I wasn't always."

"You're right." He hesitates. "I guess I just never thought you could feel that way about me."

His eyes are soft. Vulnerable. I've never seen Seth this way before.

"I never thought you could feel that way about me." I swallow. "I didn't think anyone could. After my mom left, I felt like it was my fault. And then Gen turned on me, and Fiona pushed me away, and then Jeremy was gone, and . . . I thought it was me. That there was something wrong with me. That no one could love me. Because of what I did."

"Addie." He takes my hand in his. His fingers are callused, his grip strong. He runs his thumb over my palm, over my knuckles. "I'll say it again and again until you believe it: It wasn't your fault."

"What I did to Jeremy is." I meet his eyes, but I don't let go. "And the way I was to Fiona—the way I never wanted her to do what *she* wanted, just wanted her to stay here with us—"

"So you're not perfect," he says. "So what? I have a news flash for you: I'm not, either."

I laugh. The sound is strange, too bright, bubbling up like that in the dimness of my kitchen. But it also feels like the sun breaking over the horizon, just a tiny orange streak after a long dark night—the start of something new.

"I love your imperfections," he says. "And I love you."

I don't know what to say to that.

"So what do we do now?" is what I come up with.

He lets out a breath. "We testify at Kendall's trial. And then . . ."

I grip his hand tighter. "I start at Rutgers." It feels odd thinking about my future when just days ago I thought I wouldn't have one at all. "And maybe once Davy graduates—"

Seth is shaking his head before I finish. "I think you have to stop putting your life on hold. Nothing is going to hurt Davy now. He's a big boy. You can leave if you want to—try for Stanford if you want to."

"And pay for it how?"

"A scholarship? I know Rutgers is already paid for and it's too late to transfer this semester anyway—but the point is, if Stanford is your dream, you should *try*. Try for the life that you want."

I exhale. Maybe he's right.

"I got into Cambridge," he says then. "For archaeology. My dad said I couldn't go, not on his dime, which is why I was at Columbia this past year. But I need to get out of the city. And if my grandma's money comes through, I can pretty much do anything I want."

"Wow." I try to process that. "England."

"Yeah." He hesitates. "But, you know, Stanford has a good archaeology program." He says it in a rush, like he's afraid to tell me. "Not that I'm trying to— I'm just saying, it's a good program."

I stare. "You'd move across the country—to be near me?"

His eyes flicker away from me. "Not if you don't want me to. But that's what that means to me. When I say I love you, it means I'll do what it takes." His ghost of a smile again. "But if you need space or—" He runs a hand through his hair. "Whatever you want. I'll do whatever you want." He lets out a laugh. "That sounds pathetic. But it's true." He meets my eyes again, and the hope in them is almost too much to bear.

"We don't have to decide anything now," he says. "I just wanted to let you know where I stand."

I lean into him again. His arms go around me, smelling of sweat and soap. He feels warm and safe. Two things I didn't think I'd ever be again.

I don't know what to say. So I say what I'm feeling. "I'm so tired."

"Then go to bed," he whispers.

I take his hand and lead him to my bedroom. I push a pile of clothes off and throw my bedspread over my tangled sheets.

He watches me with that half smile on his face. "I don't care that it's a mess in here. I always pictured it this way."

I can't even bring myself to retort. I collapse on the bed—then pull him down with me.

"Stay?"

"Okay."

I don't even bother changing into my PJs. I close my eyes and hear Seth get up and go out into the hallway, hear him flicking off the lights, locking the door. Against what, I don't know. The woods of Bier's End have gone back to sleep. Maybe for good this time.

And then Seth has returned, is looking at me.

"Seth?"

"Yeah?"

I take a deep breath. "I think . . . I love you, too."

The words taste strange in my mouth. But also right.

Seth's answering grin breaks across his tired face. And then he's stretching out beside me, holding me close. I shut my eyes and let myself imagine it. Seth and me, in some little room near the Pacific Ocean, wrapped up on a bed, in our own world we'd make for each other, far away from here.

It doesn't feel like it could possibly be real.

But maybe that's what Fiona would want for me. Maybe she's looking down even now, watching ideas form in my head. Allowing myself to dream.

Maybe I owe it to her to find out what I could be if I let myself try.

Or maybe I just owe it to myself.

ACKNOWLEDGMENTS

This book is about a girl who has a fierce love for everyone in her life—except herself. She thinks because she is flawed, because she's made mistakes, some of them massive, this renders her unlovable.

So first, I have to thank past me, that very young girl with all her flaws, for giving me the character of Addie, who is the heart of this story. I wish I could go back in time and tell past me that it is okay, that she is okay, that she can be loved exactly the way she is. I wish I could ease some of her pain. But I can't, and so the best I can do is hope that this book, and this message, will reach other young people who need to hear it.

It's beyond cliché to say it takes a village to bring a book together, but in my case, it is nothing short of the truth. And so:

Thank you to my agents, Barbara Poelle and Sydnie Thornton, for taking a chance on me, for loving my weird little book as much as you do, for working so hard to make it the best it could be, and for always being there to talk through plot problems and more—I cannot believe I have not only one, but two incredible advocates. It makes navigating this industry so much easier knowing I have both of you on my side.

Thank you to my editor Caitlin Tutterow for buying my book and working your magic on it. You *get* Addie and Seth, *get* this book, more than I thought possible. It would be nowhere near as good without you. Your kindness and encouragement along the way have made my debut experience better than I could have imagined.

Thank you to the entire Penguin team: to Cindy Howle, Laurel Robinson, Ariela Rudy Zaltzman, and Bethany Bryan for your careful copyediting and proofreading. To James Akinaka, Alex Garber,

Kaitlin Kneafsey, Kim Ryan, Shannon Spann, and Felicity Vallence for all your hard work getting my book into the hands of more readers. Thank you to Nancy Paulsen and Stacey Barney for making a home for me at your imprint. Thank you to Cindy De la Cruz for the beautiful interior design, and to Jess Jenkins for the gorgeous cover.

Thank you to Rebecca Barrow, the first "stranger" to ever tell me my writing was good, way back in round one of Author Mentor Match. Your guidance gave me the confidence I needed to keep going, and I will be forever grateful. Thank you to Alexa Donne for starting AMM, the place I found the very start of my writing community, as well as for all your advice through my pivot from contemporary to thriller. Thank you to Naz Kutub for your words of encouragement and for referring me to your agent, who in turn referred me to *my* incredible agents. Thank you to Laurie Elizabeth Flynn for your help with my query and your enthusiasm and support over the years.

Many people read *many* drafts of this book in the pre-querying, pre-sub, and post-acquisition stage. Thank you to my writing cohort, Sammi Spizziri, Jennie Wexler, and Kimmy Wisnewski, for your feedback on the earliest versions of this book. Thank you to my fellow thriller writers Meredith Adamo, Jenny Adams, Paula Gleeson, Cindy R. X. He, Chelsea Ichaso, and Ande Pliego for catching every detail and letting me get away with nothing. Thank you to Clare Edge and Jo Schulte for reading and for fielding various unhinged texts and voice notes from me at all stages of the writing and publishing process. And thank you to Kathleen S. Allen, K. D. Campbell, Emily Damron-Cox, Linnea Garcia, Katie Gilbert, Yuva Harish, Kalie Holford, Sarah Kaminski, Monika Kim, Holly Kowitt, Fiona McLaren, Colin Neenan, Rachel Parris, Catherine Stine, and Jessica VanAllen for all of your thoughtful critiques on whichever draft I happened to yeet your way.

Many people in turn read many drafts of the five novels, short stories, and partial novels that I wrote before *Girls Who Burn*. I'm not in touch with all of you anymore, and you are too numerous to name one by one, but just know that I am grateful for you, especially those of you who were with me at the very start, reading the worst of what I had to give and offering encouragement nonetheless.

Thank you to everyone in the group chats, be they on Twitter, Discord, or Slack. You all got me through querying, through sub, through the debut year. I don't know what I'd have done without all of your information, enthusiasm, and commiseration.

Thank you to my in-laws, Jackie and John, for letting us live with you during the start of the pandemic. I drafted most of *Girls Who Burn* from the guest bedroom of your house while you entertained my one-year-old. Without your help and hospitality, I'm not sure when this book would have gotten written. Thank you, too, to my parents, Gloria and Tom, for the additional childcare, but also for instilling a love of reading in me from a very early age and for always encouraging me to work hard and dream big. Thank you to my Grandma Pagano and my godmother, Aunt Bobbi, for fostering that love of books and storytelling even more.

Thank you to my childhood friends: Shannon, Matt, Chris, Nicole, my sisters Liz and Amy, and the rest of the kids who ran around with us playing manhunt and superman tag and *The Last Unicorn* in New Jersey backyards. The seed of this story comes from those times and those memories, and I will be forever grateful.

Thank you to all my friends and family for your encouragement and support over the years as I dreamed about and worked toward this little pipe dream I had of being an author. None of you ever made fun of me or told me I wouldn't get there, even when I thought such things myself.

Thank you to my children for making my life so much richer. Before I had kids, I used to say that if I had to choose between having a book baby and having real babies, I'd choose the book baby—but I was wrong. I'd choose you over anything in this world, again and again and again. (But I am quite glad that I get to have both.)

And last but not least, thank you to John for absolutely everything. I would be lost without you.